Welcome to the world of
Silk and Magic

Erotic stories of
extraordinary passion . . .

Lovers who may be
more than human . . .

And worlds that may be
light years away . . .

The individual novellas in this book
are also available in Adobe PDF format.
Visit our web site at
www.silkandmagic.com or
www.imajinnbooks.com

Note: The stories in this book may contain
graphic sex scenes and language and are
intended for mature audiences.

Dedication for *Eternal Passion*:
To Isabel, Countess of Buchan, a courageous and
beautiful flame. May her memory always burn brightly.

Dedicaton for *Let's Get Crazy*:
To Ellen, who cheered me on
as Angel and Eric's story unfolded.

Dedication for *Toil and Trouble*:
To familiars everywhere,
especially those in feline form.

Don't Miss
Silk and Magic Book One
with stories from:
Rebecca York
Rickey Mallory
Brandy Lee

Availalbe now from ImaJinn Books

Silk and Magic Book Two

***

Brandy Lee
Caryn Carter
M. A. duBarry

ImaJinn Books

Silk and Magic Book Two
Published by ImaJinn Books

ISBN: 1-933417-94-3

10 9 8 7 6 5 4 3 2 1

PUBLISHER'S NOTE:
This book is a work of fiction. Names, characters, places and incidents are products of the author's imagination or are used fictitiously. Any resemblance to actual events or locales or persons, living or dead, is entirely coincidental.

Books are available at quantity discounts when used to promote products or services. For information please write to: Marketing Division, ImaJinn Books, P.O. Box 545, Canon City, CO 81212, or call toll free 1-877-625-3592.

Cover design by Patricia Lazarus

ImaJinn Books
P.O. Box 545, Canon City, CO 81212
Toll Free: 1-877-625-3592
http://www.imajinnbooks.com

Table of Contents

To Carla,
Thanks for being
a good friend & for the "Toot" list
Paka
M. A. duBarry

"Eternal Passions"
by
Brandy Lee

The Dream

"Stay here with me, lass."

Husky with passion, his voice in her ear made her heart leap. She couldn't speak, could only reach for him, body rising to meet his in the thick dark night shadows that enveloped them. Never enough time, never enough privacy, only moments stolen together...raw emotion filled her with a sense of overwhelming urgency.

Reaching for him, she slid her hands down his body and found him hard and ready for her. Fingers curled around the turgid length, caressed him until she heard his groan in her ear and knew he was impatient for her. As she was for him.

"Yes, my heart," she whispered when he asked if she loved him, "for all eternity."

His hands were on her breasts, teasing her nipples into rigid aching points and setting her thighs aflame with need, and she parted her legs eagerly when he nudged her knees apart. Then he was there, sliding inside her, a swift thrust that sent shivers of ecstasy rippling through her.

Clinging to him, she arched her hips to take him all as tension tightened, awareness of imminent danger only making the moment more intense. Shadows hid the world for now, but they would lift soon enough and she'd have this moment to remember forever...

Just before release, at the very moment when climax was but a breath away, she awoke to find herself alone, her body throbbing with frustration, and sadness a crushing weight. It was only the dream that haunted her nights. He was gone. Again. Silly to even think it, but she just knew that one day she'd awaken from dreams to find true love lying beside her again...

One

"My lord, the Earl of Fife is being held in England as a ward of the crown and is unable to uphold the hereditary tradition of crowning you Scotland's king."

Wearing royal robes and vestments, Robert the Bruce nodded. "'Tis enough that I have three bishops and my four earls with me."

Lord Lennox went to one knee before him, his head bowed. "Aye, my lord."

The great banner of the kings of Scotland with its lion and scarlet lilies fluttered in a slight wind. Wooden floorboards creaked. Someone coughed. Heavy velvet curtains shifted, and ropes hummed. Music swelled from the orchestra pit.

It was not at all like Susan Keith had thought it'd be.

She stood in the wings just offstage, watching and waiting for her cue. This was her first performance. Butterflies beat in her stomach and her knees were wobbly. It didn't help that soap opera star Ryan Douglas was her leading man, either. She still fantasized about him, even after weeks of rehearsals had resulted in nothing more than cordiality between them. There was just something about him that drew her. Besides the fact he really was a gorgeous man. Thick dark hair, vivid blue eyes, tall and with a great body—oh yeah. Definite leading man material, though she'd read the tabloids enough to know he had a whole string of gorgeous ex-girlfriends behind him. Not that she'd ever have a chance with him. She was just an ordinary small-town girl who'd somehow been lucky enough to be cast opposite him for this benefit play in his old hometown of Greensboro, North Carolina. She should have figured nothing would come of it. Most of the relationships in her life had been that way, with few notable exceptions.

Adjusting the tight sleeves of her medieval costume, Susan focused on her lines instead of her personal life. As the doomed Lady Buchan who had crowned Robert Bruce as King of the Scots, she summoned up emotions that her character would feel: Excitement, passion, pride—and youthful recklessness. After all, Isabel had defied her husband and the English king to ride halfway across Scotland as a hereditary representative of her family.

Finally she heard her cue. Ryan, playing the Bruce, said, "Bring Lady Buchan to me."

Sweeping onstage, Susan went straight to where Ryan stood before a throne and dipped to one knee in a low curtsey. "My lord, I have come to fulfill the duty my brother the earl is unable to perform. It is my honor to uphold our hereditary office and crown you king."

She tilted back her head to gaze up at him with admiration, projecting the hero-worship the nineteen-year-old Isabel had no doubt felt for the attractive and magnetic king. It wasn't a big stretch at all. Ryan was as attractive and magnetic as any king could ever have been. A shiver went through her when he met her gaze, something electric and breathtaking. Every time he met her eyes she had an overwhelming sense of connection, a powerful current that bound her to him with some invisible force. It was so strange, but must just be his stage presence, though there were moments when she'd caught him staring at her, too. With her hands clasped before her, she gazed at him as he put out a hand to touch her lightly on the shoulder, and for that instant could almost believe he was the man he portrayed onstage. A king. A knight in shining armor...

Intense blue eyes held her gaze, and his voice was deep and slightly husky, vibrating through her when he spoke the lines, "You are wed to my enemy, the Earl of Buchan, an ally of King Edward and close kinsman of Red Comyn, who tried to kill me in Greyfriars Chapel. Dare you risk the wrath of your husband and the English king to crown me?"

Reaching for the hand he held out to help her to her feet, she said, "I dare, my lord king. I would risk all for a man such as you."

Their fingers touched, and at that moment a crack of lightning blistered the air. The old building shook with a rumble of thunder and lights flickered. Someone in the audience gave a small shriek that was quickly stifled. The orchestra faltered, then picked up again. Susan tried to remember her next line, glanced up to find Ryan looking offstage, a slight frown crowding his eyes. Then she smelled smoke. An alarm shrilled, and people began to panic. Voices lifted in a warning to stay calm, not to panic, but no one paid attention. Hesitating, she realized she was standing, and thought that Ryan must have lifted her to her feet. The lights flickered again then went out completely, plunging the theater into dense blackness.

Smoke thickened, screams ricocheted off drapery-covered walls, and the relentless wail of fire alarms grew deafening. Susan stumbled, felt a hand on her arm and heard a husky voice in her ear telling her to keep going, not to stop, just hold tight to him and he'd get her through this. She clung to Ryan's arm, fingers curled tightly in the velvet of his costume. Ironic, that a man she'd begun to think of as a white knight should rescue her, she thought vaguely, coughing as acrid smoke burned her eyes and nose and throat. Familiar corridors became an unfamiliar maze, and twice they bumped into scenery or walls. Chaos reigned. Screams, smoke, thunder created a collage of confusion. It grew difficult to breathe. Real fear turned her insides cold, and she tripped over the dragging hem of her gown and went down before she could catch herself.

"Susan!" Ryan bent beside her, lashed out with his sword when someone almost trampled them, the nonlethal prop still inflicting damage but saving them from being crushed. "Get up, girl. Come on. I'll get you out of here."

She wasn't sure if she said it or thought it, but suddenly she knew he'd keep her safe, knew he'd get them both out of the burning theater. It was odd, but she had a fleeting sense of déjà vu, as if she'd been here before, been in grave danger yet knew he'd rescue her. And she suddenly knew exactly what he'd say next, his words coming out of darkness and smoke and flames: "Stay here with me, lass."

A loud crack made the very ground shake, as if a brick wall was falling. Voices whirled around her and she spun with them, heard vague snatches of half-remembered conversations in strange accents, saw swift images flash before her then disappear just before oblivion came crashing down.

Scotland, 1306

"Stay here with me, lass." The voice came out of the shadows and smoke, startling her, and she paused with one hand against stone, turning to find the source. A man stepped into the flickering light of towering flames that leaped and cavorted high into the air.

Drawing herself up, she said briskly, "You may call me Countess, not lass."

Smoke from a May Day fire in the courtyard smudged the

sky, stung her nose and eyes and throat. A lazy grin flashed at her in the gloom, and he bowed mockingly from the waist. "So I can. My lady."

The last was added after a deliberate pause, and she narrowed her eyes at him. She knew him. Sir Alex Campbell, a rogue knight if ever she'd seen one. If she wasn't loath to cast a pall on the festivities, she'd make him regret his impudence. Instead, she set her mouth in a straight line and looked away to watch the sun sink slowly behind the parapets. Pale walls reflected crimson light from the sun, and the huge fire cast strange shadows on the stones of Kildrummy Castle. The knight watched her boldly instead of showing deference to her rank, yet she held her tongue.

Turning her back on the rude Highlander, she moved closer to the gatehouse despite his command to remain close. He followed her, making no pretense of tact or subtlety.

"Do not play the fool, m'lady. I've no desire to chase after you. Danger lurks beyond these high walls."

She sniffed her contempt. "When has it not? England and Scotland have been hard at war these ten years past. Now that the Bruce has been crowned king, hostilities will only increase. I'm not afraid. I shall walk where I please when I please."

"You are Lady Montgomery, are you not?"

"And if I am?" She turned back to face him, and had to look up to meet his gaze. He was tall, much taller than most, with a mane of glossy dark hair and piercing blue eyes beneath a strong brow.

"A bonny lad," she'd heard the queen's lady-in-waiting say with a sigh, then add softly, "and a devil in bed and battle, 'tis said." Just remembering that comment made her heart beat a little faster and the blood race through her veins. Despite the fair evening, her legs began to tremble and her hands to shake, and a knot tightened in the pit of her stomach.

"And if you are," he said softly, stepping even closer to her, "I am charged with your protection. You will bide by my commands, my lady."

"Will I?" she asked after a moment, tilting her head to one side to look at him through her lashes, a ploy that often reduced men to quivering confusion. The Highlander only grinned more broadly.

"Aye. You will. And you can save that simpering glance

for a lesser man. My lady."

Heat flushed her cheeks and she looked quickly away. Curse him! He made her feel like a child instead of a woman already widowed. A husband she'd hardly known had died when the English savaged their home in pursuit of Robert the Bruce. While their keep had been violated, she'd been left untouched. On the outside, anyway. A pervasive feeling of doom had stayed with her since then, so that she often found herself empty, cold and dead inside.

Yet now, with this man looming over her like Judgment Day, she felt only reckless and excited. Alive, for the first time in months. Days and weeks had passed in a blur of moving by rote, of doing what was expected, what she must, and now on May Day an odd pulsing excitement coursed through her that had nothing to do with the noisy festivities, and much to do with the handsome Scot staring down at her so insolently. So she stared back, meeting his gaze.

"Why are you set to watch me? There are others here much more important. The queen. Countess Buchan. The king's sister and even his daughter—why must you follow me about?"

"Because I drew the short straw."

Speechless, she stared at him, then saw the devilry dancing in his eyes. "Then you are the winner, I presume," she said after a moment, and he grinned.

"Aye, my lady. That I am." He moved even closer so that she could feel the heat of his body, smell the faint scent of heather and wood smoke that emanated from his garments, the plaid draped over his shoulder held with a heavy gold brooch no doubt embossed with his family crest. Her heart beat a little faster when he said softly, "And now I shall claim my prize."

She opened her mouth to say something sharp but he caught her by surprise, his hand cupping her chin as he bent swiftly to brush her lips with his own. A jolt like the strike of lightning flashed through her, made the hair stand up on her arms and sent a shiver down her spine. A devil in bed, indeed! Yea, she could well believe it. When he pulled back, she mustered cool self-control she certainly didn't feel.

"A man could be hanged for such an offense were I to cry foul, Sir Alex."

"Yea, perhaps so, though I think you will not. Not this time."

"And why not?" She stared up at him, caught between fascination and insult.

He smiled. "Because you liked it."

"I think," she said after a brief, chagrined silence, "that if you try that again you'll feel my dirk between your ribs. I'd not advise you to risk it, Sir Alex."

Still smiling, he put a hand over his heart. "You wound me with just the thought of your displeasure, my lady."

"Somehow, I think not." Flustered, she backed away from him to return to the great hall at the north side of the keep. Revelers gathered around the fire that burned brightly in the huge courtyard, and sheep had already been jumped through the smoke like May Days of previous years. She could scarcely recall them, the days of laughter and pleasure without the threat of war hanging over all their heads. It'd been so long ago, ten years past at least, when William Wallace had first rebelled against King Edward. There'd been little enough of laughter that she could recall since her marriage to David Montgomery, either. He'd not been brutal or cruel, just indifferent. A man devoted to war and hunting, not a wife. It'd not been surprising when he'd been killed.

What surprised her now was that she'd responded to a brief kiss from a rogue knight with little to recommend him but a handsome face and winsome smile. And she wanted him to kiss her again...

Two

Alex watched her walk away from him, her hips gently swaying as she picked a path across the crowded dirt courtyard to the great hall. Ever since he'd been sent at the king's command with Nigel Bruce to escort the women to Kildrummy, he'd been watching Lady Montgomery. Nigel had seen him watching her, a source of great amusement to him. The king's brother had a wicked sense of humor and a fair face, and jested that Alex's way with the ladies wooed away too many of the fairest damsels.

"Lady Gillian is a lovely widow, though not a wealthy one," he'd said, nudging Alex. "Still, her father was Earl of Wakefield so she's heiress to lands in Easter Ross that may interest a landless knight able to wrest them back from the English."

"I'm not landless," he'd said, but Nigel didn't listen. He rarely did. He'd made up his mind that Alex should court the Lady Gillian and he'd bedevil him until he did.

Alex had intended to thwart Nigel by having the lady reject him forcefully and soundly; he just hadn't thought he'd actually like kissing her. She'd seemed far too cold, too remote. Yet beneath that icy exterior lurked the heat and heart of a woman ready for a man. He'd felt her shiver, felt the swift, tentative response in her mouth as her lips parted for him. Yea, she was ripe for love even if he was not. Not for the kind of love a woman like her would require. He preferred a tumble on a bed of straw with some buxom wench who wanted nothing more than stolen pleasure. Lady Montgomery was a countess. Widowed by her husband's fondness for the boar hunt, and his foolishness for hunting alone. The English had caught him out and slain him, then taken his keep despite the lady's resistance. A waste, to leave such a woman widowed.

And a lovely widow indeed, with fair hair caught in thick plaits and bound with silk ribbons, and amber eyes like gold coins in a heart-shaped face. Perhaps Nigel was right, though he'd never admit it to him or he'd grow insufferable. The Lady Gillian could certainly tempt him to while away some summer hours with her since there was little else to do until the Bruce summoned them. He oft chafed at the inactivity, fretted to be in battle beside his king, yet knew the importance of guarding the queen and her ladies. And there might yet be compensation for his task.

A door banged and Alex smiled, then strode toward the great hall at the far end of the courtyard. Stone towers rose on each side of the roughly D-shaped castle, with the chapel on the east side and the lord's chambers in the Snow Tower on the west, and behind the north wall of the keep lay a deep ravine that protected it from invaders. The great hall snugged up against that north wall.

There was no fireplace in the great hall, only a huge brass brazier that provided heat. Low stone benches built into the walls often bore the blanket-wrapped forms of sleeping men and women. It took a moment for his eyes to adjust to the change from the leaping light in the courtyard to the dull gleam of torches stuck in sconces on the stone walls. Then he saw her, the Lady Gillian seated at a trestle table with a flagon of wine and a trencher of meat. Several other ladies chatted nearby, and he saw two of them glance sideways at him as he crossed the hall. One of them was Alyse of Inch, who had shared his pallet quite energetically a few times before he'd grown bored with her inane chatter and possessive jealousy. Alyse watched with narrowed eyes as he approached Lady Montgomery.

"My lady," he said when he reached her, and Lady Gillian glanced up at him with a cool amber gaze that made his blood race, "you are wanted in the solar."

It was true. He wanted her there, wanted to explore this newfound interest in a woman who did not leap eagerly into his embrace but held him at bay. It was a novel experience, for the women he chose usually responded to his attentions.

"Pray, Lady Gillian," Alyse said, "you'd best take your eating dagger with you if you go alone with Sir Alex. Unless of course, you wish to come back to the hall with straw in your hair."

Alex ignored her, but saw Gillian's eyes flick toward Alyse then back to him. He waited, and in a moment, she rose from the trestle table.

"Please lead the way, sir."

An unexpected pang of guilt at his subterfuge assailed him, but he quickly smothered it. She wanted only to irritate Alyse. Their conflicts were obvious. He'd learned long ago that women kept in close quarters often tended to quarrel between themselves, their petty grievances equal to major insults that no man would ever suffer without bloodshed. Some of their verbal barbs drew blood, and he'd found it amazing to see those same females in smiling conversation later. So he largely ignored any hint of strife between women. It was best not to get involved.

Once in the solar, empty at this time of night, he closed the door and turned to look at Lady Gillian. She stood in the center of the chamber, torchlight glinting on her hair with hints of red among the gold strands. A simple coronet of gilt and blue circled her head, the silk twisted into a coil that bound her hair away from her face, fashioned of the same material as the ribbons woven into her plaits.

"Who has summoned me here to the lord's solar?" Gillian asked, a little frown knitting her brow. She looked about the empty chamber uncertainly.

"A knight who admires you," he said promptly, and saw her confusion increase. Then she gave him a startled look, eyes widening a little.

"You?"

"Aye." He took a bold step closer. Faint of heart ne'er won the day. Or the lady's favors. Lady Gillian didn't move, even when he put a hand out to caress her cheek. Her skin was soft, sleek satin beneath his hand, and he couldn't resist sliding his fingers into the wealth of hair at the nape of her neck. He drew her yet closer, heard her breathing quicken, saw her lips part as if she meant to speak. Quickly, he bent his head to cover her mouth with his own, tasting the honeyed sweetness of her, heat coursing through him when she didn't push him away. She yielded to the kiss, parting her lips to allow his tongue access. Ah, he'd been right in his assessment of her as ready for a night of love…he moved his hand from her neck lower, pressing into the small of her back so that her breasts pushed into his chest.

A sudden sharp pain in his ribs distracted him but he didn't release her, only drew back to stare down into her face. She smiled.

"'Tis the point of my dirk you feel, Sir Alex. Should you wish your blood spilled upon the stones, it can be arranged."

After a brief pause, he nodded. "Aye, your point is well-taken, my lady."

"Excellent. Release me, sir."

He did, and stood there looking down at her, half-amused,

half-wary. "Anything for the lady with the sharp dagger."

A speculative light gleamed in her eyes, quickly veiled by lowered lashes before she nodded. "Anything?"

"Within reason." He could have easily taken the dirk away from her, but allowed her the fiction of having the upper hand for the moment, curious to what she would say next.

"Bar the door, Sir Alex."

That was unexpected. He arched a brow, thought about refusing, then decided to comply. When it was done, he turned back to look at her. Tension vibrated in her slender frame, and the hand holding the dirk quivered slightly although she looked determined enough. She gestured with the weapon.

"Now unbuckle your sword belt."

He didn't hesitate. Even unarmed, he could easily best her should she turn vicious. Slowly, he unbuckled the wide leather sword belt around his waist and let it slide to the floor at his feet. Then he stood there with his arms at his sides, feet spread apart for balance, watching her with slightly narrowed eyes.

"I await your pleasure, my lady Gillian."

A flush rose in her cheeks at his mockery and bold familiarity. She put out her tongue to wet her lips, a nervous gesture that he found intriguing. A pulse beat rapidly in the hollow of her throat, just above the low scoop neck of her gilt-edged gown. Even more intriguing…

When he took a step toward her, she lifted the dirk higher. "Nay, Sir Knight, you are at my mercy this eve. I am not a woman to be bedded and forgotten as you have so many others. Yea, did you not think we would discuss your amorous pursuits? Your latest conquests are often an amusing subject while we ply our needles around the fire."

"And which needles would those be," he wondered aloud, his mouth twisting in a wry smile. "Tapestry needles or wagging tongues?"

"We are adept at both. And I am more adept with this dirk than you may think." He made no answer to that, just waited, and in a moment she gestured toward him again. "Your plaide. Remove it."

"To what purpose?"

"Have you no sense of adventure, Sir Alex?"

It was the way she said it, her head tilted slightly to one side and a faint smile curving that luscious mouth that decided him. He unfastened the brooch on his shoulder that held the

plaide pinned to his sherte, then let it fall to a puddle of dark
blue and green wool at his booted feet. It left him clad in only
the brief sherte and his boots. A draft wavered up from cold
stones, but heat coursed through his body with every beat of
his heart.

Lady Gillian's eyes widened slightly, went dark gold
beneath her delicately arched brows, and her lips parted. In a
husky murmur, she said, "Now the sherte, Sir Knight."

"I wear only a noble stretch of hide beneath my sherte and
plaide," he warned, and she nodded.

"Yea, 'tis as I suspected."

It took only a moment to shed the linen sherte, and when it
lay atop the plaide, he reached for her. She did not resist, but
came willingly enough into his arms, her eyes half-closed, lips
parted in a faint smile. He slid his hands into the top of her
bodice, pulled it down to bare her breasts, heard the swift intake
of her breath as he caressed the small firm globes. Nipples
hardened against his palms, and he teased them between his
thumbs and fingers. A shiver went through her as he bent to
kiss her again, capturing her mouth, jabbing his tongue inside.
If she thought to test him, she'd soon learn her mistake. He
knew what pleased a woman, an education gathered through
many encounters over the course of his twenty-eight years.
As Lady Gillian would soon discover.

Blood pounded more rapidly through his veins, pooled in
his groin, made him throb with a familiar ache. He pressed
even closer, so that his stiff cock nudged against her soft velvet
skirts. One arm reached behind her to hold her tightly to him.
Torches sputtered and hissed in wall sconces, and the chaos in
the hall beyond the barred door receded so that all he heard
was the lady's soft moan. Unexpected but not unwelcome,
this swift capitulation. He tugged at her laces, untied them
with experienced motions and slid his fingers into the side
opening of her gown to caress her smooth skin. She wore no
undertunic, only the simple blue gown over her slender curves.

"Nay, sir knight," she gasped against his mouth when he
began to draw up her skirts to bunch them in his fist, "wait!"

He ignored her and slid his hand up the silky curve of her
bare thighs to her waist, still holding crumpled velvet. His
knuckles grazed the patch of curls at the apex of her thighs.
Releasing her skirts, he touched the springy mat of curls, slid a
finger into her satiny recess to stroke her, spreading damp heat

through the folds. Her thighs spread, muscles quivering as he caressed her, her breath coming swiftly. She shuddered, little moans sounding in the back of her throat as he found the tiny feminine nub that he knew was sensitive. Stroking it, still kissing her, he heard her dirk drop to the stone floor as she grasped his arms and held tightly.

Gently, he eased her a few steps back until she came to rest against the edge of the table holding a branch of candles that flickered in the gloom. She didn't look at him when he set her up on the table, but kept her fingers curled around his arms. He leaned forward between her thighs so that his hard cock nudged into the damp curls. Then he touched the pink peaks of her nipples, tight like tiny rose buds. She shivered, and he bent to suck a nipple into his mouth. Her fingers tightened so that her nails dug into his arm muscles. He sucked harder, cradling her breast with one hand while his other teased her other nipple. She arched into him with a long moan of need. He pressed forward so that the head of his cock rubbed against the sensitive nub of her sex, stroking it slowly at first, then faster and faster until she shuddered uncontrollably.

Crying out, her thighs closed around his cock and she bucked against him in jerky movements. He held her until she quieted, felt her finally go limp in his arms and let out a heavy breath, then he kissed her again. Her eyes were closed, and a flush rode her high cheekbones. The pulse in the hollow of her throat still beat like the rapid wings of a dove.

Trapped between her satiny thighs, his cock throbbed for release. He reached down to lift her for easier access, but she stopped him with a hand on his wrist.

"Wait," she whispered, sounding shaky, and flashed a wobbly smile when he looked up at her. "I would pleasure you as you have me."

"I intend for you to," he muttered, but allowed her to push him back a step. She slid from the table, skirts falling to cover her bare legs, and he reached for her before she stepped quickly away.

"Nay, Sir Alex, give me a moment."

Impatient, aching, he stood with his legs apart, then sucked in a sharp breath when she dropped to her knees before him. Looking up, she smiled as she reached for him, caressing the rigid length of his cock with her fingertips, little fluttery touches that sent bolts of lightning all the way to his toes. Clenching his teeth, he stared down at her, arms at his sides, watching in disbelief and delight. She held him in her hand, stroked him, her grip tightening slightly as her movements increased, and he closed his eyes and focused on the pleasure vibrating through him at her touch. When she paused for a moment, he waited, then shuddered when he felt the damp heat of her tongue along his length. It was all he could do not to explode. He groaned, a deep guttural sound that rumbled in the back of his throat. Heat scoured him, and his hands tightened into fists as he restrained the urge to reach for her.

After a moment she paused again, this time murmuring something he didn't quite catch. Lost in the thick haze of raw need, it took him a moment to realize that she'd moved away from him. He opened his eyes just in time to see her unbar the door. Too startled to react quickly, he met her hot gaze. Anger lit her amber eyes and turned them to molten gold.

"I am not one of your casual conquests, Sir Alex. It would serve you well to keep that in mind. You have not used me. I have used you."

Then she was through the door, leaving it ajar as she disappeared. Frustrated lust beat through him, and it was only when he turned to retrieve his sherte and plaide that he discovered them gone. Curse her! He'd been stranded in the solar wearing only his boots—and an erection.

And in that instant, he knew he wanted her more fiercely than he had ever before wanted any woman.

Three

Still shaking, Gillian threw his garments into an alcove then ran for the stairs. She didn't pause until she'd reached the second-floor chamber used by the queen. It was empty. Grateful for the privacy, she went to the wide stone window that looked out over the dark ravine and tried to still her rapidly beating heart. She'd never meant it to go so far. He'd surprised her—nay, her own body had surprised her with its betrayal at his touch. When he'd so arrogantly commanded her to the solar and she'd realized he meant to seduce her, anger prompted her to turn the tables. But she'd meant only to pretend response, to lure him with the hope of compliance before rejecting him. She'd certainly never meant to let him touch her so intimately.

And she'd never thought that a man's touch could feel so good, either. David had never touched her like that, indeed, had seemed to care only for his own pleasure without regard to hers at all. Thankfully, he'd not come to her bed often after the first month of marriage, complaining that she was too cold to suit him. He'd much preferred the arms of a servant to those of his wife. A humiliation that had not escaped her notice, though she'd never acknowledged it to anyone. It was too painful.

Always in the back of her mind was the suspicion that he'd been right, that she was too cold for any man to love. While she'd not been in love with David, just dutifully wed him to consolidate their estates—a futile pact in light of the fact both their estates were now in English hands—it'd still been a huge blow to realize that her youthful dreams of love would never happen. Foolish dreams, her old nurse had scolded her once, for she'd been born to better things. Why, royal blood ran in her veins, her ancestry going all the way back to the MacAlpin.

What would old Seonaid say if she knew Gillian had encouraged a rough Highland knight's attentions? She'd have used a willow switch on her for even smiling at him, no doubt. But Seonaid was long past this world's cares now, and Gillian had been abandoned to her fate along with her husband. Now she had a place with the queen. Tentative at best. She would have to keep her temper in check and not react hastily, or she would find herself disgraced.

Yet the memory of that unexpected and shattering response to Sir Alex's caresses still left her unsettled and all quivery inside. She'd never thought it could feel like that. Indeed, Alex Campbell was the first man she had touched so intimately. David had always come to her bed at night when the candles were nearly guttered, usually smelling of drink and the hunt. It'd been distinctly unpleasant. Alex Campbell had smelled like wood smoke and heather, not wine and a boar's blood. Yea, a vast difference indeed. And she had given in to her curiosity and caressed him, slid her fingers over his swollen organ and been amazed at the size and shape of it.

A shiver racked her. He'd been hot beneath her hand, soft and hard at the same time...it'd surprised her, the contrast. It wasn't as if she was exactly innocent of a man's body, but she wasn't experienced with passion. Her body's reaction had been shocking—and exciting. And she couldn't stop thinking about it. About him. How he'd felt beneath her hand, how he'd made her feel.

She leaned on the wide window sill scattered with velvet pillows. The smell of smoke drifted in the open window that looked out over the Black Ravine. A slight breeze shifted a wall tapestry, cooled her fevered skin, and made her yearn for a freedom she hadn't had since she was a small girl. She felt so trapped, by circumstances beyond her control, by the rigid strictures of her position and all that was expected of her. There were times—

"Are you planning to jump, my lady?"

Startled, she whirled around, and her heart thudded frantically when she saw Sir Alex in the open door of the queen's chamber. Putting her hands behind her to brace herself against the stone window ledge, she managed to meet his gaze steadily.

"Is that a threat?"

"More like a strong suggestion." He looked dangerous. Tension vibrated through him. He had found his plaide and it was thrown carelessly over one shoulder as if he'd dressed hastily, his sword belt holding it around his waist. He crossed the chamber in long, deliberate strides. "If you were a man—"

"If I were a man, Sir Alex, I doubt very seriously you would have found yourself in such awkward circumstances," she interrupted sharply. "You've only your arrogance to blame."

He'd come so close she could almost count his individual

eyelashes now, the heat of him washing over her when he came to a stop barely an arm's length away. The drumming of blood in her ears sounded like ocean waves, loud and crashing, drowning out everything but an intense awareness of him. Acute anticipation sizzled, so that when he put out his hand to pull her to him, the contact was almost a relief.

Her lips formed a protest that went unuttered as his mouth clamped down over hers in a fierce possession. She should have been more prepared, but her hands were trapped between their bodies so that she felt the rapid thud of his heart beneath her palm.

He backed her up against the window ledge and leaned into her so that she felt the hard nudge of his erection even through his plaide and her skirts. Intense heat bloomed between her thighs, searing and breathtaking, a promise and reminder of what he'd done in the solar. As if she needed a reminder...

Gillian grabbed at his plaide to keep from sliding to the floor. Her fingers curled into the wool and clung. He pulled back slightly, then slid his hands along the bare skin of her collarbone to the gilt edging of her bodice and lower, dragging the cloth down to bare her breasts. Cool air from the open window made her nipples knot into hard buds. Cupping her breasts in his palms, he teased the taut peaks between his fingers and thumbs. Exquisite sensation shot through her, a pulse throbbed in that damp place between her thighs, and she arched upward instead of pulled away. Instant heat flashed to the pit of her stomach. She should tell him to stop, but found herself clinging to him instead, fingers digging into rough plaide and hard muscle. Caution faded. She arched her back, closed her eyes and shuddered when he bent to take a nipple into his mouth, his tongue lashing it with erotic sensations. It felt...exquisite.

The insistent pulse throbbed between her thighs, unfamiliar and arousing as he suckled her breasts with strong tugs that made her ache with need. Then he put his hand beneath her skirt and stroked her private parts in an erotic caress, fingers rough and warm and sending shocks like lightning to every nerve ending in her entire body. He seemed to know how it felt; he focused on that most sensitive part, the tiny nub between her nether lips that quivered with anticipation at each leisurely stroke of his fingertips. Everything was a heated haze of urgency and shivering ecstasy.

"Oh...sweet Mary..."

The thick voice sounded like her own. It must be, because his mouth was filled with her nipple. She shuddered again. After a moment he lifted his head, looked down at her, his eyes as glazed as hers surely were. Desire sharpened his features, drew skin taut across high cheekbones, and his mouth thinned into a harsh slash.

In a rough voice he growled, "Ye like that, d'ye, lass?"

She should have said No, but she didn't. She just looked back at him, unwilling to admit it but unable to deny it. His mouth curled into a smile.

"Aye, 'tis plain enough that you like it—your eyes say what your lips will not."

Before she could form a single word, he slid his finger into her body and his thumb raked across the sensitive bud of her sex as his mouth captured her tight nipple again. As he rolled her nipple between his teeth and tongue, her thighs opened for him and her hips thrust eagerly into his hand.

It was lunacy to respond to him like this, when at any moment someone could come into the queen's chamber and discover them. Couplings weren't uncommon, as life in a castle offered little privacy, but she was a countess, and to be caught with her skirts around her waist and this Highland knight's hand inside her would be humiliating.

Yet she couldn't stop, not when release hovered so near, when the promise of that earlier ecstasy lay within her grasp. She bucked against his hand, shuddering, her fingers moving to curl into his hair to hold him against her breast, the delicious heat of his mouth sucking her nipple and his thumb across her sex making her reckless. So close now, so close...tension drawing her ever so near that elusive release...

Then his hand withdrew and she whimpered in frustration, only to gasp when his finger was replaced with the hard steel of his cock against her damp nether lips. He sucked harder on her nipple, lips nibbling at it as he spread her thighs wider and pulled her forward so that she leaned back on the stone ledge and pillows, then he was inside her with a swift, hard thrust that made her cry out again, a soft keening sound. Rough, delicious invasion, filling her so completely she couldn't move, could only hold on to him as he thrust forward again, this time a slow push of his shaft so deep inside her that she could barely breathe.

Velvet pillows beneath her, dark wind behind her, and hard steel inside her, all blended into a rising tide of urgency. Her body contracted around him, inner muscles squeezing his cock and making him groan, and she knew that he felt it as much as she did, that hovering need for release. He muttered something she didn't quite catch, then began to move inside her, slowly at first before gathering speed and power in a fierce thrust and drag that made her body convulse around him in exquisite reaction.

His hands moved beneath her hips to pull her forward until she lay fully back against the cushioned ledge, and his fingers dug into bare flesh as he pounded into her body. Her skirts were up around her waist and her naked breasts exposed, and yet she didn't care. Nothing mattered but that shattering ecstasy that awaited them both. Leaning over her, he stroked in and out as tension grew tighter and tighter. She lifted her legs and spread them wide for him.

He bent to her breast again, first one and then the other, sucking her nipple into his mouth in strong strokes that matched the thrust of his cock inside her, and she arched upward in heated, mindless need, whispering encouragement.

"Yes…yes…like that…oh don't stop."

Then he put his hand down between them and rubbed his thumb over that sensitive bud at the top of her sex as he shoved his cock even more deeply inside her. It burst on her suddenly, powerful and obliterating everything but waves of white-hot ecstasy that made her cry out and cling to him, her legs locking around his waist as she bucked ferociously against him.

He held on tightly until she quieted, then gave a final few thrusts and a low guttural groan before pulling quickly out of her body. A shudder went through him, and he leaned between her legs with a sigh.

"Marry, but I never thought you'd be so sweet, lass."

She didn't feel sweet. She felt—wanton. As passion faded, reason returned. Abruptly, she pushed him off her and sat up, shoving her skirts down and tugging up her bodice to cover her breasts. Alex looked into her eyes and smiled, a faintly sardonic twist of his mouth.

"And now you will be like the other *ladies* and pretend this didn't happen, I suppose."

She flushed, for that thought had indeed flitted through her mind. "I should."

"Why?"

"Why? Because it's not meet that...that we should just rut like animals in heat."

"My dear lady, we are animals. All of us. And there was no more to this coupling than just rutting. You may try to deny it, but you can't lie to yourself."

Of course, he was accustomed to coupling in corners with ladies, and she should have remembered that. She jerked at her bodice, ripping the gilt embroidery, flustered and unsettled. "You're wrong. I'm not like the others you've been with. This is...is not a common thing for me."

"Aye. 'Tis plain to see that." He put out a hand to touch her cheek, fingers lifting her chin so that she had to look into his eyes. "And 'tis plain to see there's more to you than I first thought there'd be, my lady. Perhaps I owe you an apology."

"For...for this?"

"Not for the act, no. I cannot regret that. But I do regret that I misjudged you."

Confused, she just looked at him.

Something flickered deep in his eyes, then he shrugged. "I thought you more honest than you are. My mistake, m'lady."

She wanted to protest that she was honest, but he gave her no chance. He bowed from the waist, then pivoted on his heel and left her standing alone in the queen's chamber. Only the echo of his boots on stone marked his passage, and after a moment, she turned to look out the window into the darkness and ponder her hypocrisy.

Four

Alex didn't see Lady Montgomery for several days after being with her in the queen's chamber. He endured the ribald comments of his companions—one of whom had found him naked and furious in the hallway after being stranded in the solar and been happy to share that discovery with the rest. No doubt it was all over the castle by now that the lady had divested him of plaide and pride in a neat stroke.

For some reason, he had no desire to retrieve his pride at the lady's expense. It would be a secret between them that he'd reaped his reward in the queen's chamber unless she chose to reveal it. He wasn't completely without chivalry.

Only Alyse seemed to suspect something, and he'd caught her staring speculatively at him in the hall as if she knew well enough he'd not let Lady Montgomery escape without some form of retribution. But then Alyse would certainly have exacted vengeance if put in a similar position, for she wasn't a woman to suffer lightly a blow to her vanity. He knew that well enough.

So tension accompanied evening meals taken in the hall with Alyse giving him glances sharp as daggers, and Nigel Bruce taking it all in with a huge grin and adding his own verbal jabs. The absence of Lady Gillian was duly noted.

"The fair lady from the Snow Tower has more fire than ice, 'tis said," he jested with a sly tilt of his head toward Alex. "'Tis also said that more than the summer heat has thawed the lovely widow."

"And 'tis said that the king's brother has more tongue than wit," Alex replied without looking at Nigel, and heard him roar with laughter.

"Yea, that has been said by more than one luckless soul," he said between chuckles, "but ne'er before to my face."

Alex looked up at last. "Your winsome face has saved you thus far, but I'm not as susceptible as some."

Nigel only grinned more broadly. "You may yet get your chance at swordplay once we have a large enough force to face the English."

Word had come that Robert Bruce had managed to raise more men from his own lordship of Garioch and from the estates of the Earl of Atholl in Strathaan and Strathbegie, and continued on to raise forces in the domains of the Earl of Mar, who was

the Countess of Buchan's younger brother. The English had
appointed the Earl of Pembroke—cousin of the king and kin to
the murdered Red Comyn—as lieutenant over Scotland.
Reports came of terrible tales of massacre and the looting of
estates and towns and even monasteries. In violation of the
code of chivalry, King Edward had just decreed that any woman
of the rebels was subject to outlawry, thus leaving them
vulnerable to rape and murder. It left everyone on edge,
watching the hilly horizon, waiting with dread and anticipation
for an attack that had yet to come.

"Yea," Alex said grimly, "and I pray that chance comes
soon. I weary of the wait."

"As do we all." Nigel looked suddenly somber. "As do we
all."

A flash of blue velvet caught his eye, and Alex looked past
the king's brother to the end of the hall where Lady Gillian had
just appeared. She paused, and their gazes met over crowded
trestle tables and noise. Her hair was unbound, streaming over
her shoulders, only a circlet of gilt holding it from her eyes. He
could see her hesitation, the way her hands fluttered slightly
before she curled her fingers into her palms, and knew he was
the cause of her distress.

Rising, he left the table without a word, crossing the
crowded hall toward the doors and Lady Gillian. She stood
still, watching him warily as he approached.

"My lady," he said with a tilt of his head and wry twist of
his mouth, "I have quit the hall. You may take your meal
unhindered."

"You do not hinder me, Sir Alex." She said it stiffly,
watching him with those amber eyes that made him think of
Spanish coins. "Should I wish to sit at table, I would do so
whether you were present or not."

For a moment, he didn't know what to say. He thought she
meant it, but wasn't sure. For she was certain to have heard
the rumors about them flying through the keep, and must think
he'd encouraged them. He shrugged, affecting indifference
when he didn't feel it, and put a hand on her arm.

"Well," a soft, venomous voice said behind him, "shouldn't
you take this tryst to a more private corner? Aye, but you already
have and therein lies the problem. I daresay, I certainly had no
complaints about Sir Alex, but then, I didn't expect much."

Alyse of Inch lifted a brow and smiled when Alex turned

to look at her, but a wealth of malice lay behind the smile. There was no point in responding to her barb for it'd only encourage more, and would put Lady Gillian at a disadvantage.

But then he realized he needn't have worried about the lady, for she merely looked at Alyse and said softly, "Your lamentable lack of expectation is well-known, Mistress Alyse."

Alyse flushed an ugly deep red, and brown eyes snapped angrily as she glared at Gillian. "Perhaps that is better than expecting too much!"

"Perhaps. If that were the case. It is not. Now pardon me while I seek better company."

Gillian moved away, and Alex spared a moment's admiration for her poise before Alyse commanded his attention. She turned on him, fury in her eyes and voice.

"How dare you allow her to speak to me thus!"

"I don't concern myself with women's quarrels."

"You concern yourself often enough with women's favors."

"Yea, when sufficiently tempted."

Alyse moved closer, until her breasts grazed his chest and he could smell the musky scent she wore. "And are you sufficiently tempted now, Sir Alex?"

Not in the least, but he wasn't fool enough to say that aloud. "You are lovely indeed, but this is not the time or place."

Before she could protest, he moved away, going in the opposite direction from Lady Gillian so as not to provoke more ire from Alyse. He should have known she'd be trouble. He had watched her drag Sir Cedric around by his cock once too often. No woman would ever do that to him, though some had tried, including Mistress Alyse.

Torches spit and sputtered in holders on the courtyard walls, and shadows hugged stone beyond the pools of light. Smoke, horse manure, and other familiar scents spiced the dusky air, mixed with a tangible feeling of expectation. Apprehension was obvious in the sentries walking the walls, in the way a sudden loud sound could pause a conversation or bring heads up to watch the gates. Danger made a constant companion these days.

He was halfway across the courtyard when he spied a familiar figure climbing the spiral staircase to the walls. Pausing, he watched a moment, then followed Lady Gillian. Traces of her flowery scent lingered in the close air of the stairwell.

Sweet. Light. Alluring.

In a world filled with much less pleasant scents, the sweetness of her fragrance was more enticing than he'd anticipated, triggering memory and instant caution. Yet he still followed her to the catwalk atop the walls. It was deserted save for the sentries posted at intervals. Her steps were loud on stone up here in the silence, while beyond the walls and hills the sun was a faint haze behind purple crags. This time of year, darkness fell near the midnight hour, and the sun rose again a few hours later. It was as if the season strove to make up for the long winter nights when daylight hours were scant and frozen.

He found her in the doorway of a tower, staring off into the distance where the line of trees and sky made an anonymous blur.

"Why are you following me?" she asked, but didn't sound angry, only slightly curious.

He couldn't answer. Indeed, had no answer that made sense. After a moment, she turned to look directly at him. Diffused light softened her face, shadowed her eyes, but he could still see her wariness as she looked at him, and understood it.

"I did not come to do you harm, m'lady."

"Harm has already been done."

"You were willing enough—"

"That's not what I meant, Sir Alex," she interrupted sharply. "You must know that gossip runs rife through the keep."

"And you blame me."

"No. I blame myself." She turned to look back across the parapets. "'Tis my own fault I—we—what happened. You are not to blame."

That surprised him, and he stood silent for a moment, thinking. If she'd blamed him, he'd have felt better. As it was, he felt responsible. He should not have pursued her. Widowed only a few months...living in fear, with every day uncertain, and she was only female, after all. It had to be difficult for her. Women weren't strong, couldn't bear the same rigors as men, especially gently-reared women like Lady Gillian. He'd treated her in the same way as he'd regarded Alyse, and taken advantage. Now he should make amends.

"Nay, lady," he said softly, and moved close enough to her that the sweet fragrance she wore made him yearn to touch her. "It is my blame to bear, if blame is the right word. You are—lovely. I've watched you these past weeks, wanting to talk to you, wanting to touch you as I did. But I should have remembered who you are. It was never my intention to dishonor you."

Turning with her back to the parapet, she leaned against stone, regarded him in silence for a long moment before she shook her head, a faint smile curving her mouth. "I wasn't dishonored, Sir Alex. Not the way you mean. If I played the wanton, it was my choice. You merely showed me how easy it is to forget all I've been taught my entire life, to yield to pleasure and ignore the teachings of the church, of my tutors."

"And you were taught it's wrong to find pleasure in love?"

"Isn't it? It's our duty to procreate, to produce children, but not to—"

"Lessons from old men or those with shriveled souls do not apply to flesh and blood, my lady. Life is short. Were it not for pleasure in love, it would not be worth the time spent here."

"Ah, but you have said it yourself, Sir Alex. *Love*. There was no love between us, only pleasure. That is the sin, I think. And yet I sinned gladly and imperiled my soul."

He had no answer for that, and after a moment, she turned away again to stare off into the distance. He'd never been a religious man. Never thought beyond this life, what was here and now and could be seen, felt, heard, or tasted. Yet for an instant, he caught a glimpse of something eternal, of an emotion besides fear or hate. Love had always seemed foolish. Dangerous, even. It made some men behave stupidly, and he'd not once been tempted by it. Loyalty was a far nobler emotion, that sense of connection to a place or person that bade him fight fiercely to keep it safe.

But now, with Lady Gillian, he could see why some men would fight for a woman when she had no lands to win, nothing but her person. There was more to this lady than just her beauty. Some indefinable virtue that intrigued and appalled him. He couldn't risk tender emotion, not in this world. Not when the loss of it may well destroy him.

Alex took a step back from her. She turned to look at him, eyes sorrowful and hopeful at the same time, and something inside him quivered. No. He didn't want this. Didn't want to feel anything that wasn't physical. Didn't want to feel this sudden intense need for her, the sound of her voice, a desire to see laughter in her eyes, the yearning to just hold her close and not let her go again. Utter recklessness to surrender to any kind of emotion, yet even as he thought that, he knew that somehow she'd touched a part of him that no woman ever had before.

No reason to it, no reason for it, other than an inexplicable capitulation.

And then she was in his arms, the sweet scent of her filling his world, the whisper of his name on her lips the sweetest sound he'd ever heard, and he kissed her tenderly on the lips, her closed eyelids, the lovely curve of her cheek...and he knew that he'd never want any more from life than this.

They found a secluded corner, an alcove of the keep that was quiet and private this time of the evening, and they sat upon stuffed cushions padding the stone ledge in front of a window that looked out over the Black Ravine. Deep shadows hid the trees and brush, and in the distance the pink and purple light had deepened to dusk. Velvet curtains hid them from view, muffled any sound from beyond, shrouded them in silence save their own whispers.

Gillian told him of her loneliness and years of emptiness, how she'd longed for someone to cherish her, of crushing disappointments, and he thought how brave she was for standing up to the English who'd killed her husband. She'd not cowered but met them in the hall, invoking right and privilege for herself and her household, until the commander had allowed them all to leave unmolested. An amazing feat. He held her hands, pressing them as if to give her strength when it was far too late to undo what had been already done.

She leaned into him, put her head against his shoulder, and after a moment of shared silence, she put her face up to be kissed. It seemed the most natural thing in the world, and felt as if he shared something precious.

He should have known, and maybe he had, but after a few minutes, kissing wasn't enough for either of them. Leaning into her, touching her, his weight pressed her back into the cushions. She felt so good beneath him, her skin smelling of lavender, her hair soft and silky between his fingers, the rise of her breasts above the bodice of her gown a temptation he couldn't resist.

Somehow he was lying atop her, his plaide up, his hand beneath the heavy folds of her skirt, skimming over smooth

flesh to find the vee between her thighs. She shuddered when
he brushed his hand over the damp cleft, then found the nubbin
that gave her such pleasure. A cool breeze whispered over
them from the open window, smelling of summer, heat leached
from the air by long hours of dusk. Gillian shivered, and he
kissed her lush open lips again.

Magic...it felt like magic to be with her like this, to feel
this unexpected, unfamiliar tenderness that was almost
overwhelming.

He deepened the kiss, tasting the sweetness of her mouth,
all his senses heightened to an intensity he'd never experienced
before. Everything seemed sweeter, deeper, richer, and the
very air shimmered with promise. She made him feel things
he'd never felt before, feel them in ways he'd never dreamed
existed, and he didn't want to pause to examine all the reasons
for it. He'd never been the kind of man for introspection like
some, been a man more accustomed to action than long nights
before the fire discussing philosophy and theology with
companions. Once, perhaps, he would have been that man.
But that privilege had been taken from him by the necessity
for survival.

Yet even survival was forgotten in the sweet delight of the
moment.

Gillian arched up into his hand, her hips thrusting against
his fingers as they slid wetly over her crevice, stroking her,
teasing the tiny nub until she cried out and he knew she'd
found release. Slowly, he stroked back the hair from her eyes,
held her shuddering body until she grew quiet, inhaling the musky
scent of her, the sweet fragrance she wore mixing with the
exciting scent of a passionate woman. It was heady, arousing.

After a moment, he began to caress her again, fingers
sliding over satiny smooth skin until she sighed with pleasure.

"Alex...how can something so sinful feel so wonderful?"

"God has a perverse sense of humor, perhaps."

She laughed, throatily, arching into his caress. Then her
hand reached beneath his plaide and found him, fingers circling
his hard length, rubbing over him as he throbbed against her
cool hand. The sensitive head of his cock pushed hard into her
palm, and he closed his eyes and groaned, a deep sound low in
the back of his throat.

"You weep for me, Sir Alex," she whispered against his
ear, and he thrust more fiercely, sliding slickly into her grasp.

Erotic shudders rippled through him, and he gave himself over to the exquisite sensation, forgetting everything but the moment.

Rubbing him, Gillian delighted in his response. It thrilled her to know she could elicit such strong reactions with her touch. Teasing him, she brushed her fingertips over him in light, feathery caresses, then more firmly, reveling in the way he pushed into her hand in a silent demand for more. Then she slid her free hand under him, cupping his stones in her palm in a soft caress that made him groan. His sac tightened, his erection hardened, and he nudged her legs apart with his knees, his weight pushing her deep into the cushions as he lifted himself over her.

Lunging forward, he slid inside her so swiftly she had no time to prepare. Her body closed around him greedily, stretched to accommodate his length, vibrations rippling through her when he pushed still deeper. Tension heightened, expanded, and he slid his hands beneath her hips to lift her slightly. Her fingers curled around his upper arms and she held on as he rocked forward, filling her completely. Raking her hands down his back, she scored him with her nails as she eagerly met his thrusts, crying out her need in his ear until he muffled her cries with his mouth, a hot, fierce kiss that stole her breath.

It was over quickly, the explosion fierce and high and hot, washing over her in exquisite tides that left her limp and breathless. Before the waves receded, he pulled free of her, his turgid cock wet and still ready. She sighed softly.

"No, we're not quite done yet, sweet lady," he murmured, and she looked down at him with wonder.

It was slightly embarrassing that she'd been so wanton and he hadn't lost control, but then he eased her up from the cushions and turned her around, his hands on her making her forget.

Darkness yawned beyond the alcove, sweet night air soft and bird calls melodic, their bower a secluded refuge. Alex caressed her quivering thighs, pressed small kisses on her bare flesh, slid his hands under her to pull down the bodice of her gown and tease her swollen nipples. They formed taut buds at his touch, tiny points of arousal that he ministered to until she began to squirm and a slow, heavy pulse throb between her thighs again. She lifted her hips in invitation and he accepted, sliding forward so that his cock scraped across the sensitive folds of flesh between her legs. Her thighs closed around him, and she rocked backward, movements growing frantic as she sought release. When it came, Alex quickly slid inside her again, slamming into her body as she convulsed around him in climax, so that she buried her face into the velvet cushions to stifle her screams of ecstasy.

They collapsed together, spent, embracing with her tucked into the angle of his chest and thighs, his arms wound around her as she held onto him. These stolen moments were precious, even with the danger of discovery just beyond thin curtains. It would have to end one day, but not now. Hopefully, not for a long time.

For now, she held tightly to him and prayed that whatever fate was in store for them, it would be kind.

Five

They met often in the next weeks, stealing time and privacy
where they could find it, not wanting to be noticed. Gillian could
scarcely believe her own actions, but couldn't resist the emotions
that welled up so strongly they were undeniable. It was more
than just physical, though that lure drew her to him as if by an
invisible chain. A glance across the crowded hall could leave
her breathless, pulse racing, knees weak, and skin tingling as if
he'd actually touched her. Never had she dreamed she could
feel this way about anyone, especially not a man like Sir Alex.

He was no baron, naught but a knight in the service of the
Bruce, loyal, and at times even savage, but nothing like she'd
been brought up to believe of the kind of men from the western
Highlands. There was a gentleness to him that he didn't often
show to others, but she saw it in the way he touched her lightly,
a soft caress, in the way he talked to children in the keep, or
even cared for his horse. It showed her a side of him not many
bothered to see. Especially Alyce.

"If you think yon worthy knight will be true to one woman,"
Alyse sidled up next to her to say as Gillian left the hall one
evening, "you hope for the impossible. He tups every female
he can."

Gillian turned to look at her. Torchlight spit and sputtered
in sconces on the walls, and shadows shrouded the far end of
the corridor. Alyse's eyes glittered in the torchlight. Her mouth
turned down at the corners, and she stood with both hands on
her hips.

"Are you speaking to me, perchance?" Gillian asked coolly.

"Yea, my lady fool, I am indeed."

"Be wary, Alyse, for your jealousy is evident."

"Jealous? Of you?" Alyse tossed her head and narrowed
her eyes. "Nay, my fine lady, I am not jealous of any other
woman!"

Gillian just smiled, and Alyse glared at her. When she
walked away, she felt Alyse's gaze on her, as pointed and sharp
as daggers. It did not bode well.

Talk in the hall that night was of recent events. Since the
battle at Methven, all the lowlands of Scotland had been cowed
into submission by King Edward's harsh vengeance. Nothing
and no one, regardless of rank, was spared as English troops

raped, pillaged, and murdered at will with the king's sanction. For the past weeks, ever since barely escaping, Bruce and his men had hidden in the mountainous heather of Atholl so that stragglers from the battle could join them. Now he began to gather the remnants of his forces to him again. It was essential his women be brought under his protection, however great they might be endangered, because the danger was greater to leave them to Edward's mercy. So Bruce sent for the women—his wife, daughter, sister and attendants—to be brought to him.

Bruce's queen, Elizabeth, took the news calmly. Countess Buchan, Princess Marjorie, Gillian, and the king's sisters—Mary, who was wed to Bruce's comrade, Neil Campbell, and Christina, now twice-widowed by Edward's hand—steeled themselves for an arduous journey. It would be harrowing and dangerous, for they could scarcely pass unnoticed through the county when King Edward had many supporters and spies willing to betray their movements.

"Where can we go?" Gillian asked Alex on their last evening in Kildrummy. Her hands tightened on the stones of the parapet. A feeling of doom lowered with the purple evening shadows, and she tried to escape it. "It's dangerous to leave the safety of these walls."

"And more dangerous to stay. Longshanks will know Bruce's womenfolk are here and send forces to besiege the walls. Kildrummy is one of the safest keeps in Scotland, but any keep can be breached with enough time and treachery."

She turned to look at him in the fading light. "Treachery? You sound as if you expect it to happen."

He shook his head. "Nay, but 'tis always a risk. Things happen. Greedy men will do too much to keep what they have. Only men who have nothing to lose will risk everything."

"And you, Sir Alex?" She put a hand up to touch his jaw, fingers grazing the rough stubble of his half-grown beard. "What will you risk?"

A muscle flexed in his jaw and he looked past her, so that for a moment she thought he might not answer. Then he looked back at her, with the wind blowing back the hair from his face and dying daylight a pale gleam in his eyes.

"I have nothing to risk. Save you."

For a moment she couldn't breathe. He'd said it so softly, almost as if he didn't want her to hear him, but she had. And she felt the same. As if nothing mattered but being with him, but knowing he was near and she could see him, touch him, taste him…she'd not dreamed he may feel the same. Did he?

"Alex…"

He grabbed her wrists, held them tightly in his fists, eyes suddenly fierce in the waning light. "I'd risk everything for you, Gillian. Curse it all, I don't know how or why, but you mean more to me than life itself."

Leaning into him, she murmured, "Oh my heart…I love you so."

He didn't say the words, but he held her to him so tightly she knew he felt the same. And it was enough for now.

* * * *

Morning broke, and as they left the safety of Kildrummy for the uncertainty of Aberdeen, Gillian cast a glance back at the castle. Illuminated by the light of the rising sun, it reminded her that she'd found love where most unexpected, and perhaps all would be well after all. It was a hope she intended to nourish.

Three days into the journey, a small band of Edward's men stumbled across them just before daylight. The fight was swift and intense. Flames from a slumbering campfire ate across sheaves of grass, smoke boiled upward and the camp collapsed into confusion. Tents caught on fire, women and children screamed, horses panicked and men shouted as the clash of swords rang loud and deadly over all. Gillian's heart pounded with fear.

Alex had rolled to his feet at the first sound and pulled her up with him. Neither had taken off any garments, save for their shoes. Gillian couldn't find hers in the dim light but there was no time to search.

"Gillian, go with the queen," Alex said in her ear, and led her to the line of trees where the horses were tied and men worked to free them for the women and children. "You will be safe with the others."

"Alex—"

He kissed her fiercely, then disappeared into the battle.

Heart thudding, Gillian saw that the queen and two of her ladies had the children close and were being mounted on horses to be taken to safety. It was cool and her teeth chattered. The twigs and stones beneath her bare feet cut her skin. She glanced over her shoulder. Only a few yards away lay her cloak and shoes, beneath the tree where they'd slept.

"I must fetch my shoes and cloak," she said to one of the

men holding the horses, "they are only over there."

He said gruffly, "Do not tarry, my lady. We dare not wait."

Cooking utensils had been knocked over, tents abandoned. Clothes lay strewn about. She grabbed her cloak and put on her shoes, then turned back to the trees and hesitated. There were so many…so many horses and men, all a blur so that she could only tell English from Scots by their shields. Uncertain, she looked around, and glimpsed the queen and ladies riding away. *No!*

Stumbling, she fell over a downed man, screamed when she saw his eyes stare sightlessly up at the sky. Blood smeared her hands. She screamed again, and when she pushed up and away from him, his nearly severed head bobbed as if nodding. Sobbing, panicked now, she shoved the loose hair from her eyes and looked around wildly. It was so dark. Smoke spread thick and black, choking her, and in the chaos she couldn't find her way. Red and black all around, blood and fire, clouds of smoke….

Paralyzed by fear and confusion, she stood clutching her cloak to her chest. She felt faint and terrified. Finally she forced her feet to move forward, but only to find herself blocked by men locked in mortal combat. She stopped, turned, and ran in the opposite direction. Terror lent her strength, but nothing looked familiar. The ground shook with the pounding of hooves and fierce fighting all around her. Metal clashed, men screamed, horses bellowed. A mounted Englishman rode toward her, his eyes glittering behind the nose guard of his conical helmet, sword held high. She looked around wildly but saw no escape. If she was to die, it would not be as a coward.

Chin lifted, she squared her shoulders, said a prayer to the Blessed Virgin that she keep Alex safe, and looked the soldier in his eyes as she waited for his sword to end her life.

A Gaelic curse rose above the pandemonium, and Alex ran toward her out of the hellish smoke, backlit by flame, a bloodied sword in his hand. The English soldier turned his mount toward Alex and lifted his sword high to cut him down. Gillian screamed. In a blink of an eye, the rider was on the ground, sword and arm lying several feet away as Alex snagged the frantic horse's reins to stop its flight. Eyes wild, lather flecking nose and breast, the horse shied away before he brought it back around. Alex gave it a soothing word and swung atop, then turned the mount around to come close to her.

He looked down at her with a cocky grin and put out his hand. "Come wi' me, lass."

Gillian put up her hand to catch his. With the horse dancing and flames licking toward them, he leaned down and scooped her into his arms, and galloped from the fray. They crashed through trees and splashed across a small burn until the queen could be seen not far ahead. Alex reined the horse to a halt and slid to the ground, then put the reins into Gillian's hand.

"Flee with the queen. I'll join you soon."

"Stay with me," she cried, grabbing at him, but he only grinned again and ran back to rejoin the fighting, disappearing into trees wreathed in smoke and licking red tongues of flame. Heart in her throat, she joined the queen and ladies. She was safe, but what of Alex?

They rode on, guarded by a small band of men, riding over barren hills and into green dales. No one spoke. All waited for the sound of loved ones or pursuit.

At last, in the distance, horsemen could be seen riding after them. Gillian knew her heart couldn't be the only one in her throat as they watched to see if 'twould be Scot or English.

"The Bruce," Lady Buchan said suddenly. "I see his shield."

Relief made Gillian near giddy, and the queen smiled though tears of joy streaked her face. It seemed forever before the survivors of the brief battle joined them. There had been some losses, but far more inflicted upon the enemy.

Anxiously, Gillian looked Alex over for signs of injury, but he only grinned and took her by the hand. "'Tis but scratches, my love, not an arm lost."

She raised a brow. "You're covered in soot. I'd not know if you had all your parts or not."

His grin widened and he leaned close so no one else could hear. "I still have the most important parts, my love, as I shall prove to you later when we have a pallet of heather beneath our backs and the stars above."

"You are a mad Highland rogue, Alex Campbell."

"Aye. That I am, my lady."

* * * *

Aberdeen lay on Scotland's eastern coast, the town nudging against the North Sea. It was near dark when they arrived, fading light blending purple sky and the line of blue sea together as if stitched by a master hand. It'd been an exhausting journey

with little rest and a sense of urgency overriding all, and Gillian
stumbled as she dismounted. Countess Buchan caught her, a
quick hand supporting her.

"Only a wee bit farther, Lady Gillian," she said briskly, and
her smile was kind and as weary as Gillian felt, "and we can all
rest safely."

"For a time."

"Aye," Lady Isabel agreed, "for a time. Pray we are
successful in our quest, for I greatly fear that our enemies may
yet thwart us."

It was a fear that was constantly in all their minds, whether
remarked upon or not, for the English had been relentless in
their pursuit of Robert Bruce, and would not hesitate to use his
womenfolk against him. It was, after all, war. Niceties were
discarded on both sides.

Gillian nodded understanding, noting Lady Isabel's dark-
circled eyes, the fatigue in her lovely face. They were all soul-
weary, frightened, yet determined not to yield to weakness.
Even the queen betrayed rare moments of fear, but more for
her beloved husband and child than for herself.

None had made complaints on the journey, even the children
unnaturally silent. There hadn't seemed to be any conversation
suitable. It was as if a smothering cloak had been dropped
upon the land, suffocating hope.

"There will be food and rest inside," Lady Buchan said
kindly, and Gillian smiled.

"Yea, I yearn most for a soft seat that doesn't constantly
jar my insides. It's been a rocky ride."

Laughing, Isabel accompanied her into the keep, where
they found roasted meat, bannocks and ale waiting for them. A
fire burned, welcome if too smoky. With her stomach quieted
and a soft cushion beneath her, Gillian grew drowsy sitting
near the warmth of the blaze, and struggled to keep her eyes
open.

It was only when a strong arm circled her waist and another
slid beneath her that she realized she must have fallen asleep,
and jerked back. Alex laughed softly.

"You are like to fall into the logs, m'lady, if you are not
removed."

Flushing, Gillian slid a glance toward the queen and her
ladies, and saw Isabel smile and nod. *She knew.* That wasn't
surprising, of course, as even at Kildrummy it was impossible

to hide things for long, but it was a bit embarrassing to realize that everyone knew.

Alex leaned close to whisper in her ear, "'Tis well, lovely lady, that none disapprove."

Startled, she glanced up to meet his eyes. No one, save Lady Alyse, had expressed condemnation, it was true. Perhaps it wasn't because they had been discreet, but because there was a tacit approval. It was a novel thing, to feel a sense of freedom in the knowledge that her relationship with this rough Highlander need no longer be hidden.

"Aye," she whispered ruefully to Alex, "it seems that our liaison is no longer private."

"Discreet, yea. Private—never. Come, sweet lady, and I shall escort you to a quieter spot where you may find rest."

The keep was crowded, and privacy nonexistent. Alex wrapped them both in his plaide and made a cushion of straw in a shadowed nook. It was safe here in his arms, held against the heated length of his body. His breath against her cheek in the dark alcove was a reminder that he would keep her safe. Gillian fell asleep almost instantly.

* * * *

Alex lay awake long into the night. Danger was real and close. Generations of a chivalric code meant nothing to this English king. Edward made it evident he intended to win no matter the cost or code. Never before had Alex felt such fear. Not for himself, but for the lovely lady at his side. Now he knew what it was to be crippled by emotion, by love for a woman that bade him do everything necessary to keep her safe, even against all odds. Even at peril of his own life.

Perhaps Bruce meant to embark from Aberdeen and seek aid from Norway. His eldest sister Isabel was Dowager Queen there, and would certainly offer safe harbor to the women at the least. It would be a relief to know they were safe, even if a great distance away.

It seemed that his speculations were wrong, for after meeting with the Bishop of Moray, the bishop left for the Orkneys that belonged to Norway, and Bruce and his womenfolk and a force of near five hundred men struck west to the mountainous region that lay on the borders of Perthshire and Argyll. Word had come that the Earl of Pembroke was advancing toward them, and Bruce meant to reach the Western Isles and his old friends, the Macdonalds of Islay. It was a long and arduous journey with the women's comfort to be heeded, and danger at their backs.

By early August they had reached Tyndrum at the head of Strathfillan beyond Loch Tay, and camped near the shrine of St. Fillan of Glenlochart. Bruce had a purpose for the visit to the tomb of the Irish saint, it seemed. He had come to ask absolution from the Abbot of Inchafray for desecrating Greyfriars Kirk with the murder of Red Comyn. With his army gathered around him, he knelt to receive the abbot's blessing for all to hear.

There, on a clear day with the blue sky above and the ancient stones of St Fillan's Priory behind them, Robert Bruce knelt on a green slope as the abbot intoned the rites of absolution. For the superstitious among them, it reaffirmed their faith in Bruce and their cause. The mood after was lighter and more confident, as they camped on the hillsides near the River Fillan.

For Alex Campbell, the time and place provided opportunity. Taking Lady Gillian by the hand, he asked her if she would wed him, not knowing what the answer would be but hoping for the best. For a long moment, she gazed at him, her amber eyes reflecting emotional turmoil. Then she nodded.

"Yea, Sir Alex, I will wed thee," she whispered, and he folded her hands between his larger ones and smiled.

"There is little time, my love. The abbot must waive the banns. We dare not tarry here too long, for our enemies are always close behind." He pulled her to him, breathing in the scent of her hair that still smelled sweet even after days of dust and travel. Never had he thought to wed, not even his first love so long ago when he'd been a youth still foolish enough to dream.

In the distance rose Ben Lui, a towering crag that cast a long shadow over the stream and glen cloaked in heather. Broad swathes of purple ended in brown folds of rising hills that seemed to touch the sky. To marry on the steps of the priory would be a lovely memory.

"I must request permission from the Bruce, as he is my new overlord." he said, "but I do not think he will deny us."

Robert Bruce smiled slightly, his gaze moving from Alex to Gillian and back. "She is the daughter of the Earl of Wakefield, and the widow of David Montgomery, is she not?"

"Aye, sire. Now she is the queen's lady in waiting. We ask your permission to wed before leaving the priory, if the abbot will agree."

"And you, Lady Gillian? You wish to wed Sir Alex?"

"Yea, sire, I do." She looked up to meet his eyes, and her hand found Alex's as if for reassurance. He squeezed it lightly, and saw that Bruce had noticed the gesture, for he smiled.

"I give it gladly, but the wedding night will not be what it should. We must leave early on the morrow. The Lord of Lorne has learned of our presence on his lands, and it is dangerous to delay."

Lorne was a son-in-law of the murdered Red Comyn, and would avenge his kinsman's death at Bruce's hands. He would be determined in a pursuit to the death, for the rewards would be twofold: King Edward's gratitude, and the satisfaction of vengeance.

Alex left Gillian in the queen's tent and approached the abbot near St Fillan's well. It was said to have remarkable curative powers since being blessed by the saint. Inside the priory ruins, relics were carefully kept and revered, the saints left arm and hand that had lit up a room so he might read in the darkness, and the crozier of the staff he carried, and a bell that was said to have come to him when he called. These relics were sacred to all of Scotland, making the abbot's position even more powerful.

To his chagrin, the abbot refused to conduct the ceremony or allow a marriage to take place at the priory. "I am sorry, my son, but banns must be posted and permission granted from the bride's family."

"The bride's family is unavailable. Permission has been given by the king."

Still, the abbot would not consent. Angry, Alex stormed away, stalking up the hillside to cool his temper on an outcropping of rocks that overlooked a waterfall. There had been censure in the abbot's eyes when he looked at him, as if he knew a knight was not good enough to wed a lady like Gillian. He was reaching above himself. Tossing a pebble into the water tumbling over the rocks, he grudgingly thought that he agreed with the abbot. She was too far above his rank, and in all other ways. He was aspiring to heights he should not dare. A bitterness burned in the back of his throat.

He'd been a fool. Caught up in what he wanted, he hadn't thought that the daughter of an earl would be unsuitable for the son of a laird. Not even a son who had been knighted by Bruce himself. War may have turned Scotland upside down, but it had not erased the class differences.

In the distance could be heard the noise of the camp, but here above the waterfall he heard only the shattering of his dream. Now he knew why he'd not allowed himself to be vulnerable. It tasted like ashes in his mouth to see hope slip away.

Six

Gillian found him above the waterfall. Evening light had dwindled to purple shadows. Soon it would be dark by this time of evening, the long winter nights ahead spent inside by the warm fire. Perhaps wrapped in her blankets with her husband...

"Alex?" She knelt beside him, saw from the expression on his face that all was not well. She had half-expected this. "Tell me—did the abbot refuse permission?"

"Aye." He glanced at her sideways, his mouth twisting as he said wryly, "He made it plain that a man such as myself should not look so far above his station."

"He said that?"

"Nay, he did not have to say it. I understood what he meant. Gillian—my lady—it pains me to admit it, but he's right. I should never have—"

"Don't you dare say it," she said so fiercely that he gave her a sharp look, "don't you dare say we are not meant to be together!"

"Lady Gillian—"

"I mean it, Alex Campbell, do not utter those words! For the first time in my life I have found love, and I do not mean to let you go without a fight. If you think King Edward is a fierce adversary, you will find me even more so."

For a long moment he just looked at her, then a smile tugged at the corners of his mouth and he opened his arms. She leaned into him with a sigh of relief as he nuzzled her hair. "I do not deserve you, my sweet lady. I have nothing to recommend me but my heart.'

"That is more than enough for me. Wherever you are, there will I also be, whether in the finest castle or the meanest cottage, it matters not to me."

"I greatly fear the last is more likely than the first," he said ruefully, tipping her face up to look her in the eyes. "If we lose Scotland to Edward, prison or death will be our reward. I do not wish that for you."

"Nor I for you. But I do not wish to stay in a world without you."

"Then I had best make certain we win this war against Edward, I see."

"Yea, so you should." She smiled, and he took her hands

between his and leaned forward to kiss her lips. The gentle kiss swiftly became demanding and urgent, and she responded as if their time together may indeed be short.

"Come with me," he lifted his head to say huskily, "where we are not so easily seen."

They picked their way down the steep slope beside the waterfalls, ducking beneath the branches of bay willows that grew in the shallow waters. Tussocks of moss that had gone from green to yellow made a soft cushion. Water slid and tumbled over rocks down the steep slopes, joining with a stream that ran into the river. More trees lined the stream, a barricade against prying eyes.

Lowering her to the cushion of bog moss, Alex held her gaze, his eyes burning into her as if he intended to memorize her features, as if he would never see her again, and Gillian's heart lurched. "You will never leave me, my love, say you will not," she whispered, and he brushed back the hair from her eyes.

"Never willingly, my lady love. Should miles ever part us, I will always be with you here, in your heart and memories." He lay his palm gently on her breast.

Tears sprang to her eyes, and she gripped him so tightly her fingers ached from it. "Time and distance may come between us, but never doubt that we will be together again. For all time, for all eternity."

"Yea, my lady love," he murmured, "for all eternity."

Kissing her mouth, her cheek, the arch of her throat, his lips moved like flames down to her breasts. Cool air feathered lightly over them when he pulled down her bodice, but she was warmed by the heat of his mouth, the hot rush of blood through her veins, and the steady drumming of sweet tension he aroused with his lips and hands. Achingly precious were these stolen moments, made more so by the knowledge that their time together was almost certain to be short. He would have to go fight, and she would have to remain behind. Since time began it had been this way, men marching off to war and leaving behind weeping wives, loves, and families...perhaps one day there would be no need for war, but for now that was only a dream. For now, she had to make the most of her time with Alex.

With his hands cupping her breasts he dragged his tongue around the tight peaks before he closed his lips and drew first one, then the other into his mouth, a steady suction that made her stomach knot. Delicious fever spread through her entire body. Writhing beneath him, she arched her back and lifted her hips, a silent invitation that he ignored. Teasing her breasts with his lips and hand, he slid his free hand beneath her skirts to caress the tiny nub that gave her so much pleasure. Faster, as tension stretched so tightly she thought she may explode, he rubbed her until finally release shattered like a white-hot star coursing through her entire body.

"Nay," he said softly when she roused and reached for him again, "we have the rest of the day to ourselves. Come."

As purple shadows deepened on the hills around them, he coaxed her into the waterfalls. The water was cold, splashing around them, and she squealed like a small child when he pulled her into the shallow pool that fed into the stream. Spitting out geysers of water, she laughed as he caught her beneath the arms.

"Can you swim, m'lady?"

"No, but that is why there are boats." Wiping water from her eyes, she blinked at him. "If you intend to drown me, you'll need deeper water than this."

"I'll not drown you, lass, for 'tis said that witches float."

Gillian promptly splashed water in his face, then leaped atop him and tried to duck him beneath the water. Spluttering and floundering, he choked out, "I yield, I yield!"

"Take it back, you Highland rogue. Say that you never called me a witch."

Before he could speak, she ducked him again, and when he came up this time, he caught her around the waist. Holding her tight he said, "You know I only jested, for there is none fairer or more beauteous than you, my lady. Your hair is like silk, your eyes like gold coins, your teeth like pearls, and your skin—"

"Continue and I'll duck you again," she warned, laughing at their play.

He grinned at her, and with his dark hair plastered to his head and his eyes alight with laughter, he was so handsome that her heart lurched. A comely man, indeed, strong yet so tender at times he made her ache with love for him.

"You are," he said, "a most fierce adversary. I see that I shall have to be cautious."

"Indeed." She put her arms around his neck and her legs

around his waist as he held her. Shivering at the cool wind over her wet body, she snuggled closer.

"I'd best warm you before you take sick," he said, and took her to the banks where their clothes lay airing on bushes. He sat her upon a tussock and dried her briskly with his plaide, until she complained that he was rubbing away a layer of skin. "That would be a hanging offense," he murmured, and pressed a kiss upon the pulse at her wrist.

Gillian grew still, and he wrapped his plaide around her shoulders as he knelt in front of her, clad only in what God had given him. Broad chest, strong arms, sinews and muscles defined by faint light, gleamed wetly. A fine man, yea, a fine man indeed.

His hands moved to her thighs to spread them gently apart, and she drew in a sharp breath as he slid his fingers over her skin to touch her between the legs. He bent to press a kiss upon her knee, then higher up her thigh. His lips were hot against her chilled flesh, searing her like flames. Then to her shock he slid his hands beneath her hips to lift her slightly for his tongue. It flickered over her in a caress that made her moan, and she held her breath as he moved ever closer to the tiny nub at the top of her crevice. His lips closed around it and he drew it into his mouth, and her entire body shuddered.

It was wicked…it had to be, for nothing that felt this good could be anything else but a sin. Her hands clenched into the wool plaide and the breath locked in her lungs. Alex's tongue flicked against her again and again, until her entire body convulsed and she cried out his name. Nothing had ever felt like this, nor had she imagined it could. Panting for breath, she collapsed atop the tussock, and barely felt him come to lie beside her, wrapping them both in the plaide.

Cradling her as she slowly drifted back from the heights, Alex began again to arouse her with his hands and mouth, taking his time. As tension began to build again, she grew more bold. She slid her hand under the plaide and found him hard and ready for her. Her fingers plied along the turgid length of his shaft, gently at first, then with firmer strokes until she could tell from his ragged breathing that he was as ready as she. Spreading her thighs wide, she lifted her hips so the velvety soft head of his shaft rested against her.

"Now, my love," she murmured against his ear, and he slid into her with exquisitely deliberate slowness so that she felt every inch of him filling her, rubbing against her tight heat until he filled her completely. Then he began to move, withdrawing slightly only to plunge forward again so that it seemed as if he went even deeper with each stroke, in and out as she held tightly to his arms. The drag and thrust of his hard cock inside her quickly brought her to the very point of release again, and she hovered there for only a moment before he went so deep inside her it felt like they were one person, one body, joined forever...

Trembling, she held tightly to him, unable to let him go for even a moment, wanting him like this for as long as she could, and after the briefest resistance, he gave a last deep thrust and went still. Instead of pulling out quickly as he always did, he waited too late. Groaning, he rested his head beside hers, muttering, "Sweet love...I did not mean...I should have stopped..."

"It's all right." Gillian pressed her lips to the bare skin of his shoulder. "'Twill be all right, my love." She prayed she spoke the truth.

* * * *

Early the next morn, the camp broke up and started for the Dalry pass. It was a narrow defile that barely allowed a single horseman through at a time, with rocks rising high on each side. It happened so suddenly that Alex had time only for reaction. Half-naked Highlanders swooped down from the slopes on both sides, slashing with long Lochaber axes at the bellies and undersides of the horses and bringing many down. Screams of wounded men and horses filled the air and the ground soaked up the blood of the slain. Bruce shouted the order for retreat and they withdrew, gathering around the king and all circling about the women to protect them.

"Lodge the women in yon small castle on the isle in Loch Dochart," Bruce ordered, "for if we make a stand here, we're likely to lose most of our horses and be at their mercy."

Wounded in the fray, James Douglas said grimly, "'Tis the Macdougall clan with Lorne, and I saw a few of the MacIndrosser clan with him as well."

"Lorne is determined to bring our heads to Edward however he can. We must get the women to safety," Bruce replied.

The route to the isle in Loch Dochart lay along a narrow track that ran between a steep hillside and the deep waters of the loch. Marshaling the women ahead of them, they managed

to go at a fast pace, while Bruce and a few men remained at
the rear to face the pursuing forces that caught up with them
before they reached the loch. It was a fierce fight. Again and
again the Highlanders under Lord Lorne attacked, but were
kept at bay. In desperation and anger, Lorne sent three men to
ambush Bruce at a place where the loch and the rock cliff
came so close that a horse could barely turn.

Alex saw them and shouted a warning, but from his position
could only watch as they leaped upon Bruce when he passed
beneath the rocks where they waited. One seized his bridle,
but Bruce cut his arm and shoulder from his body. The other
two jumped on him, but the king fought so viciously they could
not prevail, and were cut down. When the others who pursued
him saw Bruce's valiant feat of arms, they were afraid to follow
any longer, and he was able to join the others waiting ahead.

Even though they had saved some horses and men, the
losses had been enough that Bruce knew the risks to the women
were too great to continue on with them. The only route to the
west was blocked by his enemies, so he altered his previous
plans. He handed over all the surviving horses to his brother
Nigel and the Earl of Atholl, and bade them escort the queen
and her companions with as many men as could be mounted
back to Kildrummy Castle. Once the women had time to
recover from their exhausting journey, they were to rejoin the
Bishop of Moray in the Orkneys, while Nigel was to fortify
and defend the castle against the approaching English to hold
them in check as long as possible.

"And I will take the other men to the heather with me to
bypass my foes to the south," he said wearily, and looked up at
the somber men gathered around him. Most were bloodstained
and grime-caked, as was he. The situation was dire, and all
knew it far too well.

Alex did his best to allay Gillian's fears, knowing that to
sow seeds of doubt could well alarm all the women and make
them more susceptible to panic. He should have known she'd
see through his efforts.

Searching his face with her amber eyes, she nodded slowly.
"I understand. Will you travel to Kildrummy with us, or must I
part with you here?"

"I'm to go with you as far as Kildrummy, then I'm to leave
there and see what I can find out about Edward's movements.
It'll only be for a little while," he added when her eyes widened,

"then I'll join you before you leave with the bishop."

"Yea," she said in a faint voice, "I'll pray for that."

"Gillian, sweet love—it's only for a little while."

She leaned forward to press her face against his chest. "If only I could believe that. But I feel...I don't know, I feel somehow as if the fates are against us. Oh Alex—I cannot live without you!"

He hugged her tightly, his throat closing. "Don't say that," he managed to get out gruffly, "for we must be parted for a time. But not forever. Never that. Life could not be so cruel."

"I want to think that, but I look around and I see just how cruel life truly is, dead children and the elderly—lands wasted, the earth scorched where nothing can live on it. And I have to wonder, is it worth it? The fighting, the killing...is it worth it in the end? Is it worth losing all that you love to win?"

For a moment he could not answer. Never before had he had anything to lose so he'd not pondered these questions, but now he feared her loss more than anything he could ever have imagined. "Nay," he said slowly, "nothing would be worth losing you, not even Scotland."

She smiled. "I know you don't truly mean that, but 'tis nice to hear."

He clasped her hands tightly. "But I do mean it. God help me, I do. Never have I felt like this about a woman, not even Mary."

Her brow lifted. "Mary?"

Grinning, he said, "Aye, I was near ten and she lived across the braes, a fair lass with hair as red as an autumn apple. I swore to marry her one day, but she loved another. Near broke my heart."

"And that is when you swore off women?"

"Aye. Fickle creatures. All save you."

She put up her hand to touch the cut upon his face. He'd forgotten about it, a token of the battle just past. "It needs tending," she murmured. "Come with me. I'll see to your hurts."

Taking her hand in his, he jested, "That is not all that needs tending, my fair lady."

That summoned another smile from her, but it lacked real amusement. He wanted to reassure her, to swear that all would be well, but she would recognize the promise for what it was and know better: Only hope.

Parting was poignant, Bruce bidding his queen and their

twelve-year old daughter a stoic yet sorrowful farewell, not knowing if they would ever see one another again. They left then, with Robert Bruce watching from the hillside as the little group of women and their cavalcade of mounted men disappeared beyond the loch.

It was an arduous journey through the mountains of Atholl and Braemar all the way to the castle on Deeside. Nigel Bruce did his best to entertain them with jests and wry comments, but for the most part, they were a solemn group. Nights had grown colder, and Alex lay wrapped in a blanket with Gillian, both too numb from cold and desolation to do more than hug each other all during the night hours. Days had grown shorter, the month of August gone and September new when they reached Kildrummy at last.

The familiar walls rose starkly against the cloudy sky, rain threatening to turn the grounds to mud when the bridge was lowered and they crossed into the bailey. Men ran to take their horses and Alex helped Gillian down himself, taking the opportunity to hold her close.

"We're here," she murmured in relief, "safe at last."

"Aye, Kildrummy is the most formidable castle in Scotland, well-provisioned and able to fight even a long siege if necessary. You'll be safe here, my love, until time to join the bishop."

Curling her fingers into his plaide, she looked up into his eyes. "Will you come for me? When this is all over, when 'tis safe for you to travel—will you meet me, Alex?"

"Yea, love, wherever you are, however distant you are, I will find you and meet you, if it takes an eternity."

She lay her cheek against his chest. "It might, you know. The war goes on so long, and it seems as if 'twill never end."

"No matter. I will come for you, I swear it."

"I believe you. I'll wait for you."

"When this is over and we are together again, we'll wed in the little kirk on my father's land. It will be mine again, and after we're wed we'll live in my keep that overlooks Loch Leven. It's a small keep, but beautiful."

"'Ey there, look about now," a rough voice said, and Alex turned as the blacksmith of the keep gestured at him to move. "Ye're in me way."

"There's no hurry, Osborne," Alex said coldly. "The horses will be here a while."

"Aye, but me supper willna stay. Nor yours, I warrant."

It was on the tip of his tongue to sharply rebuke the blacksmith for being rude to a lady, but a look at Gillian's exhausted face changed his mind. With his arm around her shoulders, he escorted her into the castle hall, where a bright fire burned a welcome and the tempting fragrance of roast meat and hot bread made his stomach growl.

The long trestle table was quickly loaded with trenchers of meat and platters of bannocks. Pitchers of ale were passed along the benches to fill eager cups. Heated by the fire and bellies full at last, most quickly found their pallets or rolled up in blankets along the walls. The queen and her ladies retired to her chamber, but Gillian remained with Alex.

Drowsy, she rested her head on his shoulder and watched logs burn, squinting slightly at the acrid smoke curling up to the high ceiling. Alex held her against him, content to allow her to sleep in his arms. Even Alyse had ceased her bitter comments now, exhausted as the rest and no longer seeming to care.

Perhaps he would have slept there near the fire all night with Gillian, but Nigel Bruce sent a summons to the solar. Easing Gillian down to sleep wrapped in a blanket, he joined the men, and saw from their faces that the news was not good.

"The Earl of Pembroke is already in Aberdeen with his troops. He awaits only the arrival of the Prince of Wales and his army with their siege engines to attack Kildrummy. We dare not let the queen and her ladies linger. They must leave before first light in the morn. Atholl will take a few of his men and see them to the Orkneys by way of Dornoch Firth."

"But that is in Easter Ross," Alex said with a frown, and Nigel nodded.

"Aye, so 'tis, but they can take a ship from there to the Orkneys."

"The Earl of Ross supports the Comyns. If he learns of their presence, he may well take them hostage. Edward will use them harshly, I fear."

"Then it is up to Atholl not to be caught," Nigel said simply. "It is their only hope."

All the men were silent for a few minutes, as the danger to the women was too great to allow them to stay at Kildrummy, but still great for them to journey over a hundred miles without an army at their side. Yet it must be done. There was no alternative.

It was near midnight when Alex returned to where Gillian

slept still in her blankets, rolled up like a child, her hands clasped
and cushioned beneath her cheek. He watched her for a long
time without waking her, lost in admiration of her fair skin,
parted lips, even the heart-shaped curve to her ear...when he
could wait no more, he lifted a strand of her golden hair, dusty
now from their travels but still soft and silky in his palm. She
woke slowly, blinking her long lashes then smiling when she
saw him.

"Is't morn already?"

"Nay, my love. I'm being selfish. Our time here together is
very short, I fear, as you must leave before daylight."

Her eyes widened, catching the light from the fire and
gleaming. "*Nay*...so soon? But why must we part so soon?"

"It is too dangerous for the queen and her ladies to stay."
He told her of the earl awaiting the prince in Aberdeen, so
close to the castle, and that they must flee for their own safety,
then he held her while she wept. "Dinna greet, lass," he finally
got out though his own throat felt thick, and his voice came out
rough with the Highland burr of his youth. "Dinna greet..."

Yet still she wept, and he held her close until finally she
stopped, shuddering. After wiping away her tears, he lifted her
face with a finger beneath her chin. "Shall we find a quiet
place to say our farewells in privacy?"

She nodded, and he stood, pulling her up with him. They
picked their way around the sleeping forms scattered through
the hall. Cold shadows lay behind torchlight and the warmth of
the fire, and he guided her out of the hall and across the bailey
to the small alcove behind the blacksmith's forge. It was warm
there, though it had only straw for a bed, and he spread out his
plaide for a blanket. Clad in only his sherte and trews, he
lowered Gillian to the pallet and lay beside her. It would be
their last night together, perhaps for a long time. There was so
much he wanted to say, but words failed him. They'd said it all,
it seemed.

Silently, they undressed each other in the close warmth of
the fragrant alcove. Red-hot coals smoldered in the forge,
providing heat and light. Without preliminaries, both too impatient
to wait, he took her quickly, plunging his cock inside her warm,
damp core as she eagerly wrapped her legs around him and
lifted her hips for each thrust. Release came swiftly for both
of them, yet left them wanting more.

Slower now, he kissed her brow, her temples, her closed

eyes, then grazed her lips lightly. Moving down, his tongue washed over skin still dusty from their journey. A faint fragrance teased him, familiar and so sweet, the scent of her skin smelling still of heather. He had given her a spray to tuck into her hair on their journey, as they passed hills thick with it in bloom. A token, he said, when what he wanted to give her were jewels and fine furs instead. It was little enough to share, but she'd taken the heather as if the grandest gift in the world, smiling at him with such love in her eyes he'd been tongue-tied.

Now, knowing they were to part, he said the words that had always been so hard for him to say, even with her. "Lady mine," he whispered against her ear, "I love you more than life."

She took his face between her palms, tears shining in her eyes. "As I do you."

"Stay wi' me, lass," he said huskily, knowing she could not but unable to still the plea, "stay wi' me."

"Always. I will never leave you, no matter how far apart we may be. Until we are together again."

He would carry that with him through the days to come, a beacon of hope that never died.

* * * *

"Stay here with me, lass."

Husky with passion, his voice in her ear made her heart leap. She couldn't speak, could only reach for him, body rising to meet his in the thick dark night shadows that enveloped them. Never enough time, never enough privacy, only moments stolen together...raw emotion filled her with a sense of overwhelming urgency.

Reaching for him, she slid her hands down his body and found him hard and ready for her. Fingers curled around the turgid length, caressed him until she heard his groan in her ear and knew he was impatient for her. As she was for him.

"Yes, my heart," she whispered when he asked if she loved him, "for all eternity."

His hands were on her breasts, teasing her nipples into rigid aching points and setting her thighs aflame with need, and she parted her legs eagerly when he nudged her knees apart. Then he was there, sliding inside her, a swift thrust that sent shivers of ecstasy rippling through her.

Clinging to him, she arched her hips to take him all as tension tightened, awareness of imminent danger only making the moment more intense. Shadows hid the world for now, but they would lift soon enough and she'd have this moment to remember forever...

Seven

A sense of urgency drove the Earl of Atholl onward. They all felt it. With scant rest and even less sleep, Bruce's queen, his sisters, his daughter Marjorie, and the Countess of Buchan did their best to show no fear or weariness. Gillian remained stoic as well, though she wondered if her face reflected her exhaustion. Perhaps she was just too weary to be afraid. She had no notion of how many days or nights they'd been traveling, as they all seemed to blend one into the other. Perhaps they were near their destination, for it seemed the air had turned salty, and she was sure she'd heard seabirds.

"We must be close," Isabel, Countess of Buchan said encouragingly, "and then we shall be safely on the ships. It cannot be far now. I see smoke from the chimneys." While she spoke mostly to the queen's twelve-year old daughter Marjorie, all felt better at her reassurance.

The sun had come out to warm the day, and the hills undulated toward the sea. Close, so close. It may yet be safe soon. Gillian even allowed herself to dream of Alex, not as she'd last seen him, lit by the wall torches outside the gates, watching as they rode away, but as she'd seen him in the light of smoldering coals on their last night together. When he'd said he loved her, there had been such a look in his eyes she knew she'd never forget it. Even had he not said it aloud, she'd have known it. It made everything bearable. And later, they had sworn again to find one another when it was safe, when they could be together for the rest of their lives. That day must surely come, for how could it not?

With the warmth of the sun on her face and the wind brisk but not too cold, she rode in a pleasant reverie of the days when they'd be together again.

Then the Earl of Atholl raised a sudden alarm. A party of mounted riders came at a swift pace over the hill behind them, and it was apparent they had not come as friends.

"Ride," he shouted, "as fast as you can!" The earl and his men turned to make a barrier to give them time to escape.

Smoke smudged the sky, and a thin silver line of sea ahead gave direction as they all rode swiftly toward the village. They'd almost reached Tain on the shores of Dornoch Firth, and riding at the head, the Countess Buchan gestured for them to follow her. Gillian soon saw why, as the stone walls of a chapel came into view. *Sanctuary.*

Urging her horse faster, the gray stone walls seemed tantalizingly close yet were still so far away, with the thunder of pursuit behind them, the clash of steel swords and shouts of men. Then it happened. Gillian's mount stumbled and went down, and she sailed over its head to sprawl on the green hillside, dazed. The dark shape of her horse getting to its feet and racing away was a blurred image. She lay there only a moment before danger shrieked in her mind to get up and flee. Staggering to her feet, she felt the rumble of approaching hooves, heard distant shouts, and then a cool, clear voice: "Take my hand."

Looking up, she saw Isabel, Countess of Buchan, leaning from her horse. Without delay, Gillian took her hand, and somehow her foot found the stirrup and she clung to the cantle of the saddle for dear life, half on, half off the horse. The jolting gait made it difficult, but she hung on until they reached the chapel.

The queen stood in the open doorway, beckoning them to hasten, and they barely made it inside before the earl and his men joined them, pulling closed the heavy chapel doors. Gillian could barely speak, struggling for breath, her heart pounding so furiously it felt like a fist inside her chest. It hurt to breathe.

Isabel helped her to a stone seat at one side of the chapel. Arched windows behind the altar let in light, and candles flickered on pedestals and in wall holders. Kneeling beside her, the countess asked, "Are you well? Did the fall break any bones?"

Gillian managed to shake her head, and when she was able to speak, she said, "I'm only bruised, but if you had not come back for me—"

Smiling, Isabel said, "You would have done the same for me."

"Still, if ever I can repay you, I shall."

The countess rose to her feet. "I know you would."

The earl strode toward them, and his face was grim. "We cannot tarry here long. I fear the brigands sent by Pembroke will not respect the sanctuary of St Duthac."

Queen Elizabeth said sharply, "Surely they will not break sanctuary! This is the birthplace of the saint."

Atholl turned to her. "With all due respect, the precedent

was set at Greyfriar's Kirk when your husband slew Red Comyn in the chapel."

For a moment it was so still and silent the flicker of candles could be heard, then the earl went to one knee and bowed his head. "My pardon, your highness, I should not have been so bold as to speak to you like that."

"Most unwise of you," the queen replied coolly, "but forgivable under the circumstances. If we are not safe here, where shall we go?"

"In disguise, perhaps we can slip out in the night to the ships. There should be priests' cowls that will—"

A heavy banging on the chapel doors interrupted him, and as if one, they all turned to stare at the buttressed doors. There was to be no time, no sanctuary, not even from a saint.

* * * *

Events passed in such a blur after they were seized and taken under guard to King Edward that Gillian could scarcely recall them all. Some things stood out stark and terrible in her memory and others were only vague memories. She vividly remembered seeing the ancient Roman wall that ambled across the border between Scotland and England just before they reached Lanercost, the English monastery where the king awaited his valuable prisoners. But the audience with the king remained lost to her, only the terrible aftermath.

The Earl of Atholl was to be hung, beheaded, then burned for his part in the rebellion against the English crown. Shocked by the sentence, Gillian reeled, suddenly afraid of her fate.

Isabel, Countess of Buchan, and Mary Bruce, sister to the Scottish king, received the brunt of Edward's displeasure. For them, Edward decreed that wooden cages should be built and hung from the battlements of Berwick and Roxburgh, and that the two ladies be incarcerated in each one for all to see, exposed to the gaze of those below like animals. The only concession to their modesty were privies within the walls, and they were to have no conversation with any but the English maidservants assigned to bring them food and drink. Worse, a similar cage was to be constructed for Marjorie and jut from the battlements at the Tower of London. Christina Bruce, the king's other sister, widowed by Edward when her husband had been hung, drawn and quartered, received leniency and was sent to a convent at Sixhills. The queen was the daughter of the Earl of Ulster, and as such, King Edward dared not offend her father, a noble most valuable to him. For her, the sentence was house arrest.

Gillian, too, was the daughter of an earl, and her sentence was to a nunnery in Lincoln. It made little difference to her, somehow, for the sentences of Isabel and Mary were so much worse she could scarcely comprehend them. Yet none of them wept or pleaded, all remained dignified and composed, and she could do no less. Escorted by their guards, they parted, and Gillian's last view of them remained stark and vivid in her memory.

* * * *

At Kildrummy, days passed and the siege dragged on. Nigel Bruce and the men with him beat off every attack, inflicting such loss on their enemies that they withdrew for a time. At day's end, Alex met Nigel on the parapets overlooking the Black Ravine.

"They will come again," Nigel said, and Alex nodded.

"Aye. They're up to trickery, no doubt. Or waiting for reinforcements."

Nigel nodded gloomily. He stared out over the ravine, at the thick, almost impenetrable tangle of vines and thorns, then looked back at Alex. "I have a task for you, one that is dangerous but necessary."

"You have only to ask, my lord."

A faint smile slanted Bruce's mouth, and in the thin moonlight, weariness was evident in his handsome face. "Yea, you are always willing, Sir Alex. Do you know the back way from the castle?"

"Through the ravine? Aye."

"Do you think it possible to get away undetected?"

"Possible, yea, my lord."

Bruce put a heavy hand on his shoulder. "I have a message for the king I wish you to take. It is brief."

"I will carry it to him, my lord, and keep it safe."

"I do not intend to write it down, Sir Alex. It is but a few words. Tell him…tell him that I have done my best, and that he will be the best king Scotland could ever know."

Alex stood still for a moment. It was a strange message, almost…prophetic. "Is that it, my lord?"

"That is it, Sir Alex. See, if you will, that he hears it."

Hesitating, Alex thought there was something almost defeated in his tone, but Nigel Bruce had never admitted defeat in his life. He must be mistaken, must be reading his own doubt into the words.

"I will leave before first light, my lord."

The Black Ravine was nearly inaccessible, but not impossible. Alex had once used a path through the thicket, and it came out far down the slope away from the castle. He would have no horse, but that could easily be remedied when he came across one.

That night, Osborne, the castle blacksmith, threw a red-hot ploughshare into the stored corn. It caught fire, and flames spread from the storage to wooden buildings in the bailey, so that the entire garrison was driven to the catwalk along the battlements. Alex wanted to stay, but Nigel Bruce insisted he leave as he'd promised.

"There is not much time. The castle gate is burning and the English will soon be upon us. Leave now, Sir Alex, or you will not be able to leave at all."

Torn, Alex yielded at last to the command, and made his way to the tiny portal that led to the ravine. Noise of battle lay behind him, and before him lay the dense shadows of night. He slipped away unseen, barely escaping notice of an English troop skirting the castle to come up on the other side. All he could do now for those in Kildrummy was pray. He set his sights on finding the king, but it was over six months before he reached him.

* * * *

Robert Bruce listened intently to the final words from his brother. Alex knelt before him, exhausted, having gone from the Isles to Carrick and to the Isle of Arran but always just missing Bruce. Now that he'd found him in a cave in his ancestral lands of Carrick, he gave way to the weariness that had been a part of his life for so long.

"My queen," the king asked, "have you news of her, Sir Alex?"

"She and her ladies fled north with the Earl of Atholl, but I know nothing else, sire."

"And my brother Nigel? Thomas and Alexander? Have you word of them?"

"Nay, sire. No word of any, nor of my lady."

Silence greeted his reply, then Bruce rose wearily. "I shall pray that all our loved ones are well and safe, Sir Alex."

"Aye, as we all do, sire."

The next day, a former mistress of the king, Christian of

Carrick, came to the cave, bringing with her fifteen mounted tenants and the promise of money and supplies. And it was from her that the king and Alex heard the terrible news of his family and friends, of his brothers' fates, Thomas and Alexander and Nigel all hung, drawn, and beheaded, along with his sister's husband Sir Christopher Seton, and the Earl of Atholl. And he heard, too, of how his wife and her attendants and even his daughter were imprisoned, though now his daughter was in a nunnery instead of the cage where Edward had first put her.

Stricken, Alex asked hoarsely how fared the Lady Montgomery, and Christian replied that she, too, was in a nunnery, but he knew not where. It was a relief and a shock, and he mumbled a request to be excused from the king's presence but left without hearing it given.

Outside, he drew in a deep breath that smelled of spruce and cold air, and thought of his lady as he'd last seen her, riding bravely away, her spine straight and her head held high. He went to his knees then, as he'd not done since a lad, and closed his eyes against the pain and tears. And he resolved that he would find her, no matter how long it took. He would never give up the quest.

Eight

"Stay wi' me, lass." A voice urged her not to leave, Gillian thought hazily. A familiar voice in a familiar accent. Thick, the words were in a burr redolent of the Highlands. *Alex.* He'd come for her. At last. It'd been so long since she'd seen him. Four years? Five? No, six. She felt so strange, so sleepy and weary. It was hard to think. Difficult to recall things best forgotten. Save for Alex...yea, save for Alex. Not for a single moment had she ever forgotten him. Nor would she. He was her love. Her life. Her forever.

"Stay wi' me, lass," the voice said again, and he sounded so sorrowful that she tried once again to open her eyes. This time she succeeded, and though he was but a blur, she looked upon Alex's handsome face with a faint smile.

"You came for me," she whispered hoarsely, and he let out a great shout.

"She lives! Father Joseph, come quickly—she lives!"

A cowled priest hurried toward them, disbelief changing to joy when he knelt beside her pallet. "'Tis a miracle, my son. Our prayers have been answered."

"Yea," Alex said, sounding suddenly fierce, "'tis a miracle they did not kill her, though they certainly tried."

"Silence, my son," the priest leaned forward to say softly, "for even the walls have ears."

Frowning, she had a brief flash of iron bars, stone walls, leering guards and constant, aching cold. Then it was gone as Alex leaned over her again, his face finally coming into focus. She smiled, put up a hand to touch him, her fingers grazing the scar on his left cheek that was compliments of a sword. It only made him more dear to her. A badge of honor, of courage. Of determination.

"Rest, my lovely lady," Alex murmured, "for when you are healed we have a promise to keep."

And she remembered then that they'd sworn to take their marriage vows in the small kirk where he'd been baptized, to swear undying love for one another for all eternity. It didn't matter that the world she knew was gone, for all things passed eventually. She'd learned that. The carelessness of youth was forever gone. Now she knew how precious was each hour that passed. All the lost hours with Alex...

So she clung to his hand, wanting to tell him that during those long months and years she'd kept his memory bright, remembered their laughter and their love, and it was that most of all that had kept her from yielding to the cold hand of death. Now she felt its breath close, and knew there was little time. Tears stung her eyes, but she didn't allow them to fall. He'd not see her weep. His last memory of her would not be of tears, but of love. She cleared her throat.

"Do you still think of that bonny lass from beyond the braes, Alex?"

"Not since May Day eighteen years ago," he replied promptly and firmly. "All that lies beyond the braes is this bonny lass whose hand I now hold."

A faint smile tugged at her mouth. "I doubt Mary has forgotten you."

"It doesn't matter." He said it so fiercely she looked at him in some surprise. His hand tightened around her fingers. "You are all I want. All I need. When you're feeling better we'll go to Skye where the wind blows fair so you may recover."

She shook her head sadly. "Nay, love. I'll not be there save in spirit. No, listen to me. I've not much time. And...and I've a task for you."

Stormy eyes met hers, darkening, then he looked away. His mouth set into a tight line and his voice was thick. "What is it, my lady love?"

She summoned the strength to ask, "I must know about Countess Buchan. Lady Isabel—"

"She lives," he said. "Though in fear of her life. She escaped her prison, but is still being sought by the king's son, Edward Second."

Closing her eyes she thought of Isabel's bravery, all she'd lost for her courage in crowning Robert Bruce king, and knew what she must do. It was difficult, but she forced out the words even when Alex tried to stop her. "When I am dead give my name as...Lady Isabel, Countess Buchan. Do that...for her. It is the least I can do since she once saved my life."

"Nay...Gillian, God's teeth, no! Stay wi' me, lass."

"I fear I cannot. But Isabel's still strong despite all that's happened—oh my love, do not look at me like that. I want to stay, to be with you...but that choice has been taken from me. I feel it. Promise me. Swear an oath to me that you will do that for her—for me."

Stricken, Alex looked at her for a long moment, and she saw the hope die in his eyes. "Aye," he said finally, his voice thick and fierce, "I shall do as you ask me do, but hear this—I am not far behind you when you leave this world. I will love you forever, through all eternity."

"Yea," she whispered, "for all eternity. We shall have our chance at happiness there."

"Nay, we shall have it here. Stay wi' me, lass. Stay wi' me!"

It was cold, so cold, and the stark room began to fade away, receding into some distant blur that ceased to matter. All that mattered was the hard, bright hope that they would meet again beyond the braes...

Alex saw her slip away, held her hand until the last breath slipped gently from between her lips to frost the chill air of the abbey room. Then he bent his head in grief and savage anger, curbing the sudden need for violence. He didn't know how long he sat there beside her pallet, until the priest put a hand upon his shoulder and he looked up.

"My son, she is in God's hands now," he began but Alex jerked abruptly to his feet, frightening the much smaller man into scuttling backward several steps.

A grim smile curled his mouth as he tossed the priest a purse of coins. "Here, Father, payment for masses to pray for her soul."

"And her name, my son?"

Sucking in a deep breath, he said flatly, "Lady Isabel, Countess of Buchan."

A debt repaid to both.

When he turned to go, the priest said, "Will you not wait for her burial?"

If she'd lived, he would have lingered, but all that was left was the lovely, still figure that bore little resemblance to the fiery woman he had known and loved. Only the shell remained.

"I cannot," he said. "My king needs me." And he must hurry to Bannockburn to join him.

* * * *

The English were defeated. Alex realized it dimly, lying beneath his dead mount as the battle turned to a complete rout.

Oddly, though he knew he must be dying, he felt no pain. Only a sense of regret and bittersweet triumph. They had won their freedom, but he had lost what made his world worthwhile. *Gillian...*

"Sir Alex!" A man knelt beside him, lifted his head gently, then wiped blood from his brow so that Alex could see James Douglas. He managed a smile and a whispered question.

"We...took...the field...?"

Douglas nodded. "Aye, that we did. The English are in full retreat, King Edward has fled, and Stirling will soon be ours. Scotland is free, lad. Free!"

Alex tried to grin, but nothing seemed to work right. It must be near dark, for the sun had dimmed and shadows shrouded the land. Despite the heat of the summer air, cold gripped him. The hilt of an English sword still protruded from his side, yet he felt only a strange lassitude and numbness. He wanted to tell Sir James that his sword should be given to his younger brother, but all that came out was "Gillian...stay wi' me, lass..."

Nine

Stay with me, lass....

Susan's eyes snapped open and she sucked in a deep breath of air that provoked a violent fit of coughing. Her throat was raw and her lungs ached, and someone was yelling for a nurse.

"Stop it, dammit!" she got out, and heard a startled laugh. An acrid taste in her mouth made her nauseous, and as her vision cleared, she saw Ryan Douglas peer at her with a grin.

"Guess that's the thanks I get for saving your life. No, don't try to get up. The nurse is on the way."

Staring at him, Susan suddenly remembered everything: The play. The fire. Kildrummy. *Alex...*she began to shiver uncontrollably, and Ryan's grin turned to alarm.

"Hey, don't go into shock...hang on. Here. I'll put this blanket over you. I called the nurse. You were hit in the head by the falling wall. Just don't move around much, okay?"

As if she could. For when she looked at Ryan, she saw Alex. It was the eyes. Not exactly the color or shape, but deeper than that. It was crazy. She'd been unconscious and had a very real dream. Or hallucination. But it'd been so detailed, and seemed to take so long...and was still so vivid. The emotions were still so sharp, grief mixing with love and passion, that her heart ached for all that had been endured.

When Ryan turned back to stare down at her with concern, he reached for her hand. The contact sent electrical currents pulsing through her, and from the look on his face, she knew he felt it, too. His eyes widened, darkened, held her gaze as if searching for answers.

"It's you," he said finally, huskily, as if just awakening from a long sleep. "You're here."

"What...do you mean?"

He sucked in a sharp breath. "My dream. This is going to sound crazy, but since I was a kid, I've had these dreams. Sometimes they're brief, but they're always so vivid, and they always end the same way even though different things may happen in them. There's this woman in my dreams, lovely, sweet, passionate—and I lose her even though I'm begging her to stay with me. I call out to her but she slips away, sometimes into this gray mist, sometimes across the water, and sometimes, she just fades into memory, but I feel her loss so deeply that I know I must find her again." He laughed, an uncertain sound, and looked away toward the glass partition that led to the hospital corridor. "It always feels like I've lost the love of my life when she disappears. When I wake, I feel abandoned. It seems I've searched for her my entire life. Now, somehow, I get this sense that you'll understand."

"I do." It came out in a whisper and when he turned to look down at her again she said, "I have the same dreams. But I once promised you we'd have eternity together, didn't I?"

Ryan gave an inarticulate sound and his grip tightened on her fingers. "Is it—?"

"Gillian. Aye, my love, now and forever."

"You know her name."

"I know her life. I know her love—don't ask me how or why but I know all of it. It's as if it were only yesterday at Kildrummy…"

"Oh my God. It *is* you."

They stared at each other, while the muted beeping of the machines marking her heart rate and blood pressure made the only sound for several minutes.

"Is it possible?" Ryan asked at last, and she shook her head.

"I don't know. I never thought so before, but now—I just had the most vivid dream, and you were in it, not as Robert Bruce, but as—"

"Alex Campbell."

A shiver tracked her spine, and his grip tightened. "Yes," she murmured, "yes"

Holding her hand, he said softly, "I guess I've been looking for you all this time, but when I first saw you, I didn't believe it could be true. Now…now I know."

She drew in a deep breath. "Then we've found each other at last."

"Do you think it's real?"

He nodded. "This time, it's real. This time, it's not just a dream of a time long past. This time, we'll be together for all eternity."

She smiled, for she knew it was true, knew that against incredible odds, against everything she'd ever thought possible, their love had come full circle and they'd been given another chance.

Leaning over her, Ryan kissed her, long and deep, a soul-kiss that said she'd come home at last. Eternity beckoned.

* * * *

July in Scotland was fair and beautiful. Warm days with bright sun, and short, cool nights with the peaks of Ben Nevis in the distance. An ancient kirk of the Campbell clan lay tucked into a copse of trees and near forgotten by time and man, but Ryan had found it. There, in the beauty of the still wild Highlands where once war had raged, peace reigned. And there, in the ruins of the kirk, they were wed, as once they had promised to be. Susan wore sprigs of heather in her hair, and Ryan wore a Campbell kilt and a Douglas bonnet, in honor of both clans.

Later, they lodged in a solitary cottage overlooking Loch Leven. It was simple but comfortable, yet they had no need of anything but each other. They'd waited for this moment, the time when they were wed, to consummate their love.

Now, as he looked into her eyes, Ryan knew that his dreams had come true, that the fair lass he'd loved and lost so long ago had been returned. All these years he'd searched for her, but not realized who he was looking for until he'd found her. It was a miracle.

"Are you happy?" he asked huskily, and the tears in her eyes and smile on her face said as much as her words.

"More happy than ever I thought I could be. Ryan...to have found each other after all the centuries—it seems impossible."

"Love makes everything possible." He drew her to him, and bent his head to kiss her. She tasted so sweet, her lips parting for him. "Stay with me, lass?"

"Yes, my heart. For all eternity," she whispered, and he knew that this time it was true. This time, they'd have their eternity together.

* * * *

Because it seemed to draw them, they went back to the falls near St. Fillan's priory where they'd so briefly shared an afternoon long ago. It was ruins now, moss-covered stones jutting up from bright green grass. Susan barely recalled the way it had been, but Ryan walked the ruins as if he'd been here just the day before. The expression on his face was one of pride and sorrow. It was a mixture of emotions she understood.

Everything was so strange, the blend of past and present bewildering, sad, and joyous at the same time. No one would

ever believe them if they told it, so they'd not shared the truth
with anyone. Even their family and closest friends. If it
somehow leaked out, the tabloids would make soap star Ryan
Douglas and his unknown new bride seem foolish and publicity
hungry, or worse—crazy. Sometimes Susan worried about that
herself. It didn't seem true. It still seemed more like a dream.
A wonderful dream.

They'd traveled so much of Scotland since being married
in the Campbell kirk, revisiting places Robert Bruce had made
famous. Except Bannockburn. Susan couldn't bring herself to
go with Ryan to Bannockburn where he'd died so long ago.
She didn't know why. Surely, if anyone, she should know there
was another life after death. That the soul traveled many
journeys, and saying farewell didn't always mean forever.
Maybe one day she'd go with him there, but now she just
wanted to visit places where they'd been happy.

They'd already visited Kildrummy Castle, ruins now as
well, but with the Snow Tower still intact enough they could
remember stealing time together in curtained alcoves. And in
the solar where Lady Gillian had left Sir Alex Campbell standing
in nothing but his boots. Others at the ruins had looked at them
strangely when they dissolved in laughter, probably wondering
what they found so amusing in lichened stones.

But now, here, at St. Fillan's priory where they were the
only visitors at the ruins, Ryan's face reflected a far different
mood. Susan sat on a flat stone and waited, watched him walk
places in his memory that only he could know. Finally he turned
to look at her. He smiled.

"We're married despite that stubborn priest."

Susan laughed. "It took a few hundred years, but you got
your way after all. Time hasn't changed your stubbornness,
either."

Grinning, he strode across the grass toward her. Her heart
lurched. Sunlight made his dark hair gleam. He wore a kilt, not
the Douglas tartan but the Campbell, though in Bruce's time
the patterns didn't matter. Wool had been dyed with plants
native to the area. Cockades in the men's bonnets signaled
their clan.

When Ryan reached her he lifted her easily from the stone.
"I always thought we'd come back here one day. Care for a
trip down memory lane?"

"I thought that's what we've been doing."

His grin turned wicked, and the light in his eyes made her nipples harden. "I have another memory in mind. Remember the falls?"

"The—*oh!*" She smiled. "Oh yeah. I remember a *lot* about the waterfalls."

It didn't take long to find their way to the waterfalls. Bay willows still grew in shallow waters, and currents slid and tumbled over rocks to meet with a stream that'd end up joining the river. Mossy tussocks cushioned rocks, and the air smelled cool and clean.

Ryan came up behind her where she stood on the mossy banks. "How about a repeat?" he asked in her ear, his tone low and raspy.

Susan leaned back against him. "What if someone sees us?"

"They won't. We had to cross a farmer's land to get here ourselves. The only visitors are likely to be sheep."

"Or cows." She shivered when he bent his head to kiss her on the neck, then he lifted her hair and loosened it from the French braid that kept it from her eyes. He shoved his fingers into her hair and spread it out on her shoulders.

"Beautiful," he said huskily. "Like spun gold." His hands moved down her arms to her wrists, and he pulled her firmly against him. Even through his kilt and her Levi's, she felt his erection nudge against her. Her pulses quickened. The air got thick and hot.

Before she had time to come to her senses, he had her windbreaker, boots, jeans, tee shirt, and bra off and on the ground. She sucked in a sharp breath when his palms cupped her breasts and his fingers teased her nipples. Heat from his hands warmed her bare skin.

Dipping his hands to the waistband of her bikinis, he slowly pulled them down, trailing kisses along the arch of her spine. Cool air brushed over her and she shivered, but not from the cold. Ryan knelt behind her, gently lifted first one leg, then the other, to free her from the bikinis. She thought he'd turn her around then but he didn't. Instead, he licked a leisurely path down her thighs to the bends of her knees, one hand reaching up to touch her between her legs.

It was oddly erotic standing there naked with him behind her fully clothed. Moss was soft between her toes, springy and cool. A wind swayed willow branches and dragged long strands

of her hair across her face. Pulsing heat blossomed when he
stroked her clitoris with his thumb. She closed her eyes. Heat
turned into breathless need, and she spread her thighs wider.
Ryan slipped a finger inside her, then two. Susan gasped.

"Touch your breasts," Ryan murmured, his lips moving
against the back of her thigh.

Quivering, she slowly put her hands up to her breasts. The
movements of his hand grew faster and the sense of urgency
escalated. Nipples hard, she rolled them between her fingers
in a rhythm that nearly matched the rub of his thumb over her
clit and the thrust of his fingers inside. Climax burst on her
quickly, white and hot and strong.

Before she collapsed, Ryan stood up and held her against
him with his arms just under her breasts. The kilt was gone.
His bare cock nudged her buttocks. It was wet and hot and
hard. She leaned into him, breathing slowly growing even.

Then, as so long before, Ryan gently lowered her to a
cushion of bog moss and brushed her hair from her eyes. He
kissed her mouth, the slope of her cheek and arch of her throat.
When she closed her eyes, he kissed her eyelids, then blew
softly into her ear. She shivered.

He laughed softly. "I think we've done this before, my
lady."

Opening her eyes, she looked up at him with a smile.
Emotion beat hard, all past sorrows fading as she took his face
between her hands. Beard stubble grazed her palms, and she
caressed the grooves on each side of his mouth with her thumbs.

"A time or two, Sir Knight."

The laughing light in Ryan's eyes turned darker, more
serious. A slight muscle leaped in his jaw. "I thought once I'd
lost you forever," he said hoarsely. "You were always just a
dream to me...sometimes when I look at you, I can't believe
we're together again."

"At last."

He took her hand and kissed her palm, looking up at her
through his thick black lashes. "At last. Now. Forever."

She smiled.

He cupped her breasts in his palms and dragged his tongue
around the pebbled peaks, and sucked first one, then the other
into his mouth. Her stomach muscles knotted, and a steady
beat pulsed through her all the way to her uterus. It contracted
with each suction, and fever spread through her entire body.

Arching her back, she lifted her hips in open invitation. Ryan teased her, licking her all around her nipples then closing his lips on them to suck for a moment until the pulsebeat between her legs got so hard and strong it almost hurt.

"Ryan..."

"Not yet...not yet."

He moved lower, tongue dragging over her ribs, then dipping into her navel. When she reached for him to put his hard cock inside her, he took her wrists in his hands and held them out to the sides. His tongue licked over the soft brown curls on her pubis mound, lower...lower...and flicked against her clitoris. She moaned and parted her legs wider, lifting a little. He blew softly on the damp crevice, cool air quickly followed by the heat of his tongue. She writhed, panting, needing him but loving the torture. When he sucked the tiny pink nub into his mouth she almost screamed. It took only a few strong pulls before orgasm washed through her again.

Still not releasing her hands, Ryan moved up and over her. The expression on his face was so intense, almost fierce, and while her vagina muscles still contracted he pushed his hard cock into her. She cried out with pleasure. It felt as if he'd pushed all the way to her ribs, so big and hard and welcome...panting now, she lifted her hips to encourage him, and he thrust more deeply inside when she'd have sworn he couldn't. It felt so good...everything whirled around her, the musical splash of the falls, the soft whish of wind through willow limbs, the fine mist of water spray on them, the feel of the cool green moss below her...and Ryan a part of her, as close as a man could get to a woman, body and soul and past and present all melded together.

Pounding into her, the exquisite drag and thrust of his shaft brought them both to a swift climax. Ryan groaned and lowered his head so that his face lay in her hair spread over the moss. He was still hard inside her, and after a few moments, he began to move again, slower this time, dragging out the luxurious intimacy. Afterward, they fell asleep in each others arms, there on the moss beneath the willows, the burn chuckling and birds serenading the celebration of reunion.

* * * *

When they woke, purple shadows deepened on the hills around them. Ryan sat up first.

"Beautiful dreamer," he teased, "we've still got to walk

back to the car."

She opened her eyes and looked up at him, smiling sleepily. "It's July. It doesn't get dark until after midnight."

"Lazy girl."

"If I could stay right here and not move for a week, that'd be fine with me." Blinking, she sat up, and he reached out to push a strand of loose hair behind her ear. Pale brown strands mixed in with the soft gold color, a natural shade that couldn't be duplicated. It felt so soft in his palm, like silk.

Emotion choked him so that for a moment he couldn't speak. Then he said lightly, "I'm afraid we shocked the sheep."

Susan glanced over at the sheep chewing their cud and staring at them from a small rise. "I bet they have a tale to tell the farmer, then."

He grinned. "We can give them a few more tales before we leave."

She arched a brow. "Hm. That sounds tempting."

"Come on. It's been a few hundred years since we've bathed in these falls. Let's see if it's still as cold."

"Ryan—no!"

Ignoring her, he pulled her into the burn, taking her out to the middle where it was deeper and laughing at her when she squealed. When she found her footing on the bottom, she hit the water with the edge of her palm and splashed him.

"I can swim this time," she warned. "Don't think you can take advantage of me again."

Sputtering from the unexpected dash of water, he pretended to be off-balance, then caught her by the back of her leg and ducked her. She came up dripping and coughing, wiping water from her eyes to glare at him. Her nipples were beaded and pink, her lashes thick with water. She put her hands on her hips.

"Now it's war."

"Bring it on," he said.

They played until they were tired, then sat out on the moss again. He put his wool kilt over her shoulders when she shivered, and held her against him. Stars blinked dimly against the darkening sky, and a thumbnail moon gleamed on the eastern horizon. Neither spoke, just let the twilight and companionship surround them.

Then Susan said into the softness, "There was a child, you know."

He went still. "A child?"

She nodded. "Long ago. A daughter. I saw her only briefly before she was taken from me. I held her close...she had dark hair and blue eyes, and a mouth like a rosebud. When I put out my finger to stroke her cheek, she curled hers around it and held on so tightly...then the nuns came to take her away. I never saw her again."

Ryan didn't know what to say. Suddenly he felt keenly the loss of a child he'd never known existed, though it'd been seven hundred years ago.

"A child," he repeated softly. "Why didn't you tell me that day I found you?"

"There was nothing you could have done. I wanted to spare you the pain I felt at parting with her. If you had...had survived at Bannockburn, the priests were to send you a message from me with all the information I knew about her. I couldn't put that burden on you before a battle."

For a few minutes he didn't say anything. Then he pulled her into the shelter of his arm and chest. "We found each other after all this time. She'll find us."

Susan looked up at him with such love in her eyes a hard lump clogged his throat.

"I believe she will."

The Dream Fulfilled

"Stay here with me, lass."

Husky with passion, his voice in her ear made her heart leap. She couldn't speak, could only reach for him, body rising to meet his. Raw emotion filled her with a sense of overwhelming joy.

Reaching for him, she slid her hands down his body and found him hard and ready for her. Fingers curled around the turgid length, caressed him until she heard his groan in her ear and knew he was impatient for her. As she was for him.

Waiting only heightened the anticipation, so she moved down in the bed, kissed the flat plane of his stomach, and cradled his balls in one hand while her other moved feather light over his hard cock. He was more than ready for her. His balls tightened in her palm, his hips arched as he thrust into her fist eagerly, and he made a wonderful, sensual sound low in his throat. Then he reached for her, hands finding her breasts in the dim light of the room that looked out over Loch Leven. His fingers teased her nipples until she caught her breath and looked up at him. He had the same look in his eyes that must be in hers, a light of passion and need and emotion.

Heart beating in time with the steady throbbing between her legs, she put her tongue out to rake it over his shaft, up and down, doing circles, then flicking against the tip.

"God...Susan..." He started to sit up but she gently pushed him back down.

"Not yet...not yet."

She parted her lips and took him in her mouth, lips sliding slowly down the thick shaft as far as she could, then sucked on him as she worked her way back up. His cock filled her mouth, hard and ready, juices flowing. She released him for a moment, flicked her tongue in a teasing caress over the tip, then slowly took him in again, even farther this time.

Ryan groaned. His fingers plucked at her nipples, spread over her breasts in an erotic caress that made her inhale sharply. He obviously liked that, the feel of cool air along with the heat of her mouth. Cupping his testicles in her palm, she gently rolled them while she sucked hard on his cock, until she knew by the tightening of his balls and the arch of his hips that he'd neared climax. Instead of pulling away, she held him still, let his juices burst into her mouth, then lubricated his pulsing shaft with them before she rose to her knees and moved over him.

He was still hard, ready, and she spread her legs with a knee on each side of his hips. He was hot and wet, and so was she as she poised briefly. Holding his eyes, with his hands on her breasts and his hard cock eager for her, she slid down the thick length until she was so full with him she could barely breathe. Life throbbed inside her, so hard and alive, the memory of days past and anticipation of days ahead bringing tears to her eyes. This was all she'd ever wanted, to be with him, to know their time together would last long in this life and forever in the next.

Closing her eyes, she rocked forward, slowly at first, then faster and faster. He'd moved his hands to pull her slightly forward so that her clitoris hit his pubic bone with her every motion. Then he caressed her breasts again, his strong fingers plucking at the nipples, rolling them as she moved ever closer to that elusive peak.

Then Ryan paused with his hands still on her breasts, his voice thick and husky. "Susan—my lady Gillian, my dearest—will you love me always?"

"Yes, my heart," she whispered, "for all eternity."

With the smell of heather in the warm, soft air that caressed their naked bodies, and the lilting, timeless wail of bagpipes drifting across the glen, release came, washing over her like a white-hot star, obliterating all around her as she held tightly to him. She lay there, drowsy, replete, and happier than she'd ever thought possible.

Ryan lay a gentle hand on her soft, rounded belly. She smiled. Soon there would be three of them, together at last.

Just a new beginning...

"Let's Get Crazy"
by
Caryn Carter

One

She was going to die.

Maybe not tomorrow or next week. Maybe not even next year. But she was going to die sooner than she should.

"Ms. Duvernay?"

Dr. Frazier's hand on her arm brought Angel's head up, leveled her gaze with his usually bright blue eyes, clouded now with concern.

"I'm sorry I had to hand you such upsetting news. It's just that—"

It was just that what had come back from the laboratory didn't look good. Not good at all.

Dr. Frazier gave her arm a comforting squeeze. "There's still a chance it's not what it seems to be. With a disease this rare, this new, diagnosis isn't easy. There's always a chance for error."

She knew he was doing his best to lift her spirits, to give her something to hold on to. To soften the blow. She appreciated that, but she had always preferred to meet the unpleasant things in life head-on. It was better to swallow the bitter pill fast, her mother always told her. Get it over with quickly, then forget about it and go on to something else, something sweeter.

And that's what she would do now. Swallow the bad news fast, then get the heck out of here and try to come to terms with the rest of her life.

"I'm going to set up another test with Carlyle Labs. No place is better equipped to deal with something like this than they are. I'll ask them to put a rush on it, since you need to know before you have to leave the country again."

She nodded, too clogged in the throat to speak. It was one thing for the mind to accept a decision, another for the emotions to follow suit. She wouldn't be dealing with this without a few tears. And she wasn't one to cry in public.

She needed privacy. She needed to be home.

* * * *

Sunday morning, Angel watched the sun come up over Madison Avenue from her bedroom window. She'd spent the entire night exactly as she'd spent the remainder of Saturday after she left Dr. Frazier's office. Worrying. Thinking. Planning.

Crying.

Trying to accept the grim news she'd been handed. Trying to understand the how and the why of it. Trying to halt those dreaded words that scrolled past her mind like a blinking neon banner.

Leukemia. Rare. New. Words she'd likely be hearing and living with for the rest of her natural life. The rest of her *short* natural life, if the new test results came down on the wrong side of the scale.

No matter how sensitive Dr. Frazier had been, leukemia was still cancer. And there was no comfort in the fact that it was a new, rare form. If anything, its newness and rarity made her more anxious because there would be less knowledge in the medical community to access.

Maybe if she took a different approach she might alleviate some of the anxiety.

Maybe she could look on the bright side.

Well, okay, there was no bright side. But maybe there was opportunity here. Opportunity to do some of the things she'd always thought of doing but never seriously entertained because...well, because basically she was a chicken when it came to pushing the envelope. But if ever there was a time to throw caution to the wind and push the envelope, this was it.

Let's see, there was skydiving. How many times had she envied all those brave souls who jumped fearlessly from airplanes and vowed to join their ranks one day? And what about rappelling and white-water rafting? How many times had she considered those gutsy sports?

Of course even if she made up her mind to try any of those things now, the seriousness of her condition might not let her follow through on them.

Although Dr. Frazier had assured her that even in the worst case scenario, once they began treatment she'd likely feel good for quite some time, one never knew. On the other hand, truth be told, she didn't feel the least bit sick now. Just a little tired, which was what had sent her to Dr. Frazier in the first place.

But did she feel well enough to indulge in strenuous activities she'd shied away from in good health? Her short-lived, buoyed-

up spirits took a nasty nose-dive and she was down in the
dumps again. She couldn't even look forward to experiencing
something with an edge of danger in it for whatever life she
had left.

Perhaps if she gave it more thought she could come up
with something that would be a grand adventure, something
exciting and daring, and yet not demand so much of her
physically. Something like...like having a night of sex with Eric
Sweeney.

Just the thought had adrenaline rushing through her
bloodstream like water over a dam, lifting her up, taking her
down, and pushing her forward, calmer, yet still rampant with
energy.

Here was a real possibility. A real chance to do something
daring and daunting, maybe even a little dangerous, but in a
good, life-affirming way. After all, what will be, will be. She
had no power to change the verdict. The only power she had
was to change herself. Clichéd, but true.

She sighed heavily. Should she do it? The answer came
quickly.

She would take the chance and go for the gold.

After all, what more did she have to lose?

Two

When Angel slipped into a booth at Manhattan's Heritage Jazz Club Monday night, every nerve in her body tingling with excitement, Eric Sweeney was just finishing the last song in the set.

She still couldn't believe she was actually here. Couldn't believe that she'd put on one of her sexiest dresses and come alone, as Eric had asked her to last Friday when he'd managed to capture her attention and let her know he was interested in her. Interested? From the way his hand had found its way to her thigh, he was more than interested.

She'd come here the first time with two other employees of the language resource firm with whom she was sharing a corporate apartment until she went back overseas on her next assignment. Both of the women were working temporary jobs for the company in Manhattan and went to the club often so they already knew Eric.

Before the women even introduced Eric to her they'd both candidly admitted having the hots for him. Each in turn would have probably gotten naked and let him do her right there on the table in one second flat, given half the chance.

But Eric hadn't been interested in either of them. She was the one he'd chosen to spend time with in between sets. He'd admitted he was turned on by her bubbly personality and her sexy body, and he'd whispered into her ear his desire to get to know her better.

She *had* been bubbly the first time they met. And she was still bubbly on her return visit last Friday because she hadn't yet made her second visit to Dr. Frazier.

Angel yanked her thoughts back quickly, anchoring them firmly in the here and now and reminding herself sternly of her decision to take a night of pleasure with Eric Sweeney and enjoy every last minute of it. That is, if he really *had* offered her that pleasure.

She'd asked herself a dozen times since Friday if he'd really implied he wanted to spend the night with her, or if it was just her overly active imagination wishing it was so. Did this unbelievably handsome, incredibly talented man, who could probably have any woman in the room with just the snap of his fingers, really want her?

As so often happened when she was on sensory overload, Angel's mind hopped, skipped, and jumped through the several languages she spoke fluently to the one she happened to be most familiar with at the time.

Magnifico. That one four-syllable word said it all. Once again Angel marveled that the Italians had such a way of saying the most with the least, especially when it came to things of breathtaking beauty.

And Eric Sweeney was breathtakingly beautiful, if a man could indeed be considered beautiful. From his tawny shoulder-length hair, held back tonight by a strip of black leather, to his deep sapphire eyes, and straight down to his perfectly sculpted, sensuous lips, he was perfection. Even his nose, which was slightly off-center, added to his incredibly masculine, breathtakingly good looks. Angel's heart raced faster than Eric's fingers as they played the final quarter notes of the set.

Before she could calm her racing pulse or figure out a way to let Eric know that she was here, he was already off the dais and down in the audience. Damn. For once she should have done the sensible thing and let him know she'd be here tonight.

Instead, she'd come here looking her sexiest, hoping her feminine charms—two of which had almost escaped her décolleté neckline—would take him by surprise and knock him off his feet.

But that, she realized, could only happen if he saw her. And what were the odds of that happening when the club was filled to capacity and she was hidden off here in a corner all by herself?

Well, she decided, she'd come this far and she darn well wasn't turning back. Not before she pushed the envelope as far as she could. And not before she at least had another face-to-face with *Mr. Magnifico.*

If necessary, she'd take the bull by the horns and go after him herself. Ummm, yes, exactly what she'd do. But not without first moistening her lips and brushing a bit more color on her cheeks to compensate for the dim overhead lighting.

Angel hadn't yet found the tube of lipstick in the bottom of her purse when someone slipped into the booth beside her. She knew it was Eric even before he spoke.

"Hello, Angel."

Eric's baritone voice was as smooth and rich as the classical jazz he coaxed out of his baby grand. Like everything else about him, it sent shivers up her spine and already had her stomach looping in knots.

Whatever it was that his body communicated to hers, it was the most powerful, invisible aphrodisiac she'd ever experienced. It called out to something both primal and spiritual inside her. She could only imagine what sex with him would be like. And imagine. And imagine. And—

"How do you like it?"

"Like it?"

"Your drink." He signaled for a waiter. "I'm going to order you a margarita, and I need to know if you like it with or without salt."

She was already in awe of him. He'd actually remembered she drank margaritas!

Eric placed his hand over hers, and Angel drew in what she hoped was a silent gasp. His touch was ten times more arousing than his voice, and what it did to her body she didn't have to imagine. The little throbs of pleasure between her thighs were all too real.

"What are you having?" she managed, her voice tight from having to concentrate on hiding how hot she already was for him.

"Soda water for the time being. I never drink alcohol until the break before my last set. I'm one of those weird people who mellows out real quick after only one drink."

Angel added that bit of information to her "Things I'd Love To Do With Eric Sweeney Wish List." She'd just love to mellow out with him, since she was one of those "weird" one-drink people too. Mellow out skin to skin, she added to "The List."

"Soda water's fine for me as well," she told him, thinking that if he asked, she'd drink Drano with him at that moment.

Good heavens! Was she losing her mind? Certainly it was eroding at the very least. Just because she was teetering on the edge of the cliff didn't mean she had to jump over it. There was always that slim, one-in-a-million chance that this new lab...

She did a quick three-sixty and swung her thoughts back to Eric as he gave their orders to the waiter who had materialized out of thin air and vanished just as quickly. And when he gave her hand a light squeeze and leaned in close, she just knew that if he moved any closer she was going to puddle-up right here.

"There's something important I need to know, although I'm already pretty certain of the answer," Eric said, bringing her hand up to his lips for a soft, butterfly kiss on her palm. "There is no Mr. Angel, is there?"

Was he for real? In her experience, most men would hit on anything in a skirt and worry about a little detail like that later. She liked it that he didn't. She shook her head.

"There's no Mrs. Eric, either," he said, as he winked at her over her fingertips.

Angel felt her heart settle down in relief at that bit of news, only to have it start rattling again when, his sapphire eyes piercing hers like a laser in the shrouded light, Eric whispered against her hand, "I was afraid you might not come back."

"I told you I would."

"Sometimes people say things they don't really mean."

"I don't."

"Good. Because there's something else I need to ask you." She hoped it was a short question because every time he spoke his breath fanned across her fingertips and she got goose bumps on them. Goose bumps on her fingertips? She was really losing it.

Eric held her gaze. "You know I'll be leaving in a week for Europe."

Yes, she knew that. He'd told her when they talked for what seemed like hours last week that he had to be in London by the end of the month for another engagement. Just as she had to be in Milan in two weeks. Correction. Just as she *hoped* to be in Milan in two weeks.

"Will you spend the weekend with me before I leave?" he asked.

Angel took a fast breath and considered the possibility that she had totally misunderstood him. At the same time, she was certain she had heard him correctly. But perhaps a weekend might not mean the same to him as it did to her. His idea of spending the weekend with her could mean spending time together in the day, separating at night and getting together again the next day. Nah. She didn't really believe that.

Better to have no misunderstandings, though. "The entire weekend? As in Saturday and Sunday?" After the question was out, she held her breath.

Eric smiled and was just about to answer when the waiter set their drinks in front of them. "How about let's get crazy and make it Friday night to Sunday night?" he whispered when they were alone again.

"Day and night?" She wanted absolute clarification.

"That's pretty much what I had in mind."

Her hand was still in his, so she brought both down to rest on the table. His fingers fascinated her, and she quietly studied them by the light of the candle in the table's center. They were long fingers, almost femininely soft at first glance, but even within his light grasp she felt their strength.

Not surprisingly, she found his fingers every bit as magnificent as the rest of him. She could only imagine what they would do to her, how they would make her feel when they…. She forced herself to quit the fantasy and get back to reality. There were still questions that needed answers before she agreed to what he'd proposed.

She was about to ask one of those questions when Eric glanced at the diamond-studded gold watch on his wrist and frowned. "My time is up. I'm back on for another forty-five minutes. Will you wait for me?" He lifted her hand to his lips and let them linger there while she went nuts from the candlelight dancing in his eyes. "Will you?"

"I'll be here when you finish."

"Promise?"

She didn't have to think twice about her answer. She knew even before she'd arrived at the club that if he really wanted her, when she left here tonight there would be some type of arrangement between them. There was no sense playing cat and mouse. Especially when she knew the mouse wanted to be caught.

"Cross my heart."

She would have to be crazy to leave now. One night of pleasure had just turned into an entire weekend of what promised to be the greatest sexual adventure of her life.

* * * *

Eric's music was as close to him as his own skin. He could afford to let his thoughts dwell on the beautiful woman in the corner booth as his fingers mechanically played the last song of the set.

The idea of taking a lover for a brief, intense affair wasn't new to him. He'd first come up with the idea six months ago. It was to be a very special thirty-fifth birthday present to himself. He'd even planned to carry through with it during his gig here in the States. But every time he found a woman that piqued his sexual interest, he'd talked himself out of it.

Until he met Angel. Angel with the raven hair and the molten, obsidian eyes. Angel with a body that would tempt the devil himself.

There was something about her, something that attracted him more than any of the other women he'd only halfheartedly seduced during his tours around the world. He wasn't able to put his finger on exactly what it was, but he damned well had every intention of finding out.

Since that first meeting, scarcely a week ago, he'd known this was the woman with whom he wanted to cross all barriers and explore every sensual pleasure their bodies had to offer. She was the woman of his fantasies. The woman who would be open and honest enough with her body to climb with him to the heights of carnal bliss. The woman who had kept him hard day and night since their first meeting.

He could still feel the warm flesh of her thigh against his hand even as his fingers flew across the smooth ivory keys. Christ, how he'd ached to slip his hand beneath her skirt and press his fingers against the soft down of her sex.

Touching Angel the other night had been a test. If she'd made the least objection he would have moved his hand. It wouldn't have deterred him from his goal, but it would have indicated he needed a new approach. She hadn't objected at all, though. In fact, she'd placed her hand over his and without a word let him know he was welcome to leave it there awhile longer.

Her invitation had taken him by surprise. So much so that he'd had to temper the rush of heat that encouraged him to pounce on her like a rutting animal, and he'd acted instead like a completely aroused, but sensitive male. After a respectable length of time, he'd removed his hand from her luscious thigh, turned it over to capture hers and bring it to his lips for what he hoped was the kind of kiss that told her how utterly desirable he found her.

He'd then asked her to come back. Alone. And she had.

Because she had, he'd felt no need to put off the question that was the reason for all of this. He'd put it to her straight. He wanted to spend the entire weekend with her. She'd seemed a bit surprised, but she hadn't turned him down. And she wouldn't. She couldn't. It was unthinkable, unbearable, for him to even consider that now that he'd finally found the woman with whom he wanted to celebrate a birthday of nonstop sex she'd refuse him.

He played the last notes of the night in a rousing crescendo. Not unlike the finale on a concert stage. Or the way his blood thundered through his veins at this very moment. He had not felt this exhilarated, this alive, in a long, long time.

After a short good night to the crowd, he hurried to the corner where he'd left Angel, his heart thumping against his ribs. Had she kept her word and waited for him?

His stomach pitched at the sight of the empty booth, and the thumping of his heart turned into a sharp pain. He slumped onto the leather seat, needing a drink in the worst kind of way. He looked up to search for a waiter only to find Angel standing in front of him like a vision straight from heaven.

"I thought I'd make it back before you finished," she announced, setting her purse down on the table. She looked at the seat opposite his, then back at him. How dense could he be?

He slid toward the middle of the curved leather seat so she could join him, biting back a moan as the crotch of his silk trousers dug into his erection. This woman—this Angel—had already completely bedeviled him.

Man of the world that he was—or thought he was until he met Angel—he had never had a woman set him on fire like this. Much as he wanted her, needed to get inside her, it unsettled him. It must be his long hiatus from sex, he decided, that had him ready to come without her even so much as putting a hand on his cock.

The same waiter who had served them before returned. Eric ordered a margarita without salt for Angel and a double scotch and water for himself.

Courageously, he slid an arm around Angel's shoulder and inched close enough that their thighs touched. At the contact, she pulled in a sharp breath and parted her lips, the tip of her tongue glistening in the soft candlelight. He dipped his mouth down to hers, tangling her tongue with his as she deepened the kiss.

His spirits soared. She was going to accept his proposition. If she wasn't, she wouldn't be kissing him like she wanted to draw all of him into her mouth. Oh god, if only that were true. If only she would give him the opportunity to find out. He couldn't wait any longer.

Ending their kiss, Eric put a finger under Angel's chin and lifted it until her eyes were level with his. "Is your answer yes, then?"

She dipped her head, caught the tip of his finger between her lips, drew it into her mouth and suckled it. "Yes," she said, swirling her tongue around his fingertip.

If he'd had any doubts before about the ability of the woman he'd chosen to tutor him in the finer points of lovemaking, they were now completely dispelled. Any woman who could get him this hot with just a kiss and a sensuous lick of his finger had undoubtedly mastered a hundred and one ways to please a man. And he would bet that along the way she had learned just as many ways for a man to please a woman. He would be a very willing pupil in that regard.

What he learned from Angel this weekend could only help him be a better sexual partner to Joan, if they decided to enter into an exclusive relationship when he returned to London.

From the beginning of his and Joan's relationship, which was nearing the five year mark, sex between them had never produced rockets, or even firecrackers, for that matter. He'd always blamed the lack of passion in their lovemaking on the fact that the demands of his career left him little time or energy for anything but release when they slept together.

He often wondered if she compared him to other men she'd been with, knowing full well there had been others. By mutual agreement, they'd both dated other people when he was out of the country. When he was home, however, they were always an item. They had come to expect it. Their friends and families had come to expect it. And lately his friends and family had come to expect there would one day be wedding bells for him and Joan.

Which was why, when he accepted this six-month gig in the States, he and Joan had decided to use the lengthy separation from each other to rethink the direction of their relationship. To see if they really wanted to take it to the next level when he returned home.

Thus, the motive for this coming weekend with Angel.

Before he committed the rest of his life, sexual and otherwise, to Joan or anyone else, he had to find out if he was capable of experiencing mind-blowing sex with the right partner. Or if the deficiency in his and Joan's relationship went deeper than sex.

And the woman next to him was going to make finding out not only easy, but extremely pleasurable.

Angel nudged his finger from her mouth and lowered her lashes seductively, erasing all thoughts of any woman but her from his mind. "I have a couple of conditions," she said, amending what he thought at first was an unqualified yes. A little of the euphoria he'd felt earlier was replaced by a tiny prickle of apprehension. Still, she *had* agreed.

"Name them", he whispered, his breath sticking in his throat as little aftershocks from her erotic play on his fingertip continued to race through his body.

The look on Angel's face turned serious. "We have our liaison in a neutral place."

He nodded, his throat still too constricted to speak. "And when it's over," she continued, "we don't ever try to contact each other again."

Was that all? His heart nearly burst from joy. She had laid down the very conditions he intended to place before her. How much luckier could he get? This woman was perfect for him. "Agreed," he said, adding, "I have a condition of my own."

"Name it."

"We don't divulge our identities to each other."

She drew her brows together. "But we already know each other's names."

He brought his finger back up to her mouth, wet it with her tongue, and then dragged his finger down to the tiny indentation in her chin. "First names, yes, but not last names. I've never asked for yours and Sweeney is my stage name."

Did he notice a flicker of uncertainty in her eyes, or was it merely the flickering candlelight?

"Agreed," she said so quickly any apprehension he'd felt disappeared.

He trailed his finger along her jaw to the dangling silver pendant at her ear. "When can we choose the place?" He moved the earring back and forth with his finger, fascinated as it twinkled in the candlelight.

Angel tilted her head and initiated another kiss, this one lasting for what seemed to him an eternity, while her tongue teased his in a whirl of erotic dances. Releasing his mouth, she laid a hand on his thigh and his cock strained painfully against the fly of his slim-cut pants. Surely she must be able to sense the pressure at his crotch, the agony on his face. Would she put her hand on him, soothe him just a bit? Oh, if only...

Instead, she reached up for another kiss, this one quicker but no less erotic than the one before. "I'll be back Wednesday night. We'll both have two whole days to think on all of this." She tilted her head to the side and grinned. "And to be certain it's what we both want."

His heart fell and the euphoria that had quickly returned took another nose-dive. Was she playing straight with him, or toying with him? Building him up only to let him down? Her hand inched up his thigh, close enough to his cock that if she moved a finger half an inch she would be touching him. His heart pumped so hard his chest felt as if it would explode.

"I know I'm not going to change my mind," she said, trailing her hand down his thigh to the underside of his knee.

"Nor I," he managed to whisper despite the hammering of his heart, the thundering in his ears and the fierce throbbing of his cock.

Damn, if he wasn't on his way to a climax. What the hell had happened to him? He knew he was horny, but this was unbelievable. He would certainly have to take himself in hand as soon as possible or he wouldn't last one second with her when they were finally alone together.

He wanted another kiss and was just about to take it, when Angel suddenly took a quick gulp from the as yet untouched margarita and slid away from him towards the other end of the booth. She had her bag in her hand and was on her feet before he could stop her.

"Wait." He reached out and put a hand on her arm. "Can't you stay and finish your drink?"

She shook her head. "Got to run. I'll come back Wednesday night so we can finalize everything."

And then she was gone, walking away from him, leaving him with a stone-hard erection and a head full of fantasies he couldn't even begin to sort through.

To make the transition from his aching need for sexual release to a state of stoic self-control before he left the club, he forced himself to think again of the woman on the other side of the ocean.

* * * *

Two days later, Angel left Eric at the club and slipped into her car. She put the air conditioning on full blast and rested her forehead on the steering wheel.

In ten minutes, she was cooler on the outside, but she was still burning up on the inside. If Eric Sweeney could affect her this way after just a couple of kisses, a little groping by both of them, and a lot of erotic promises on both their parts, she wondered how she was going to get through a full weekend of wild, hot, sex.

In spite of the heat still flooding her insides, a long shiver shot from her spine straight to her scalp. She needed to get home where she could gather her wits and assess exactly what she had just agreed to do.

She reached for the gear shift, but stopped before she engaged it. It wasn't safe for her to drive in this condition. She was still too unraveled, her thinking too fuzzy to trust her reactions on the road just yet.

When she'd first given in to the fantasy of becoming Eric Sweeney's weekend lover, she had felt almost like a little girl playing make-believe. Now, she felt like she had grown up all of a sudden and discovered that make-believe was real. What she had just agreed to do was real. And certainly the possible medical condition that had given her the courage to consider this fantasy in the first place was *very* real.

As real as the things Eric Sweeney had said just a few minutes ago, which led her to believe he expected her to be an aggressive, uninhibited, accomplished lover. Leaning close to her, his fingers splayed at her hip, his warm breath at her neck just below her earlobe—the most sensitive spot on her body, no less—he'd vowed he couldn't wait to give himself up to her experience and guidance.

He was going to give himself up to *her?* If he only knew how inexperienced she was he would probably laugh himself right out of their arrangement.

She'd been tempted to level with him, tell him all she was looking for was a great sexual experience with someone who wasn't interested in becoming a part of her future. Someone like him, who seemed to want the same thing.

But she'd decided not to burst his bubble. This weekend she'd be everything he expected her to be. In the time she had left before they got together she'd bring herself up to speed on all the ways to be a great lover.

Necessity was the mother of invention, she reminded herself. And while she knew there were few things left to be invented where sex was concerned, there were probably still a few techniques that remained untried by someone. Surely, no matter how experienced Eric might be, he could not have been the recipient of them all.

She recalled a book she'd flipped through in a book store her last trip home to Manhattan. There was a section where the author had listed all the various concoctions a person could whip up to stimulate a lover. Things like lotions and oils, Jell-O, whipped cream and of all things—peanut butter. Crunchy peanut butter at that.

That particular technique, she recalled, had not only held her attention for a full five minutes, it had had her blushing and squirming right there in the aisle. She loved peanut butter, but heavens, how long would it take to lick all that thick, crunchy goo off someone? Especially off someone's delicate, private places.

She wouldn't have to be content with just peanut butter, either. If she gave it some thought she was certain she could come up with some interesting ingredients of her own. Honey was one of them. Honey and peanut butter. Ummmm. Her mouth was watering already.

She had her work cut out for her these next two days. Not only did she have to assemble a much sexier bedroom wardrobe than she presently owned, but she'd have to go back to that book store. Then she'd have to gather all the items she'd need to practice her newly found sensual arts on Eric the Magnificent.

By the time their *sexcapade* was over, she'd definitely be his match in bed. Heck, if she used that peanut butter and honey correctly, she just might come away from this weekend with Eric Sweeney believing she was the best in bed he'd ever had.

With a satisfied sigh, Angel decided she was ready now for the trek home. While she drove, she made a mental list of the things she had to do before she met Eric to begin their weekend of erotic pleasure.

First thing tomorrow, after she had the new blood test Dr. Frazier had ordered, she'd shop for everything she wanted to bring with her this weekend. That would leave Friday morning clear for a trip to the beauty salon and a manicure. She might even have time for a pedicure before lunch. Once all those things were taken care of she'd be free as a bird until Monday.

Free to enjoy what promised to be the best, most erotic, weekend of her life.

She could hardly wait.

Three

"I believe you have a message for me from Eric Sweeney," Angel told the clerk behind the Registration Desk of the Continental Hotel.

"And your name, madam?"

"Angel."

The man moved away from the counter to the wall of pigeonholes behind him, where written communications between hotel guests and visitors were kept. He came back to his station, handed Angel a folded slip of paper and turned his attention to an incoming guest.

I'm in Suite 3212. Call me when you're on your way up. I can't wait to see you. E.S.

3212? The thirty-second floor? Angel's gaze flew to the bank of elevators to her right. The thirty-second floor was the Penthouse. *The Penthouse?* Not hardly. Eric must have made a mistake. He must be as nervous as she was and written an extra digit. She looked guiltily at the bellman waiting for her with the cart holding her two suitcases and the small box wrapped in brown paper.

"I'm afraid I have to make a call before I go up. Can you direct me to a house phone, please?"

"Follow me," the young man said, stepping in front of her and leading the way with the luggage cart. At the first hallway they came to, he waved his hand for her to enter. Half a dozen phones stood idle.

Her heart drumming against her ribs, Angel lifted the receiver of the first phone she reached and dialed the numbers on the paper in her trembling hand.

"Hello."

She would have recognized that voice anywhere.

"It's Angel." She couldn't believe she had spoken so calmly, casually, like this was going according to plan.

"I'll be waiting." Eric's voice flowed over the line, sensuously soft, the way it did when they were together and he had his mouth to her ear. She nearly collapsed. Might have, if the bellman hadn't been standing there waiting. But somehow she got the room number out of her mouth, followed the young man to a private elevator, which required a key, and rode with him in shocked silence for thirty-two floors.

Eric was waiting at the open door when they arrived and ushered them in. Once her luggage was deposited against the wall and the bellman compensated with a generous tip, he took both her hands in his.

"I'm so very glad you're here," he said, rather modestly, Angel thought, for a man who had not only initiated this once-in-a-lifetime tryst but had supplied these lavish surroundings as well.

Surroundings she was just now able to comprehend fully. And so taken aback was she by the splendor that surrounded her she never even considered a response to his declaration.

It was all too much to be taken in with a swift glance. It took several sweeps around the room for her mind to completely grasp the setting into which she had just been welcomed.

Bouquets of flowers were everywhere. Sweetheart roses, daisies, irises. Several arrangements of long-stemmed red roses. Every available table was laden with blooms.

The room itself was beyond anything Angel had ever imagined existed outside of her dreams. A cobalt blue carpet, so thick and plush she sank up to her ankles in it. Delicate gold-leafed furniture upholstered in various shades of blue brocade—her very favorite color—from the palest color of the sky to the deepest, darkest midnight hue.

She pulled in a breath of disbelief. At the opposite side of the room, the two large windows were covered in heavy cream-silk brocade, draped to the sides with tasseled ropes of blue and interwoven with heavy strands of thick gold braid. The walls were adorned with gold framed mirrors and paintings that looked like originals. The magnificence surrounding her was like something out of a fairy tale.

And this was only the living room. Angel had never been inside a Penthouse suite before, but she was sure that none of the three sofas in the room opened up into a bed. There had to be at least one other room beyond. Maybe even a couple more. From her limited vantage point, she knew this suite was the size of a large apartment.

"Do you like it?" Eric was staring down at her, his hands still gripping hers.

"This is a penthouse." Stupid thing to say. He knew what it was.

He chuckled softly. "Yes, I know. But do you like it?"

"I don't understand. You shouldn't have done this. This is

all too…"

He laughed again, not at her, she could tell, but at her obvious amazement. "Elegant? Expensive? Extravagant?"

"How can you afford this?" A tactless thing to say, perhaps, but she couldn't find the words to adequately express what she meant, what she felt. And then an awful thought came crashing down on her. He could be a shady character. A criminal.

Surely no musician, not even one who played in an upscale Manhattan nightclub, could afford anything like this. It dawned on her then how little she knew about Eric Sweeney. He'd already admitted he used a stage name. Suddenly, she was terrified. What had she done? What had she gotten herself into? More importantly, how could she get herself out of it?

Then Eric ran his hands up her arms as smoothly as he ran them over his keyboard. Her insides turned all soft and warm, and all she wanted to do was melt into him. That frightened her even more.

"What is it, Angel?" Eric asked in the silky, sexy voice she had come to love and recognize as distinctly his. "Doesn't this please you? I wanted so much to make you welcome, to do everything I could to make this the most memorable weekend of your life." He pulled back, his brows creased in a frown. "You look frightened."

"I am," she admitted, quickly. "All of this terrifies me. It isn't at all what I expected. You…this, you…isn't what I expected. I think I made a mistake. I think I should leave."

* * * *

Eric's insides fell like an elevator with a snapped cable. He hadn't considered this kind of reaction from Angel. Hadn't considered that someone unaccustomed to this kind of luxury would be frightened, even put off by what might look like a crass display of wealth by an egotistical man out to impress a woman with resources he didn't possess. It didn't occur to him to do things any differently than he would have if he had met Angel under different circumstances.

If he had met her when he was himself—Eric Swensen, world-famous concert pianist.

But that was foolish thinking. He *was* himself. Inside, he was always himself. It was only the outer trappings he changed to accommodate whatever realm he happened to inhabit at any particular time.

He'd played the part of a writer in need of solitude in

France, an artist in Greece, an investment broker on his first vacation in five years in Spain. He'd even been a beach bum in Hawaii, when, in a moment of unexpected panic, he'd felt an emptiness in his life and had desperately needed the open sky to soothe his troubled spirit.

On his trips around the world he may have been an imposter on the outside, but he had always been himself where he knew it really mattered—deep in his soul. He'd never thought of himself as dishonest. He had only done what was necessary to survive.

Should he have done things differently this time? Come clean with Angel because she was so unlike any of the women he'd sought out simply for a few hours of sex? Because, beyond the physical allure of her face and her body, in spite of all the other men she must have known around the world, there was an innocence about her that puzzled him.

He studied Angel's face carefully. He saw fear in her eyes and in the tight thinning of her lips, and she was staring up at him as if she were expecting some kind of assault. My God, was she afraid he'd harm her? He slid his hands higher up her arms and gripped her shoulders firmly but gently.

"Angel, listen to me. I'm sorry if all of this has come as a shock to you, but I swear to you I've come by the money for all of this through legal and honest means. And some shrewd investments," he added, aware that she knew there was no way a night club musician could afford all of this on his income alone.

A smile lifted the corners of her mouth, and he felt her relax a little beneath his hands. She took another look around the room, wide-eyed, still a little uncertain, but the fear had been replaced by open admiration. "Wow, you must have invested in gold."

He allowed himself to relax a little, too, and countered her smile with a broad grin. "A modest trust from my grandfather got me started." Not altogether a lie. His grandfather had bought Eric his first baby grand when Eric was only ten, which to the old man's way of thinking had been the beginning of his grandson's career.

"I just didn't expect—"

He laid a finger gently across her lips, and then he took both her hands in his. "The fault is mine. I should have prepared you. But now that you're here, please try to relax and enjoy it.

I want to show you the rest of the suite. But first, let me get you something to drink. Some champagne?"

Angel took a deep breath. He could almost see her mind and body surrender to the sincerity in his voice. At least he hoped that's what he saw. The thought of her distrusting him brought a strange sorrow to his heart.

"The flowers are beautiful," Angel said, sliding her hands from his and walking farther into the room. She stopped at one of the tables adorned with a cut-crystal vase of pink roses and a lacy fern and passed her fingertips lightly over the delicate blooms. Lowering her head, she drew in a long, deep breath of the fragrant blossoms. Then she looked up at him, a return of the trust she had shown him this past week in her eyes. "I think I'm ready for that drink, now."

He crossed the short distance to her and slipped an arm around her waist. Turning her toward him, he curved his other arm around her shoulder, drawing her to him. The blood in his veins was hot even before he touched his lips to hers.

He had to fight the clawing need inside him to keep from pulling her down to the plush carpet and begging her to begin their first wild night of pleasure right then. Instead, he kissed her more gently than he wanted to, and he only deepened the kiss when she willingly parted her lips and stroked his tongue with hers.

His heart beat so wildly in his chest he feared he wouldn't be able to speak or even breathe. Lucky for him, Angel pulled away, a look on her face he couldn't decipher. But he knew it wasn't fear anymore, and for that he was thankful.

He had expected her to be a little more self-confident and in control, not quite so timid—almost shy. But perhaps this was her way, and they were, after all, in a much more intimate setting than on any of the previous times they'd been together.

Besides, she was here, wasn't she? And willing to stay from the looks of it now. He wouldn't push or press her. He'd think of her as a beautiful piece of music and let her set the beat. He would pick up on her mood and follow her lead.

For the next two days—and nights—she would be the maestro.

* * * *

Angel didn't know how or why it happened, but as quickly as her fears had risen, they subsided with one touch and the soothing sincerity in Eric's voice. The man literally turned her insides to liquid—in more ways, and in more places, than one.

How much Eric Sweeney was worth financially was his own business. Since this weekend was his idea and he was paying the tab, he could darn well spend as much as he liked. The important thing was deep down she did trust him. If she didn't, she would never have agreed to spend the weekend with him in the first place. He had every right to keep personal things from her. Wasn't she exercising the same right by keeping the news of her illness from him? Neither of them owed the other anything but this weekend.

On the strength of that conviction, Angel gathered all the courage she owned and decided whatever the news she received next week—and she knew it would not be good— she still had the weekend with Eric Sweeney to look forward to.

And right now she had the next second to look forward to, because Eric was standing in front of her, close enough to touch, offering her a glass of champagne.

She allowed them both a few sips from the crystal flutes before she took Eric's glass from him and set their glasses on the marble coffee table.

Delighting in his surprise when she slipped one arm around his neck and curved her body into his, Angel ran a hand down the front of his fly and cupped him lightly.

And, oh, my! He wasn't the only one surprised. She wasn't expecting such a handful this early in the evening.

Eric's body tensed and his breath whistled as he sucked it in between his teeth. "I've wanted you to touch me like this for days." He rocked against her hand, drew in another quick breath and moaned deep in his throat before he pulled the air into his lungs.

Angel tilted her head back so she could look into his eyes. She felt playful, giddy almost, like she'd had more than just a taste of champagne. "We've only known each other 'for days,'" she teased. After one very gentle squeeze, she released his weighty testicles and ran her hand up the front of his fly, pressed it against the erection that was already a prominent bulge.

She was ready for his lips when they descended on hers with breathtaking force. He crushed her against him, and she closed her hand on his penis, already pulsing against her palm through the thickness of his fly. Her breath whooshed from her lungs. She wanted to unzip his pants right then so she could feel the fullness of him in her bare hand.

Then, as if a fog lifted from her brain, she realized just how brazen she was acting. Even a genuine, highly-sexed, experienced, know-it-all woman would show more restraint, more finesse, than this. He must think she was nothing but a common tramp. She would have to take her time with this, take it slower, maybe—

Before she could finish her thoughts, Eric clamped his hand over hers, stilled it and pressed it hard against his sex. He took a few audible breaths and brought his forehead against hers. "You are even more wonderful than I imagined you'd be. I'd like nothing more than to strip you naked right now and carry you to bed, but I really want us to take it a little slower. *I* need to take it a little slower."

Relief flooded through her. "So do I," she admitted, grateful for even a short respite from the clippety-clop of her heart. "I don't know what came over me. I can't even blame it on too much champagne. It's just that you're..."

He was sliding her hand up his fly, and none too quickly, she noticed. "I'm what?" he asked, stopping when their hands reached his waist.

"You're too damn sexy," she blurted out. Laughing at her own honesty, she slid her hand from his and flattened it against his chest, discovering that the beat of his heart was as erratic as her own. "And I seem to be in an unusually silly, reckless mood."

Reckless because you've nothing to lose and everything to gain, she reminded herself. You're here to enjoy everything about Eric Sweeney there is—his boyish good looks, his quiet, gentle manner, his drive 'em crazy body that had yet to make an appearance. A body she already knew would put Greek gods to shame.

Just as importantly, her conscience pressed forward, you're going to let him enjoy you. You're going to be everything he thinks you are. You're going to give him everything he wants, everything you've led him to expect from this lavish, never-to-be-forgotten weekend. He bargained for over-the-top, on another planet, mind-blowing, erotic sex with you. And you're going to deliver what you promised.

Eric lowered his mouth to hers, brushed her lips with his, and buried his face in her hair, his mouth at her ear. "I love the mood you're in. I wouldn't have you any other way. But please," he whispered, "slow down just a little. I've waited a long time to find a special person like you. Perhaps a little too long. I..."

Angel moved her head to the side so that the corners of their lips touched, wrapped her arms around his waist and hugged him tight. "Your request is my command. Besides, I barely tasted that wonderful bubbly stuff, and I would like to see the rest of these palatial surroundings." She took a playful swipe at the corner of his mouth with her tongue and reached down for the neglected flute of champagne.

Eric's sigh of relief didn't escape her notice. He really did want her to take it slow. And from the hefty erection she'd felt just moments before she knew it wouldn't be easy for him to do so. Once again, she admired his restraint at a time when most men would have her naked and stretched out on one of the more than adequate sofas in the room.

Eric carried his glass of champagne to the far side of the room, drew the drapes closed and turned on a few more lamps until the room was bathed in a soothing, golden glow.

She made herself comfortable at one end of the luxurious sofa. Tucking her feet under her, she kept her eyes steady on Eric, not willing to let him out of her sight for one second longer than she had to.

On his way back to her, Eric stopped abruptly, smacked his forehead with his hand. "Good heavens, I forgot about the food. I take it you're hungry?"

"Famished," she told him. "I followed your mandate. One of the last things you told me Wednesday night was to come with a good appetite." She smiled and lifted the flute to her lips again.

"So I did," Eric agreed. "And I've taken care of everything. I placed an early order with the kitchen and told them I'd call when we were ready." He picked up the phone closest to him on a long, high table in front of the windows. "They assured me it would take only a few minutes to assemble everything and send it up." He punched in a couple of numbers, but before he brought the phone to his mouth, he placed the receiver back on its cradle.

"I've ordered a cold meat tray with crackers, assorted fruit, cheeses, sorbet and coffee. And another bottle of champagne. Does that sound good to you? Is there something I missed, something else you'd prefer?"

It sounded perfect to her. She'd skipped breakfast and

lunch, had existed the entire day on coffee and cola but now with the champagne relaxing her, she actually felt like she could eat something substantial.

"Everything you've mentioned sounds great," she assured him. "I can't think of another thing I'd want." Except you, she wanted to add, but instead, thanked him out loud for his thoughtfulness.

She could tell by the smile that spread across his face that he was pleased with her response. It took so little to make him smile, and it did so much for her when he did. She felt that warm, tingly feeling winding its way under her skin like it had the first time she'd gone to the club alone.

Eric settled himself on the other end of the sofa, next to the table that held the champagne bucket. "Can I top that for you?" He nodded to the half full flute in her hand.

Angel leaned forward and handed him her glass, waited while he added more champagne, then retreated back to her corner, acutely aware that he was still keeping his distance from her.

He topped both their glasses and they sipped in silence, watching each other over the rims of the crystal flutes. Sexual tension stretched between them like a taut electric wire.

"Do you mind if I kick off my sandals and stretch my legs a bit?" she asked, shifting her body slightly on the sofa.

"Not at all. I want you to make yourself as comfortable as if this were your very own home. If there's something you need or want, or something you're uncomfortable with—including me—please let me know immediately." He took a generous drink from his glass before he set it down on the coffee table. "This weekend is for you every bit as much as it is for me. I want you to remember that."

Angel let out a soft murmur of contentment as she slipped off her shoes, stretched her legs as far as she could and ended up with one of her bare feet against Eric's thigh. She felt the involuntary jerk of his body and pulled her foot back as if it had touched fire. "Sorry about that. I thought I had more room."

He reached out, grabbed her foot and brought it back to rest against his thigh. "No need to be sorry. I'm just a little jumpy. Anyway, I love your feet. They're as beautiful as the rest of you," he said, skimming his fingers lightly over her instep and around her ankle.

Closing his eyes briefly, he gave a sigh of annoyance and

shook his head. "Dammit, Angel. The last thing I want is to get you all uptight because you're worrying about doing something wrong." He leaned forward and held out his arms. "Come here."

She sat up eagerly and scooted over toward him, moving easily into his embrace. "Angel, Angel, Angel," he crooned. "My knee jerk reactions have nothing to do with you. It's my problem." He pulled back a little so he could see her face clearly. "It's been more than six months since I've been with a woman. I'm afraid I'm on the edge...afraid I'll remain there until. . . Damn it all, I'm not handling this very well, am I? I'm probably embarrassing you to death. Hell, I'm damn well embarrassing myself, if you want to know the truth." He looked away, but not before she saw his cheeks bloom with color.

She put her hand on his chin and gently turned his face back toward her. It was so easy to empathize with him, especially since she'd been teetering on the edge herself ever since she met him. It would not be difficult at all to do anything she could to make this easier for him.

"Would you like us to have sex now, maybe take the edge off, then we could. . ." Before she could finish, a medley of low chimes sounded.

"It's our food," Eric said, a pained look on his face. "And at the most embarrassing moment for me." His face, already flushed, turned a deep red. She understood his predicament immediately, jumped up quickly and was halfway to the door when he called out, "Sign for me would you? And add a twenty-five dollar tip."

Once the food had been set out and they were alone again, Eric beckoned to her with outstretched arms. "I know you're starving, but would you mind coming over here for just a minute before we eat?"

Would she mind? Not in a million light years.

She hurried over to him and sat down on his lap. Once she was comfortable, he slid a hand behind her neck and brought her mouth down to his. "If I don't kiss you now, I think I'll die."

When he took her mouth it was with so much hunger Angel felt as if she were feeding his very soul.

Eric explored the hot, moist flesh of Angel's mouth with wide sweeps of his tongue. The deeper he probed, the more she welcomed his parries with a force equal to his own.

His head felt light-years away, yet his brain registered every sensation that stormed his body. He had never before been this hot from just kissing a woman. It was pure heaven. And hell.

He would have kept on kissing her until he passed out from lack of air, but his cock was about to burst from this pleasure that had him nearly out of his mind. Every nerve in his body rebelled against the thought, but he knew he had to release her now. If he didn't, he'd lose all control and come.

With a groan, he wrenched his mouth from hers, squeezed his eyes shut and threw his head back on the pillowed sofa. Angel's soft, rounded buttocks still pressed against his cock, but now that their lips were no longer joined, his arousal was holding steady, the most he could ask for considering the way his blood was churning through his veins.

Angel passed her fingertips over his brow and placed light kisses first on his eyelids, then at the corner of his mouth, and finally at the base of his throat.

Then he felt her body slide down along his, heard the rasp of his zipper and opened his eyes to Angel's raven hair spread across his thighs. Before he could take a deep breath, his cock was in her hand, her fingers wrapped around its base and she was working him up and down with a slow, easy rhythm.

* * * *

Angel hadn't planned her next move any more than she'd planned her next breath. All she knew was Eric needed release and the tip of his engorged penis was beckoning to her.

Realizing what she was up to, Eric tried to lift himself, tried to discourage her. "Angel, no. You don't have to do this now." But when she ignored his plea and took the sensitive head of his cock between her lips, he could do nothing but fall back on the sofa and give himself up to the sweet, furious pleasure of her mouth.

He was larger than she thought at first and she had to shift him around with her tongue before he fit comfortably in her mouth.

Eric shuddered, made a halfhearted attempt to lift himself again. "Angel, what about you? What about. . ."

She lifted her head only enough to let the tip of his penis slide from her mouth. "Shhh," she commanded, her hands rubbing the length of his thighs in an effort to soothe him.

She had just wrapped her lips around him again and was

readying herself to treat him to some special maneuvers with her tongue when hoarse moans from deep in his throat caused her concern. She eased him out of her mouth and looked up at him.

His face was flushed nearly as red as the tip of his penis, and his hair that he kept so neatly bound in back had come undone. His condition, Angel assessed, called for quick emergency treatment.

Gently, but insistently, she pushed and guided his hips until she'd coaxed him flat on his back. His penis stood nearly straight up and jerked uncontrollably. She gave it one admiring flick of her tongue before she made her next move.

Quickly she rose, threw one leg over Eric's thighs and brought her other leg up to straddle him across his knees. The generous size of the sofa afforded enough room for both of them to be comfortable.

Eric lifted his head, his beautiful tawny curls fanned out like a golden-fringed shawl around his shoulders. "Angel, please let me see you, touch you...Oh, Jesus, Angel..."

She didn't let him finish, didn't bother to comment. She just took him in her mouth again. And while she swirled her tongue around the hot, velvet head of his penis, she started steadily stroking him with her hand, increasing the tempo of the strokes as the pulsing under her lips signaled Eric's orgasm rushing toward her.

His body stiffened, he took a couple of fast, harsh breaths that rushed back from his lungs in short, panting bursts. And then she tasted the warm, salty-sweet essence of his ejaculate as she filled her mouth with the length and breadth of him, suckled him until his body jerked hard, once, twice, shuddered, then went lax. Only when he moaned his contentment did she slowly release him.

Eric whispered her name, outstretched a trembling hand to her and urged her forward. The instant she spread herself on top of him, a wild, hot clawing ripped at her belly and she began rocking against him. She had been so focused on bringing satisfaction to him she had totally ignored her own building desire. But it could no longer be ignored. The urgent, pounding pulse between her thighs demanded release.

And Eric's hands sliding down her hips were on their way to bringing her that ecstasy.

Four

While the room and reality settled back around him, Eric lifted Angel's skirt and bunched it up around her waist. The soft, rounded beauty of her buttocks yielded under his hands and he pressed her to his body, his flaccid penis beginning to stir again.

How was this possible? How could he be thinking of coming again so soon? She had just sent him through the roof, drained him dry and he was already feeling the first twitch of arousal. His joy knew no bounds. Angel was everything, and more, that he'd waited for. And he hadn't even been inside her yet. Hadn't even seen her naked yet.

He worked a finger under the elastic of the flimsy scrap of satin panties until he felt her dense, wet curls. A slight move to the center and he found her opening, hot, drenched and waiting for him so he slipped a finger inside, found no resistance, and slid it deeper. Angel let out a yelp of pleasure and ground herself against him with determined force.

"You like that inside you, Angel?"

Her body arched and she pushed against his finger, trying to get it deeper still. "Yes, oh yes, this does feel good."

He slipped another finger inside her and brought his thumb into play, moved it around the slick, hot opening until it met her swollen clitoris. Then he rubbed it gently, but with enough force to cause a delicious friction for her. She applauded his efforts eagerly with a long moan of satisfaction.

His cock was doing more than just twitching now. It was beginning to stiffen. But before he got them both in a situation he didn't want to face just yet, he figured he'd better do something about it quick.

"I know another part of me that's dying to make you feel as good as you made me feel," he said, removing his fingers from her hot sheath to grasp her buttocks firmly with both hands. He held her in place and slid down the length of the sofa until his mouth was directly under her mound. She let out a high squeal of pleasure when his tongue took its first lap of her moisture.

And oh, she was the sweetest thing he'd ever tasted, sweeter even than the juiciest, most exotic mango, thought by many to be the most delicious fruit in the world. With every thrust of his tongue she squirmed and squealed, and the more she encouraged him, the more he drank of her nectar.

He was fully aroused again, and he cursed himself for not having the forethought to prepare for such an eventuality. As glorious as coming in her mouth had been, he wanted to be inside her, wanted to feel that heat wrap itself around his cock and launch him to that place where his mind and body would shatter. But, much as he hated to, he'd have to wait for that ultimate carnal delight until they had protection.

Even as his mind accepted the responsible decision, he felt the thunder inside Angel, felt it roar through her body, vibrate against his lips. Her sweetness mixed with the musky scent of desire and her sexual release washed over him, filling him with a special kind of headiness.

As Angel rode out the last of her orgasm, she reached behind her, grasped his cock that was now at full mast and worked him deftly with her fingers until he too rocked from the thunder of release. Again.

He could hardly believe he'd come so soon on the heels of what she'd coaxed from his body just minutes before. Yet, even blissfully sated, he couldn't keep from imagining what it would be like later when he finally got to slide his cock inside her. Already, he had surpassed any previous sexual experience he'd had with anyone, including Joan.

Not quite sure what to make of that realization, and not really caring to pursue it at the moment, he turned his thoughts to something much less carnal, but no less necessary.

"I had planned to get some food in our stomachs before we actually got this weekend underway," he said, after Angel scooted higher up his body and his breath wasn't coming out in gasps anymore. She nestled her head in the valley between his cheek and his shoulder and he spent the next few minutes just enjoying her scent. She mumbled something unintelligible, nuzzled her cheek deeper against his shoulder, and he hugged her close.

"Although to tell the truth with the condition I was in when you walked in that door, I don't think I would have managed to get one morsel of food down my throat anytime soon." He dropped a kiss on top of her head, drew her closer still.

Snuggling lower, Angel let out a long sigh of contentment against his chest. "I'm glad your condition has eased. So has mine. Quite considerably."

"You knew exactly what I needed, although I feel I must warn you that I'm not always so compliant, or so easy to control."

Angel tilted her head and looked up so she could see his face. "Are you telling me you're a tiger in the sack?"

He growled playfully and nipped the tip of her nose.

"I'll let you decide that for yourself when the time comes. Which reminds me, we really should be thinking about food before it gets too late." He lifted himself to a sitting position and hauled her up with him. "I'm going to make a quick trip to the john first. There's a guest bathroom in that little alcove over there." He pointed to an arched opening across the room. "Unless," he said with a wink, "you want to accompany me and get a tour of the bedroom at the same time."

Angel worked her skirt down over her hips and then walked her fingers up his chest while he struggled to zip his pants. "I do think your naughty side is beginning to show." Her voice rang with laughter.

Eric slid an arm around her waist. "You haven't seen anything, yet. And we still have forty-eight hours to go." His hand slid down to her bottom and gave it a gentle squeeze as he echoed her laughter.

"So we do," she said and bent down to nibble at his throat before she pushed herself to her feet.

Eric watched her sashay across the room, already feeling light years away from the other world he inhabited. Treating himself to Angel's whimsical, playful spirit would be the best birthday present he would ever receive.

And when the weekend was over he would know if he and Joan faced any problems that couldn't be solved. He would know, and hopefully so would she, whether tying the knot was in their future.

In any event, at the moment he couldn't hold back the depressing thought that next year he would have to celebrate his birthday without Angel. All the more reason to make every second of this birthday celebration count double, he told himself, shrugging off the dismal thought.

* * * *

Angel was glad for the few minutes of privacy in the guest bathroom. She needed time to pull herself together after the unexpected sexual encounter with Eric. Every time she thought about having oral sex with him, the blood rushed to her face so fast she felt faint. Not that she hadn't had oral sex before. Or that she hadn't planned on it happening with Eric over the weekend. She had. She had just never before allowed herself to experience this degree of intimacy with a man until she'd already had sex with him.

But then, she had never before allowed herself to spend a weekend with a man she barely knew, either. Nor had she ever had to face a weekend that could be the beginning of a death sentence for her.

Shaking off a chill, she leaned over the pink, shell-shaped marble sink and looked herself straight in the eyes in the oval, gold framed mirror. Nothing in her life made any sense right now. Everything was upside down.

Damn right it was. And everything fun in her life might be over in the next few days. Compared to that little fact, letting a man tongue her clit and giving him a good head job was small potatoes. She splashed more cold water on her face, as much to rejuvenate her spirit as to cool herself down.

She turned off the water and rearranged her hair, paying particular attention to her appearance. She liked what she saw. The haircut and style was the best she'd ever gotten. Her eyes were brighter than she'd ever seen them. And her skin glowed like she was the picture of health. Who would ever think to look at her that she might be on the brink of...

She slapped at the marble vanity top with one hand and picked up the tube of lipstick she'd set down with the other. No. She would not do this. She would not allow herself this morbid self-indulgence. Not when she had Eric Sweeney in the other room and the most incredible two days of her entire life stretching before her. Forcing her hand steady she applied the ruby-red lipstick in long, even strokes, and then she passed her tongue over her lips for extra shine. She had no time to waste.

Soft music wafted into the bathroom when she opened the door. She smiled. In the other room, the most devastating man she had ever known was waiting for her. Waiting to give her pleasure with his body, waiting to take pleasure from hers. She'd be a damned fool to pass up this fantasy come to life, especially since it might well be her last.

When she joined Eric in the dining area, a fresh bottle of champagne was waiting in a gold ice bucket. Against the wall, a serving counter held meats, cheeses, fruits. The dining table was already set with delicate crystal and expensive china. Eric pulled a chair out for her as she approached.

"You've pulled your hair back again," she said, initiating a neutral topic of conversation.

"Habit," Eric responded, sliding the chair beneath her and waiting until she was comfortably seated before seating himself. He offered her the tray of fruit. She took a few strawberries then helped herself to a selection of the meats, along with some crackers and slices of the most delectable cheeses she'd ever seen.

"I'm afraid we were a little too long getting to this. The cold meats are warm, the hot coffee is probably beginning to cool and the sorbet is undoubtedly melted," Eric said apologetically as he filled his plate with generous servings of each of the assorted selections.

"Everything looks scrumptious," she assured him. "And I'm hungry enough to eat the proverbial horse, so I'm not about to complain about something as insignificant as the incorrect temperature of food." She slathered a thin, crusty piece of bread with some pâté, popped it in her mouth and rolled her eyes upward in delight. "Wonderful," she said, licking every last crumb from her lips.

"I love when you do that," Eric said, setting his fork aside.

"Do what?"

"Pass your tongue over your lips that way."

"What way? Like this?" Angel teased, gliding her tongue from one side of her mouth to the other.

Eric sucked in a gasp. "It makes me hot just watching you."

Involuntarily, she squeezed her thighs together. He got hot watching her lick her lips. He made her hot just by telling her she made him hot. What a combination they were.

She folded a thin slice of smoked salmon over a toasted mini-bagel she had already covered with the creamiest herbed cheese she'd ever seen. After taking a dainty bite, she lifted the flute of champagne to her lips, locking eyes with Eric over the rim.

He was staring at her with the same hot, ready-to-explode look he had before she'd gone down on him. She clenched her thighs tighter. Damn, she wasn't any more interested in food now than he seemed to be, but she was determined to add some sense of civility to this weekend. She might be sex-deprived at the moment, and craving a weekend of hard loving, but she wasn't depraved. At least she'd never considered herself so. Yet, the way she felt and acted around Eric made her doubt her own sense of good conduct.

She picked up her cup and saucer and held it out to Eric. "I think I'm ready for some coffee now." He looked at her with a pained expression and for a moment she thought he was going to refuse her request, but then he pushed his chair back from the table. He stood with considerable difficulty, Angel noticed. And then, as he made his way to the silver carafe on the serving table, she saw why.

His fly strained at the seams from his very sizeable erection. Poor man. She wanted to giggle, but didn't dare. She only allowed herself a few seconds of a self-satisfied grin. Women had it so much easier than men in that department. No way could he tell she was as uncomfortable as he was.

While Eric filled her cup, Angel kept her eyes focused on the thin wisps of smoke swirling up from the still hot liquid. From the looks of it, the coffee hadn't cooled off any faster than either of them had.

"Everything was delicious," she told him, once he was seated again.

Eric poured coffee for himself. "I'm glad you enjoyed it." She didn't miss the obvious strain in his voice and the fact that he avoided looking directly at her.

"Am I allowed one personal question?" she asked, taking a sip of coffee to smooth out the tension she felt arcing between them again.

"Depends. What is it you want to know?"

"I was just wondering if you had ever been married." As soon as the question left her mouth she wanted to pull her tongue out. She set the cup down with a loud clink and waved her hand at him. "Forget I asked that."

Eric set his own cup down, and this time he did look at her. "No, I've never been married. And the reason I haven't taken the plunge yet is a long story that has as much to do with my overburdened career as it does with a fear of repeating the mistakes of my parents."

Eric picked up his cup again, but kept it hovering over his saucer. "Actually, I have been thinking lately of getting married. In fact—" Thinking better of it, he didn't finish the sentence, put his cup down and pushed it aside. "What about you? Ever taken the plunge yourself, or even thought of it?"

She'd been expecting an echo of her question. "Oh, sure, I've thought of it. But like you, one look at my parents and I changed my mind. For a different reason though, it would seem, than the one you've expressed."

"Oh? How so?"

"Well, I gather from your answer that your parents' marriage wasn't exactly made in heaven." He nodded so she continued. "Just the opposite with mine. My parents have been so deliriously happy for all of their married life they've set a standard I could never hope to achieve." Suddenly, she felt confined sitting behind the table, so she pushed away from it and stood.

"I'd rather not deal with the calamity I see in most marriages. Besides, I love the work I do, and I can't imagine any man agreeing to my living a whole year in a foreign country without him. Or of finding one who would relocate with me." That had certainly been the case with Paul Barron whom she'd met last summer on her yearly trip home to Manhattan.

Beginning to feel awkward just standing there, Angel walked back into the living area, stopped at a table holding a beautiful silver sculpture of two lovers entwined in an erotic embrace. In a reflective mood, she ran her hand along the smooth, round edge of the statue's base. "I guess you could say the jury's still out on whether or not I'll ever take a walk down the aisle."

The statement was meant to be one of those impersonal, clichéd remarks people make simply to keep the conversation moving, so she wasn't prepared for the sudden cloud of doom that settled over her, bringing her mood down low again.

She was so caught up in the depressing thought that she was unaware Eric had crossed the room until she felt his warmth behind her. And then as quickly as her mood had dipped, it rose, and wordlessly, she turned and moved into his arms as naturally as if she'd done it a hundred times before.

* * * *

Eric had no desire to continue the discussion of marriage while he had Angel in his arms. He had no desire to talk or think of anything even remotely connected with his life outside this room.

He didn't want to talk about the concert stage, his tenuous

relationship with Joan, or the decision he faced concerning his career. He didn't want to speak or think of anything except this moment and all the moments to come in the next two days.

"Penny for your thoughts," Angel said, nuzzling her head under his chin.

"Hardly worth even that," he answered, tightening his embrace and feeling himself stir as she arched into him.

Angel's body began to sway in time with the soft, soothing music that filled the room. "Such beautiful music," she murmured as Eric's body picked up the beat from hers and followed her lead.

He pressed a kiss on top of her head. "You like classical music?"

"It's my favorite."

He dragged his lips down to her temple, then to the corner of her mouth. "Really?" he asked against her lips, his tongue already aching to tangle with hers.

She shifted her mouth slightly so that their lips were perfectly aligned but with a breath of space between them. "Really. My parents were almost as fond of classical music and classical literature as they were of the languages they taught. They introduced me to all three before I entered kindergarten."

Her warm breath tickled his lips, teased his tongue. Saliva pooled inside his mouth. He swallowed quickly. "You were lucky to have such wise and wonderful parents." And he was a very lucky man indeed to have her in his arms. To have had her cross his path just when he had given up hope of ever finding someone like her.

They swayed together for a while, like two parts of a whole, their lips a breath away and their gazes so intent on each other neither saw the other so much as blink. And then Angel suddenly stopped moving, slid her arms up his back and looked at him with the most serious expression he'd seen on her face all night. "Eric?"

"Yes, my angel, what is it?"

"How many glasses of champagne have I had?"

It took a moment of thought before he answered. "Three, maybe. Why?"

"I was wondering if you were as mellow as I am."

He hadn't realized it until now, but his constant state of sexual arousal had definitely toned down to the I-don't-care-what-happens-next mood he usually found himself in after a couple of drinks.

"I'm mellow, but not so much so that I can't feel what your body is doing to mine." He had a sudden, disconcerting thought. "I hope you're not in such a mellow mood you can't tell. Or that you don't feel the excitement, too." He held his breath. What if she wasn't as turned on by him as he was by her?

He needn't have worried. She took one of his hands from her waist and brought it up between them to fit his palm over her breast. He could feel the tight peak of her nipple even through her clothing, and he squeezed it gently, bringing forth a whimper of pleasure from her and a sharp jerk of his cock that he had no doubt she felt.

She pulled in a short, involuntary gasp as he released her breast and slid his hands beneath her blouse. The soft, warm silk of her skin against his hand made him think of the delicious, sweet folds between her thighs that he had not only touched, but tasted, and he wanted to cry out with his need to do it all over again. To do that and more. He needed to enter her, to empty himself inside her, to make her ache with her own need, to climax with him.

Dizzily, he closed the space between their lips and crushed his mouth against hers, one tiny sharp edge of her tooth piercing the inside of his lip. He hardly felt the pain. He was so turned on his entire body was aware of nothing but the heat that raced through his veins and the drumming of his heartbeat in his ears.

At last his tongue was inside her hot, wet mouth, her tongue sparring with his for dominance. Willingly, he gave her the upper hand and let her greedily suck away at his tongue until he thought she might tear it from his throat. Then she relaxed, gave a little moan and with a tease from the tip of her tongue invited him to take over.

He kissed her deeply, suckled her tongue, gave them a second of much needed rest and then slanted his mouth over hers and plundered her mouth until his lips felt bruised and he worried that he had been too careless with her. He pulled back, breathing hard.

"I'm afraid I may have kissed you black and blue," he confessed on a hoarse whisper.

"That was one of the soundest kisses I've ever received," she said, cocking her head to the side and giving him a smile with her raspberry red lips. "But I doubt it wounded me." She treated him to a quick, butterfly kiss.

"Only one of the soundest?"

"All right, the soundest, sexiest, most soul-searing kiss I've ever had in my life." Her tone was bantering, meant to be as light as his, but he wasn't so totally lacking in experience that he couldn't detect the quiver of sexual excitement in her voice. And that knowledge gave him the hardest erection he was ever likely to get.

He passed the pad of his thumb lightly over her swollen lips. "Be honest, now. Do they hurt?"

She shook her head briskly and gave him a wide smile of reassurance.

He passed an even gentler thumb back over her lips and gave them a feather kiss. "I got carried away. I'm sorry."

"Apology not needed. I got rather carried away myself." She reached up and touched her fingertips to his lips as gently as he had stroked hers.

His hand had somehow become wedged between their chests, his palm against his heart which was beating triple-time. As if his very life depended on it, he knew he couldn't stand one more second of this torture.

"Angel, let's go to bed."

"I thought you'd never ask." She sagged against him, the fabric of her skirt pleating and rubbing against his now very painful erection.

He did something then that he'd never done to a woman before, not even to the woman he'd left behind in London. He scooped Angel up into his arms. But before he could take a step, she looked over his shoulder and pointed to the other side of the room.

"I need to take that box with us."

He lifted an eyebrow. "What for?" Suddenly, a thought popped into his head and he chuckled aloud. "Angel, did you bring some naughty, kinky stuff with you?"

He was half-joking when he asked her about the contents of her little brown box, but the devilish smile that immediately spread across her face gave him pause. He set her down gently.

"Don't move an inch," he warned with mock sternness, as he walked across the room, one hand pressed against his bulging crotch, and picked up the box.

When he returned from his trip to retrieve the box and saw the naughty smile still on Angel's face, he couldn't hold

back his own smile of delight as he lifted her into his arms
again, carried her to the bedroom and fell with her crosswise
onto the luxurious king-size bed.

Five

Eric rolled them both over on the enormous bed and settled himself on top of Angel, pinning her beneath him. His body fit intimately against her soft, sloped curves. He moved his mouth over hers forcing her lips to part, drew her tongue deep into his mouth, let his mind and his body swell with the delicious taste of her.

Beneath him, he could feel the increasing beat of her heart against his chest, see her rising desire in the shuttering of her eyes, and hear the subtle catch in her breath every time his erection made contact with the arch between her thighs. He felt one step away from being out of his mind with the need to get inside her.

He wanted her like he could never remember wanting another woman at any time in his life. He needed her like he had never needed any woman, ever. And the thought that he was going to have her soon set his teeth on edge and the blood spiraling through his veins like a cyclone. He could think of nothing but what heaven it was going to be when she finally sheathed him.

Angel shifted her mouth to the side and hastily pulled in a breath, then let it out just as fast. "The box," she gasped with barely enough air to speak.

Box? To bloody hell with the box. Reluctantly, he pulled back enough to watch her reaction. "Not now, Angel. All I can think of is getting your clothes off and getting inside you." And to do that he couldn't think of anything she might have in that box that could make him any hotter or more ready than he was right now. Maybe later, maybe tomorrow...

"Okay," Angel sighed, "if that's what you want, I won't argue about it." She slipped her hand between their hips and latched on firmly to his crotch, causing him to momentarily lose his breath. "I definitely won't argue," she echoed, running the heel of her hand up and down his shaft.

Oh, damn it all, in spite of how quickly she'd covered it up, he hadn't missed the flicker of disappointment that crossed her face when he dismissed the box. Yet, here she was not only being a good sport, but giving his boner a massage on top of it.

Never one to hide his frustration very well, Eric sighed

deeply and none too quietly. After admonishing himself for his thoughtlessness, he reminded himself that this weekend was meant to be about learning new things, about being adventurous and discovering what turned a woman on. Maybe he'd never given a woman enough space to be herself before, maybe...

He flinched inwardly at the thought of what he was about to do.

Groaning aloud, he rolled off Angel and onto his side, shielding his throbbing cock with his hand. "I'm sorry, Angel. Go get the box." He gave her a nudge on the hip for reassurance. "Go on."

"Are you sure?" She rolled to her side so their eyes were level.

He wanted to tell her he wasn't sure of anything right now except wanting to fuck her until he collapsed from exhaustion, but she deserved a more polite response than that. Even if he lied through his teeth. "I'm sure. Fetch the box and let's get on with it."

She gave him a sheepish grin, brought a finger up to his mouth and traced the outline of his lips. "You'll have to do a little work for me first."

Oh, lord, now what? Whatever she had planned had better be bloody well worth the agony she was putting him through. He was sure every ounce of blood in his body had settled in the head of his cock and the whole thing was going to blow off.

She moved closer to him and all his thoughts evaporated in the scents that tickled his nose. Soap, perfume, shampoo, desire. And God, she was beautiful on top of it. Just looking at her— at her dark, silky hair brushing her shoulders, her skin flushed and slightly damp across her brow, her eyes shiny as polished obsidian—made him crazy. He wanted to crawl on top of her so badly his stomach clenched in pain.

"Work?" he croaked. "What kind of work?" It hurt his throat to speak through all the tension in his body, which had somehow lodged there.

"We have to get you naked and this beautiful bed covering out of the way."

Their noses were tip to tip now. She had inched closer while she spoke. He couldn't resist kissing her again, so he put his hand on the back of her head and drew her in until their lips touched. He nibbled, sucked, and drew her lips between his teeth. Tortured himself.

"If you get me naked I can't guarantee you'll make it off the bed to get that box of yours," he growled, trying to devour her mouth.

"I'll get it first then," she said, sliding out of his grasp, "while you take care of the covering." She was off the bed, across the room and had the box in her arms before he knew what had happened.

With a grumble he pulled back the heavy bedspread and worked his body over it until he was lying on nothing but the silk sheet. He lifted his head just enough to see Angel better. "What about you?"

"What about me?" She set the box down on one side of the long wooden table at the foot of the bed, moved an ornate vase of flowers to the other side.

He swallowed to relax the muscles in his throat. "Are you getting naked too?"

Angel tilted her head to the side and feigned a thoughtful pose. "Hmmm. I hadn't thought that far." She ripped a piece of the clear tape from the top of the box, caught another piece at the side and stripped it away too. She reached inside, took out two small jars. "I think this is enough for now."

Eric rolled to his back and watched her as she moved to the side of the bed at his feet. She put the jars on the bedside table, lowered the lamp to a soft glow, slipped one black leather loafer from his foot, and did the same with the other.

"To show you what a good sport I am," Angel said, smiling coyly at him. "I'll shed my clothes first. Well, most of them." She undid the top button of her blouse, passed her tongue over her bottom lip, moved to the next button, wet her lip again, and continued the routine until he could see the cleavage between her breasts and the narrow strip of satin below it. He pulled in a breath and let it out in short, none too silent shudders.

Angel slipped out of her blouse, dropped it behind her on the floor, unfastened her skirt and dropped it as well. He couldn't take his eyes off her. She was a vision straight from heaven. Full, round breasts barely contained by the flimsy black lace, narrow waist, full hips. The satin panel between her legs barely covered the dark, curly thatch that protected her sex. He turned his fingers into his palms to keep from rising up and grabbing her.

She leaned over him then. Her hands started to work on

his buckle and then proceeded to the zipper. He squeezed his eyes shut. "You could give me a little help with your shirt," she whispered. His pants and his briefs slid down just as he tugged his shirt over his head.

She rid him of his socks before she climbed up on the bed and straddled him across his knees. His mind raced back to the living room and what she'd done to him the last time she'd knelt across him this way. His cock jerked and he gritted his teeth against the pain in his groin.

When her tongue touched the tip of his cock, he knew he was about to die. No doubt about it. He was never going to get inside her because she was going to kill him first.

He sucked in another breath when her tongue flicked over him again and then she reached behind her and twisted back around, one of the jars in her hand.

It couldn't be what he thought it was. He craned his neck up as far as he could. "What's in there, Angel?"

She twisted the lid on the jar, bent down and gave the tip of his cock another stroke with her tongue, looked up at him with a grin that sent a shiver down his spine. "Just peanut butter."

"Oh, Christ, Angel, don't tell me…"

"Crunchy peanut butter," she told him.

Dear merciful Jesus, crunchy? "Angel, honey, won't that hurt? Sweet lord, look at me. I'm already in pain here."

"Not to worry," she assured him, as she swiped a peanut butter covered finger from the base of his shaft to the tip of his penis. "I'm going to mix it with honey. It'll slide right on. I love crunchy peanut butter. It's my favorite. I won't leave a drop on you, I promise." She put her finger in her mouth and sucked it clean, then reached back around, set the jar down and came back around with the other jar.

When the first drop of honey hit the crown of his cock and drizzled down his shaft, he let out a harsh, low moan. No doubt about it now. He was a dead man.

* * * *

Angel's heart was racing like a wildfire through a forest and she felt sick to her stomach. She had never been in a situation like this before. What if she fumbled and bumbled around? Made a fool of herself?

Why in the world had she ever agreed to this weekend? She should have leveled with Eric from the start, like she almost did a couple of times. Told him the truth about herself. That while she liked sex, she had never had the wild, mind-blowing kind that she read about in books. That she was hoping to find that incredible, mind-shattering experience with him. That she wanted more than anything to spend a whole weekend having sex with him, but that she'd never played a seductress before. Had never done anything more with peanut butter than spread it on a piece of bread. Had never used honey for anything before except sweetening her tea.

Now, here she was, spreading crunchy peanut butter and honey all over Eric Sweeney's *magnifico* penis, following her finger with little swipes of her tongue, while he uttered soft expletives and swore she was going to kill him with her sweet mouth. All the while begging her to stop—then begging her not to.

And she was enjoying every minute of it as much as he was.

After one unusually acerbic oath from Eric, Angel paused in her ministrations and looked up at him with concern. "Just fighting hard to keep control," he reassured her. "But I can't go much longer," he warned, reaching out to grasp a handful of the cast aside bed covering.

Angel gave him a knowing smile and returned to the work at hand. A few more strokes and she would be ready to drive him over the line. Only she wanted to stop just short of that. While she was driving his desire to the limit, she was doing the same to hers.

She'd been so driven she had not spent time exploring the rest of Eric's masculine attributes. Determined to correct that unintended omission, she let her gaze travel from the rigid, peanut butter and honey covered shaft in her hand up to the thick, wiry nest of curls covering his groin. The hair there was darker than the tawny curls on his head and narrowed when it reached his navel, fanned out upward to cover his chest with even denser, darker curls.

The beauty of Eric's body turned her on even more, and she wrapped her fingers around him, squeezed his pulsing erection as the muscles in her belly clenched. But when his body jerked against the sudden pressure, she knew for both their sakes she had better bring this first little episode to a fast end. She released him quickly and replaced her hand with her mouth.

"Oh, baby," Eric moaned, grasping at the bedcovers with

renewed force. "That feels so good, so damn good…aaahhh…"
The moan faded to a guttural whimper as Angel's tongue slid
down his shaft to his testicles, lapped up the gooey mixture
that had settled there, then continued up to the tip of his penis,
licking and sucking every inch of the way.

Her tongue was twirling around the swollen head of Eric's
penis, licking off the last of the concoction when he reared up,
grabbed her by the arms, hauled her on top of him and brought
her mouth down hard on his.

He shot one of his hands down between her legs. "You're
wet, Angel. Wet for me," he moaned, slipping a finger inside
her while he pushed her panties down with his other hand. She
moved and squirmed, lifted her legs each in turn to get the
panties off, and the tightening in her groin slid into a steady
ache.

Eric's mouth moved down from hers and dipped to her
breast, sucked her already tight, peaked nipple through the lace
until it stuck to her skin from the remnants of the honeyed
mixture he'd drawn from her mouth. She wanted to scream.
The ache between her legs had become a thrumming that was
quickly spreading throughout her body.

"Get this damned thing off," he growled impatiently, moving
his finger inside her with determined thrusts while groping with
his other hand behind her back for her bra hook. She felt her
orgasm building and quickly brought both her hands around to
her back, brushing Eric's fingers away. It was a struggle, given
her awkward position, but she got the hook undone and wriggled
her arms from the straps, just as Eric slipped his fingers out of
her, grasped her hips and rolled her over and under him.

He reached under the bed pillows, retrieved a foil wrapped
condom, opened it and quickly covered himself before he
entered her.

It seemed so very natural to wrap her legs around his waist,
to open herself to him and meet his first penetration with the
same eagerness she'd felt for him in her fantasies. To draw
him within and tighten around him, to feel his hot, pulsing flesh
move restlessly inside her.

It was beyond anything she had ever imagined. To be on
the receiving end of Eric's foreplay, to be the recipient of his
hungry mouth at her breasts, to surround him with all the hot,
aching need she had kept bottled up inside her for so long.

Eric gave her nipple one last tug before he shifted his mouth to her other breast. With each pull of his lips the thrum deep inside her built. Her fingers found his hair, worked forward from the dampness at his forehead and threaded through the long, wavy strands. He took his mouth from her breast and brought his face up close to hers. There was an almost feral look in his eyes. She locked her arms across his back, crushing him to her.

Her breath hitched in her throat, an involuntary reaction to the increased tempo of Eric's strokes. He was driving her to a fever pitch and her body was demanding release. She tightened her legs around his waist and arched to meet his deepening thrusts.

Then suddenly, Eric stilled. His body tensed, she could feel the bundling of muscles in his shoulders, across his back. Perspiration broke out across his forehead. He closed his eyes, clenched his jaw.

"Eric? Wh—what's wrong?" Had he lost interest in her? Had his desire ebbed? He was still hard inside her, but. . .

He brought his forehead against hers. "I need to know how it feels to you. Is it enough? Too much? I don't want this first time to be—"

She almost cried from relief. Was that all? He was worried about how much or how little he filled her? "You feel wonderful, Eric. And first time or not, I want all of you. I've dreamed of this every night since we first spoke." She wanted him to know without any doubt he was everything she'd wished for. Everything she'd expected. And more.

She wished she could tell him that this weekend had already started out to be the brightest memory she'd carry into a very uncertain future. That this could well be the last time she would be this intimate with a man for a long while. Maybe forever. That of all the men she had known in her life there was no one she would rather be intimate with at this moment in time than him.

But, of course, she couldn't share those thoughts with him. Not with the agreement they'd made that this weekend, no matter how special or spectacular it was, would remain just that. One weekend.

She was already beginning to feel a twinge of regret that after Sunday evening she would never see Eric Sweeney again.

* * * *

Eric took Angel at her word. At her command. At her

wish. And drove into her as smoothly and as deeply as the natural restrictions of their bodies allowed, marveling at the perfect fit, as if the very intimate parts of their bodies were sculpted to fit perfectly inside and around each other. He had never fit this well with another woman. Had never been in sync with another woman quite this way.

She bucked up to meet him, her inner muscles grasping him in tiny, quivering spasms. "You feel so good, Angel," he murmured, "I like the way you rise up to meet me. I like feeling your legs locked around me." He pulled in a ragged breath, held it, and then he released it in short, shuddering gasps. "I'm near the edge though," he warned. And cupping the round firm cheeks of her ass, he cried out as his flanks quivered, urging him to spill himself quickly inside her.

He knew the moment her climax began. He felt her grasp him and try to draw him even deeper inside. They rocked together in a frenzy, him thrusting, her rising to meet him, and then she cried out his name and his own orgasm rushed forward. They came together as they had coupled, in perfect unison, like the most beautiful piece of music he'd ever played.

He lost count of how many climaxes he had. He stopped counting after three. What he couldn't stop was the rush of tenderness that washed over him when the roaring in his ears had stopped and his mind had started to clear.

At some point, he had rolled to his side taking Angel with him, and she was snuggled up close to him now, her breathing almost as even as his. One of her arms was draped over his hip. He stroked her back tenderly in widening circles.

It startled him to see how comfortable they were with one another. A phenomenon easily explained, he reasoned, by the fact that they had no commitment to each other beyond bringing each other pleasure for the next two days.

Angel purred contentedly. He planted a kiss on her damp forehead, fanned a breath across her brow. She purred some more. "You certainly sound contented."

"Ummm, I am," she admitted, curling up closer to him, her hand moving lightly over the rise of his hip. "You?"

He let out a low, throaty sound, a cross between a purr and a growl. "Contented and sated. You were worth waiting for."

"So were you." She moved her head lower and buried her face against his chest, chuckling. "Your chest hairs tickle."

She rubbed her nose from side to side on his furry chest.

"Is that good or bad?" He planted another kiss on her forehead, this time letting his lips linger.

"Good. Very good." She kissed his chest close to his nipple and even though he hadn't fully recovered from his very recent climax he felt a slight stirring in his groin.

Reluctantly, he slipped his arm from beneath her and inched away, lifting up on his elbow. "I think a trip to the bathroom is in order. Don't move. I'll be back before you can blink an eye." He rolled off the bed in a hurry, because he was tempted to pull her up close again and he knew he shouldn't just yet.

In the bathroom he disposed of the condom, turned on the tap, threw cold water on his still flushed face, then thought of Angel and the flush that was still on her cheeks when he left her. He dampened one of the fluffy, blue monogrammed face cloths and went back to the big bed and the adorable angel that waited for him there.

Angel was still in the same position as when he left her, on her side, one arm underneath her body, her other hand under her cheek. He climbed on the bed, wash cloth at the ready, but stopped when he saw her eyes were closed.

"Angel?" He kept his voice barely above a whisper.

"Hmmm?"

"I have a cool cloth for your face. Okay?"

"Um-hm."

She sounded on the edge of sleep, so he touched the cloth lightly to her face, smoothing the hair back from her temple. "Are you tired? Do you want to sleep awhile?"

"Very tired," she mumbled. "I could sleep just a little while. You mind?"

As an answer he slid his arm under her shoulder, hauled her with him to the top of the bed and laid her head on two of the plump, silk covered pillows. Then he reached down for the silk sheet, curved his front to her back spoon-style, and settled down with her, pulling the sheet over them.

In no time her breathing signaled she was asleep, and he moved his body as close to hers as he could, swallowing back a lump that rose in his throat when another wave of a peculiar tenderness crept over him.

He closed his eyes and tried to differentiate her heartbeat from his own, but it was impossible. As with everything else they'd shared, their pulses were inseparable. He drew in a long, lingering sigh. If she had come to him in his other life, at a different time, they might have been soul mates. But his time with her was limited. And that alone made it painfully precious.

   She murmured something in her sleep. He convinced himself it was his name that had crossed her lips. And on that conviction, he gave himself up to his own need for rest. His last waking thought was that if she were dreaming of him, he would be one very happy man.

Six

"What exactly do you do?" Eric asked Angel as he trailed a finger down her cleavage. "I know you're a language specialist, but I don't know exactly what that means."

It wasn't yet eight in the morning. They were lying across the bed, wrapped in plush Navy blue bathrobes. They'd returned only minutes before from a half-hour soak and more incredible sex in the Amazonian-sized bathtub that took up one entire corner of the lavish bathroom.

They had awakened twice during the night and had sex as explosive as their first encounter. Maybe more so, Angel considered, because with each joining they had learned yet more ways to experience the pleasure that seemed to spring naturally between them.

She lifted her arms above her head and stretched, careful not to show any sign of discomfort. There were places on her body that were as tender as a newborn's cheeks, her legs ached like she had run a marathon, and her thigh muscles had begun to reflex involuntarily. Payback, she told herself smugly, for the vise like grip she had come to master when she locked her legs around Eric's hips.

She'd give up her tongue though, before she'd ever let out so much as a whimper about her aches and pains to him.

"I work for one of the largest language resource companies in the world," she told him, proudly. "Usually I work as an interpreter for executives with business interests abroad who have neither the time nor the inclination to learn the native language. On the side, I do translations. Business documents, medical records. Things like that."

"Is that the kind of work you intend to do for the rest of your life?"

"As far as I can tell at this point, yes. Except lately I've really thought a lot about one day opening my own business here in New York City." That bit of information slipped out before she could censor it. She guessed it would take some time to readjust her thinking to reflect the uncertainty of her future. In any event, she refused to dwell on that now. Like the legendary Scarlett, she would worry about that tomorrow.

Raising herself to her elbow, she looked down at Eric. "What about you? Where do you work in London?"

"Oh, here and there." Eric cupped a hand behind her head and pulled her forward, took a nip at her chin. She caught the tip of his nose between her teeth on his way up to her mouth.

"Here and there, where?" she asked ducking the intended kiss. He sprang to a sitting position and ruffled her hair.

"How about some breakfast before I give you all the boring details of my work?" He stood, reached for her and hauled her to her feet. "I have a great idea. But it's only great if you think it's great, too."

"Oh?"

"I thought we could get a light breakfast down the street. Maybe a bagel and some coffee. Then walk over to Central Park, take a short stroll, hop a cab, go to the Museum of Natural History. Later we could have lunch at a favorite haunt of mine that has the best pizza in Manhattan."

The mere mention of food was enough to sell her on the whole package. She reached up and pecked his cheek. "Count me in."

"I hope you brought some comfortable clothes."

"A sundress and sandals. I'll have to get the wrinkles out first, though."

"Okay. Tell you what. I have a couple of calls to make while I'm getting dressed. Do you think you can do your de-wrinkling and be ready in about thirty minutes?" He made a playful grab at her behind on his way to the bathroom. "I can use the phone in the master bath. Can you dress in the guest bathroom?"

She assured him she could and went in the opposite direction to retrieve the dress that she had never even hung in the closet because, well, because Eric hadn't allowed her a spare minute since she'd arrived the evening before. She let out a low, happy chuckle. Not that she was complaining.

One hour later they were swallowing the last bites of their bagels and waiting for the remainder of their coffee to be poured into Styrofoam cups to go.

They walked the few blocks to Central Park hand in hand, Eric adjusting his long stride to her shorter one. They chattered about their favorite Broadway plays, stopped to look in shop windows. Angel even pulled him into a tattoo parlor simply because she had never been inside one before and felt safe entering it with him at her side.

After strolling leisurely for a time through Central Park,

Eric bought a bag of popcorn from a nearby vendor and they stopped at a bench to rest, sharing the popcorn like giddy teenagers on a first date, feeding each other, wiping the butter from each other's mouths.

"Still game for the museum?" Eric asked when the last of the popcorn was gone.

She let her head flop lazily against his chest, the sound of his heartbeat already a familiar sound. "I'm game if you are."

Eric hailed a cab and they spent the ride to the Museum pretty much as they had on the park bench, his arm around her shoulder, her head resting under his chin.

By noon, they were both hungry so they cut the visit to the museum short, hailed another taxi and headed to the restaurant for lunch.

The maitre d' addressed Eric by name as soon as they stepped inside, and he escorted them to a corner table. Then he snapped his fingers once and a waiter appeared seemingly from nowhere. "Margarita without salt for the lady," Eric told him. "And a double scotch for me."

Angel was impressed. "You must come here often," she said, "or else you're a big tipper."

"Jonathan just likes beautiful ladies," Eric said, lifting her hand and dropping kisses on each of her knuckles. "But I do have a confession of sorts to make. I phoned in our order to Jonathan before we left the hotel. Told him the minute we walked in to have the kitchen get started on it." He turned her hand over and kissed her palm.

"And how do you know what kind of pizza I like?" she asked in a teasing voice.

"I don't, so I told Jonathan to have the kitchen make three medium pies, each one different. One of them is bound to please you. Whatever is left we can take with us. Or not, as the mood strikes."

"Eric," she chastised, "you are far too extravagant." But deep down she loved it that he went way beyond the call of duty to please her.

They were halfway through their drinks when the pizzas arrived along with a giant bowl of salad and a bottle of red wine. They ate their way through two pizzas and didn't leave a scrap of salad behind.

Eric downed the last of his wine, leaned over and dabbed at the corner of Angel's mouth with one of the red-checkered napkins.

"I hope we don't have trouble getting a cab, because I don't think I'll be able to carry you home. Don't think I could even carry myself home, to tell the truth." He put a hand across his stomach and rolled his eyes, indicating he was filled to the max.

"I'm stuffed, too" she admitted.

He winked, leaned over and put his mouth to her ear. "Good. You're going to need your strength." He eased back a little and winked again. "That is if you're still up to more play."

"Have I yelled 'uncle,' yet?"

"No, can't say that you have."

"You can expect more of the same."

Eric grinned, but behind the laughter in his eyes Angel saw the first sparks of desire. He signaled for the check and while he waited to settle the bill, she took off for the ladies room.

She was on her way back to the table when she spied Eric near the front door talking to Jonathan, so she headed their way.

"I hope everything works out for the best and your wife is up and around very soon," Eric said to the maitre d' just as she reached them.

Angel caught the flash of pain that crossed the man's face, and though he was a stranger, she felt sympathy for him.

They said their good-bye's with a promise from Eric to return soon. He put his arm around Angel's waist, opened the door for her and ushered her to the curb. "Our cab awaits, m'lady."

With anyone else she might have been surprised, but in the short time they'd been together, she had already learned to expect the unexpected from Eric.

"Penny for your thoughts," he said, after they were settled in the back seat of the cab.

"Actually I was thinking of the maitre d' back there. You and he seemed to be on very friendly terms."

"The day after I arrived here, Mike, the owner of The Heritage Club, sent me to that restaurant for lunch. Jonathan was the first person I met when I walked in the door. I guess we just kind of hit it off. It's my favorite place for lunch. I eat there three or four times a week." He sighed and pulled her closer to his side. "It's one of the places I'm really going to miss when I leave New York."

"He seemed sad," Angel said, her mind still on the maitre d' and the sorrow she'd seen in his eyes.

"His wife has been very ill. The doctor's still aren't certain what's wrong with her. I think it's the not knowing that's the hardest for him to bear."

It was as if a dark cloud had passed over the sun just then, casting a shadow over what had been, until that moment, the beginning of another day she would never forget. But now she was reminded again of what still awaited her when she left this fantasy land and stepped back into reality. Eric was right. It was the not knowing that was hardest to bear.

"Is something wrong, Angel?"

Puzzled, she looked up at him. "No. Why do you ask?"

He brushed a lock of hair behind her ear. "I thought I felt you tense up a bit."

"Just had a chill," she said, and the lie didn't bother her at all when she saw the relief that washed over Eric's face and the heat that sparked in his eyes.

If she was reading him right, there would be little sleep in the big penthouse bed again tonight.

A nerve jumped low in her belly, setting off the first tiny flame.

The ride back to the hotel seemed to take forever. And she didn't have forever with Eric. The hours were winding down too quickly to the time they would walk away from each other, forever.

* * * *

Eric began undressing Angel the moment the door closed behind them. She had dressed with the warm September afternoon in mind—sundress, demi bra, the scrap of satin that passed for panties. All three fell to the floor as quickly and quietly as autumn leaves on grass.

In no time at all he had her stretched out naked across the unmade bed. When he'd rented the penthouse, he'd left strict orders with housekeeping that no one was to enter the suite this weekend unless specifically requested by him. The most he'd allow was room service when he and Angel dined inside the suite, and that was confined to the living area.

The bedroom was strictly off limits. He didn't want even the hint of another human's presence, no matter how remote, to intrude on the world he and Angel created inside this room. For every second of the two days they were together he wanted this space to be as far removed from the real world as if they were on another planet.

"Absolutely the most beautiful sight I've ever seen," Eric murmured as he stood at the side of the bed, trying to quell the rise of desire that already had him fully aroused. It was still a mystery to him how Angel had happened into his life at just this time.

"Don't move," he whispered.

Angel followed him with her eyes as he made his way to the table at the foot of the bed. She watched intently as he dug inside the box that held the goodies she had brought. "What are you up to?" she finally asked, unable to contain her curiosity one second longer.

Eric knew from the flare of excitement in her eyes that she was well aware of what he was up to and had merely asked the rhetorical question to titillate him further.

"Getting dessert," he said, his tone as matter-of-fact as if he had just taken a store-bought confection out of the refrigerator.

They'd both had too much pizza to even consider dessert at the restaurant, so when he'd suggested they put it off until they were back at the hotel, she had eagerly agreed. Of course, he hadn't let on what kind of dessert he had in mind.

Holding up one of the small jars from Angel's wares, he turned it several times inspecting its contents. "Hmmmm. Lemon curd. Wonderful. Lemon pie is my absolute favorite."

He moved back to the side of the bed, leaned down and kissed Angel in the crease of her thigh, kept focused on his plan or else he would unzip his pants and drive his already throbbing cock between her labial folds before he'd decently primed her.

She writhed and arched her hips when his tongue skimmed the flesh on her inner thigh, told him in a husky, sensuous voice how naughty he had become.

The joy in her voice thrilled him, shored up his confidence in the erotic idea that had come to him during lunch.

He opened the jar, set it on the bedside table, unfastened the strip of leather that held his hair back and let his hair fall to his shoulders the way Angel preferred it.

Then he shed his clothes down to his briefs, afraid to free his cock until he was ready to enter her, because one touch of the inflamed tip against her heated skin and he would have to abort his plan and thrust inside her whether she was ready for him or not.

And he refused to be that savage, no matter what restraint he had to put on himself. He had promised Angel this weekend was for her as much as for him. He wanted everything to be perfect for her. He would see that it was, no matter what the cost. But right then, right at that moment, he needed his body closer to hers.

He climbed astride her and bracketed her hips with his knees, lowered his mouth, and parted her lips with his tongue. He took deep kiss after deep kiss until, afraid he would bruise her, forced himself to lift his mouth from hers.

She didn't make it easy for him. Crossing her arms fiercely around his back she struggled to close the gap between their bodies, pulling his down, arching her own upward, testing him beyond the limit of his endurance.

His lips still hovered over hers but he couldn't allow himself to kiss her again or he would lose what little control he still had.

"Not so fast, my sweet. I've just begun to make love to you." How had he managed to sound so casual, his voice so modulated, when his insides were on fire and his nerves on edge?

Quickly, before she could stall him, he levered himself backward to reach the bedside table, dipped his finger inside the open jar and scooped out a generous glob of the smooth lemon mixture.

When he began lightly covering a dusky, peaked nipple with the cool, lemony custard on his fingertip, he heard Angel's breath catch in her throat. His own breath hitched until he forced the air from his lungs and gave his head a quick shake to clear it.

Beneath him Angel moved restlessly. "What about me," she murmured, "don't I get a taste of you?" In reply, he gave her nipple a strong, deep suckle. He drew his head back far enough to see her face and noted the heat in her eyes that he knew was for him, a heat that would soon consume them both.

"You've already had your turn," he told her, and because he remembered the rapture of her mouth wrapped around him, and how this was for her and not for him, he dipped his head and took a quick swipe between her breasts with his tongue to quiet her.

Panting, she tried to speak, but the unformed words slid

into a moan when he took her other nipple between his thumb and forefinger, strummed it to a peak as hard as its twin, then slathered it with the sweet concoction and drew it greedily into his mouth.

When her body shuddered hard, flexed and shuddered again, he knew it was time for the pièce de résistance. With his mouth still at her breast, he slid his hand down her body through the soft curls between her legs to the cleft they protected.

She was hot, wet, and already open for him when he slipped a finger inside. Her body lifted, strained against his hand. "I can't take much more of this," she warned, arching her body higher, finally letting it sink to the bed again when he ignored her pleas and plunged yet another finger inside her.

He wished he could spend the rest of the day exploring more ways he could touch her, taste her, and bring her to an ecstasy even higher than he'd done before. But in the short time they had been together he had come to know her body as well as his own. They were both a hair's breath away from climaxing. And he wasn't quite finished with her yet.

Moving quickly he discarded his briefs and slid to his knees on the floor in front of her. Grasping her ankles he pulled her toward him, draped her legs over his shoulders and fit his mouth against the swollen, distended folds of her sex. His hands moved up to her buttocks, securing her more firmly to his hungry mouth.

He delved deep into her opening with his tongue, and while she writhed and bucked against his mouth, moaning he was driving her out of her mind, he reached over and dipped his finger once again into the open jar on the bedside table.

Angel stopped resisting his plunder. Her body was flushed and glowing with the moist sheen of heat that covered it, and she yielded more readily to him, her rising moans of pleasure driving him to take her higher, faster.

Replacing his tongue with his finger, he smoothed the cool, creamy mixture over the inflamed folds of her labia and when he put his mouth to her slick, wet opening again, the taste of lemons mixed with the scent of her arousal nearly spun him out of control. He tasted and drank from her as greedily as a man having his last meal, and she let him partake of her until her own control snapped.

She came with a hard, wild pulsing against his mouth, and he held her there until her moans turned into sighs and her body slackened in release.

Rising, he positioned her higher on the bed and sheathed himself quickly. She came again with his first thrust, and he came with her, their bodies slapping and pounding against each other like the battering winds of a hurricane.

Words were inadequate for the force that rocked them, so they rode out the storm in silence, holding fast to each other until their passion was spent and they were at peace again.

* * * *

Still basking in the afterglow, Angel rolled to her side, Eric still lodged inside her, his arm under her waist holding their sweat dampened bodies close. His mouth began worrying hers in small nibbles.

"You still taste of lemon," she told him, gliding her tongue over his lips.

He stroked her shoulder, the back of her neck. "And of you."

"And of me."

"I'll never be able to smell the scent of lemon again without thinking of you. Of us."

Nor will I. She couldn't say it aloud. Couldn't admit to a time when just a scent would be all she'd have to remind her of this weekend. All she'd have to remind her of him.

And that was when she felt the first, deep ache of longing. Of missing him already. Of feeling something that was more than sorrow for the anticipated loss of his physical presence. An overpowering urge to keep him near made her draw his body closer to hers.

The ringing of Eric's cell phone shattered the tender moment between them. He withdrew slowly and lifted to an elbow to take the call. Then he put a hand over the mouthpiece.

"I'll take this in the bathroom while I clean up. Before I leave though, I want to know if you'd like to go dancing tonight. We could have dinner first."

Damn. She knew she should have brought something dressy to wear. "I didn't bring any evening wear. I thought...I didn't know..."

"Not to worry. I think there's a boutique in the hotel. Heard someone inquiring about it when I registered. We'll go down as soon as I'm finished and get you decked out from head to toe."

She started to protest, but he was already heading toward the bathroom, one hand gripping the phone, the other holding his flaccid, latex-covered penis.

And in the moment of that shared intimacy, she was gripped by the awesome fear that she could well be falling in love with a man whose last name she didn't even know.

Seven

As Eric lay in bed, Angel sleeping peacefully in his arms, memories of the evening flashed before him like a kaleidoscope, every scene as vivid as if he'd stepped back in time.

He'd had to practically drag Angel to the boutique to get an outfit for the evening. And he'd accomplished that miraculous feat only after he'd convinced her it was really his fault for not telling her of his plans beforehand. No manner of convincing, though, would get her to buy his favorite ensemble, the most expensive dress in the shop. But he'd been only too happy to settle for second best, because on her it looked first rate no matter the price tag.

After dinner at a private club, they'd danced for hours, their bodies indecently close, teasing, tempting each other with promises of every ecstasy the night still held.

They'd practically torn the clothes from each other's bodies the instant they stepped into the suite. He'd taken her the first time up against the door, then once again on the floor. They'd laughed about it later while lying naked in each other's arms in the big bed, deciding it must have been the champagne they'd drank all night that had heated their blood, made them crazy.

He knew better. In the dark, unable to sleep, he couldn't hide from the truth.

He was greedy where she was concerned. He wanted as much of her tonight as he could hold. He was building memories for all the tomorrows he'd spend without her.

Angel stirred, rolled toward him, and her knee brushed against his ever present hard-on. "Are you awake?" she whispered.

"Either that or I'm having one hell of a dream." He nuzzled the top of her head, breathed in the perfume of her hair. She curled into him, her knee brushing his expanding erection.

"Have I been asleep long?"

"A couple of hours."

"Did you sleep?"

"Nope."

"Why not?"

"Couldn't get rid of this hard-on."

She slipped her hand to his crotch and cupped him. "Why didn't you wake me?"

He ignored her question and posed one of his own. "Would

it be a breach of our agreement if I asked you where you're going when you leave here?"

She hesitated for a moment before she answered him. "Back to Italy."

"Italy's a big country."

"Milan."

He covered her hand with his as she curled her fingers around his shaft and worked him up and down with slow, steady strokes. "I didn't wake you because I liked getting hard just holding you." He increased the pressure of his hand around hers, had to take a quick breath before he asked her, "Ever been to London?"

"Twice. Why?"

"Just wondered." He was too hot now to talk, or even think about anything but getting inside her. Reaching between her legs with his free hand, he found nothing between his flesh and hers.

"Roll over on your stomach," he urged, waited until she was stretched out flat beside him before he rolled on top of her and bracketed her thighs with his knees.

While he trailed the tip of his tongue from the dip at her waist to the nape of her neck he grasped his fully primed cock and rubbed it between the cleft of her buttocks, heating his blood to a fury and wringing shivers and muffled pleas for his entry from Angel.

She rose to her knees and he lifted her buttocks and entered her. His first thrust took them both over the edge, and he pounded against her until he was empty and she had collapsed helplessly, but sated, beneath him.

The silk sheets never cooled down the remainder of the long, erotic night. The last night they would ever spend together.

* * * *

Eric carried the two Sunday newspapers to the sofa where Angel had already settled herself in one corner.

"The Times or the Washington Post?"

The remnants of brunch had been cleared from the room and a fresh pot of coffee brought up. She reached over to pour herself a cup. "The Post." She stirred in a teaspoon of sugar and a thimble full of cream. "Unless that's the one you'd prefer."

Eric handed her the Post and slipped the other paper under his arm. "The Post was a perfect choice. I'm a Times reader." He poured a cup of coffee, made himself comfortable at the other end of the sofa and watched as Angel sipped coffee with one hand and dismantled the Post with the other, tossing unwanted sections to the floor until she reached the comics. She was a delight to watch even in the midst of something as banal as ripping through a newspaper.

She leaned over to set the cup on the table and the V of her robe opened. His breath stilled in his throat at the sight of her breasts, the dark nipples relaxed in the center of their milky white universe. His tongue tingled with a retained sensation he hadn't been able to shake since his first taste of her.

He pushed aside the thought that he'd never see her in such an erotic situation again, unfolded the Times and pulled out the financial section, allowing a low sigh to escape his lips. There were other things he'd rather be doing with Angel now than reading a newspaper, but he'd decided sometime before dawn that coming down slow from the sensual high he'd been on since Friday night was the common sense thing to do. A sudden burst of laughter from Angel yanked him away from his thoughts.

He peeked at her over the top of the paper. "I sure hope you're laughing at something humorous in the paper and not at me." He ran his fingers through his hair. "I've spent very little time on this unruly head of hair that you insist I keep unfettered."

That was no lie. Other than the couple of times they'd ventured outside and the meals they'd taken right here in this room, they hadn't paid much time or attention to anything other than having sex. Not that he was complaining. After all, that's what this weekend was supposed to be all about. Wasn't it? For him to gain knowledge and experience, to release the erotic part of him he'd kept hidden all these years?

Angel lifted her gaze from the paper in front of her, looked up at him, and shook her head. "No. I'm not laughing at you. It's Peanuts." She poked the paper with her finger. "And I love your hair in wild disarray. Makes you look kind of primitive."

She went back to the funnies, and in a matter of seconds she was laughing all over again, this time with even more enthusiasm than before.

He closed the section he was reading and looked in Angel's direction. "Care to share? I'm over here with a very boring financial section, about which there is nothing funny, I assure you."

Angel shook the paper open and turned it to him, marked a spot with her finger. "It's this Peanuts cartoon. He's trying to get the dog to eat his homework so he can get out of doing it. I could have used that ruse a couple of times in my life."

He set his paper aside and moved to the middle of the sofa. "Come over here and let me have a look."

Angel scooted next to him, opened the paper, pointed to the cartoon, then immediately went to the next comic strip and began tracing the panels with her finger, speaking the lines aloud, laughing as heartily as before. He found himself laughing right along with her.

Before long they were cuddled up in the middle of the sofa, each with one side of the funnies, taking turns reading the panels out loud, giggling as if they were kids.

And that's exactly what he felt like. A child who had suddenly been allowed to play. He couldn't ever remember laughing this much as a youngster. Not ever. A sudden, intense longing for the lost years of his youth caused his stomach to roil. But that was then, he reminded himself, and this was now. Now he could play any damned time he pleased. And he loved playing with Angel.

"From now on I'm going to begin my day with a good laugh from the funnies," he vowed, stealing a quick kiss before she went back to reading again.

"You certainly need something to even out that totally boring New York Times, if that's how you start every day." She lowered the paper and looked up at him. "Do you start every day like that?"

"Just about." He felt a flush creep up his neck at the idea she might think him really stuffy. "What about you? Is this the way you usually start your day?"

"On Sundays. Weekdays, I keep up with the news via television. Like you probably do."

Hardly, he thought. Most days he had barely enough time to shower and shave in the morning before he began his day. Between long rehearsals, concert performances and special engagements in Eastbourne & Brighton, working almost daily with his PR person or his booking agent, he was lucky to have a couple of free minutes a day to call his own, much less time for anything even remotely frivolous.

That's what had been so wonderful about these past six

months. He had answered to no one but himself. He'd never felt better and had enjoyed a sense of freedom he'd never before experienced in his life. Since meeting Angel he'd enjoyed all of these things tenfold.

And in just a few hours—in less than half a day—it would all be over.

Angel looked up at him. "Didn't you read the comics when you were a kid?"

"No"

"Not ever?"

"Not that I can remember. You did, I gather."

"All the time. Every Sunday my parents would take turns translating them into a different language. Between them they spoke nine different ones."

"So that's how your skill with languages came about?"

"Yes. I learned my love of diversity and languages—my mother is Spanish, my father French—from them. Among other, very important things."

"Like what it was like to live in a household where people were happy and in love?"

She shimmied closer to him and rattled the newspaper in front of them.

"We still have a lot more to read, especially if you want to watch that football game this afternoon."

He'd suggested they might want to watch the Steelers play the Bengals only because he didn't want her to start thinking about leaving too early. Even with as much as they'd shared physically, and as close as they'd become emotionally, he didn't want to come right out and tell her all he really wanted to do until the very last moment before she left was fuck her until she couldn't stand up straight.

He put his hand behind her neck, turned her to face him and was swamped by a rush of tenderness so great his chest ached. And he suddenly realized he didn't want to just fuck her. He wanted to make love to her. He brought his mouth down to hers and drew back to look into her eyes to see if what he felt was mirrored in hers. He was certain for a moment neither of them breathed.

"Would you mind terribly if I knocked all this paper to the floor and made love to you right now?"

Without taking her eyes from his, she batted the paper out of the way, opened her robe, and drew him down on top of her.

* * * *

Angel inched her sandals from under the sofa with her bare foot, slipped them on and headed for the guest bathroom. They'd showered and dressed in the master bath after lunch in preparation for the football game and her departure that evening, but all of her personal belongings were still in the smaller bath off the hall.

She did a mental check as she tossed the items in the flowered travel case: toothbrush, toothpaste, comb, make-up remover. After she collected the few items of clothing from the master bedroom she'd be all packed, ready to go.

As soon as the football game had ended, she'd begun preparing for the departure she knew was going to be one of the most difficult of her life. She didn't want to leave. Pretending otherwise was not going to make it any less painful.

When she came back into the living room, Eric was still in the same spot on the sofa as when she'd left, staring, she thought, disinterestedly at the television screen.

She considered for a moment the possibility that their parting was not going to be any easier for him than it was for her. After all, they'd spent the last forty-eight hours together with no more than a couple of hours away from each other. There were probably a lot of couples, married or otherwise, who had not shared the closeness they'd had these past two days. There was bound to be some separation anxiety clawing at both of them.

A thick lump formed in her throat. This was not the way she wanted this weekend to end. Snatching a couple of napkins from the table, she smiled inwardly, gave herself an imaginary pat on the back and tossed the napkins playfully at the back of Eric's head. "You still owe me ten bucks for picking the losing team."

He harrumphed, got up and walked into the bedroom. He came out, took the same position on the sofa and waved the ten dollar bill over his head.

She sauntered over to the back of the sofa, plucked the bill from his fingers, leaned down and ruffled his hair. "You really shouldn't keep that beautiful golden mane tied up like you do."

He caught her wrist, kept staring ahead at the television. "Sure you can't stay just a while longer? We could have dinner sent up. Or we could go out."

Don't do this to me. Don't make this any harder than it

already is. Aloud, she said as calmly as if she were talking to one of her clients, "All good things have to come to an end, Eric. I think it's time I split." My God, how could she sound so blasé when her heart felt like it had just been squeezed dry? When had the physical pull that had attracted her to him turned into something so much more?

"I'd better take a last look in the bedroom to make sure I don't leave anything behind." She left the room before he could come up with another suggestion of what she could do in the bedroom that would be a heck of a lot more fun. Like getting on her back one more time and not wanting to get up. Ever.

When she walked back into the living room she was hit with a strong dose of nostalgia, and she paused for a long, last look at Eric. How would she ever be able to forget him? Would she ever want to?

"If I leave my little box of goodies behind will you dispose of them for me? I really don't feel like hassling with them on the way home."

She set the overnighter down on the floor. Eric pushed himself off the sofa. He looked weary. Dejected.

"Angel, why don't you at least let me ride down with you?"

"I told you before, Eric, I came up by myself, and that's the way I'm leaving."

She'd never be able to walk away if she had to see him standing there, waving good-bye to her. She wanted to remember him here, in this special place that had belonged only to them.

"Hey, don't look so downcast. Did we have a wonderful weekend or not?"

He moved quickly over to her and tried to take her in his arms. But she pulled away, stood on tiptoe and kissed his cheek. "Good-bye, Eric."

He let his arms fall from her shoulders, and she hurried to the door without another look back. It was over. But in her heart of hearts she knew it never would be. Somewhere between that first look into his eyes and this last good-bye she had fallen deeply, irrevocably in love with him.

* * * *

Eric let himself inside his hotel room—his home for the past six months—and sank down on the nearest chair. After settling the bill for the Penthouse suite, he'd opted to walk home rather than take a cab. He'd walked six blocks farther than he'd had to. He'd needed time to think. To decide on a course of action he'd considered, tortured himself over actually, for the past twenty-four hours.

He pushed himself up from the chair, went to the bureau in the bedroom and rechecked his airline ticket.

He'd wait until tomorrow, until Angel had had a good night's sleep. Until he had given himself one more night to be certain he was doing the right thing.

But he already knew what the right thing to do was.

* * * *

When her cell phone rang at seven in the morning the day after she'd left Eric at the Penthouse, Angel was still curled up in the wicker chair where she'd been all night. It took a moment before she realized she'd turned the bedside phone off as soon as she stepped into the apartment the night before.

With a heavy sigh she got up and walked to the dresser where she'd tossed her purse, dug inside for her cell phone and was hit with a sudden clutch of panic. Few people had her cell number. And only two she could think of who would call her this early in the morning.

Something was wrong with one of her parents. They'd received no answer on her land line and had resorted to the cell. She put the phone to her ear, all but choked on hello, and held her breath while she waited for one of her parents to speak.

"Angel?"

Eric.

She forced air into her lungs, but there still wasn't enough for her to breathe and talk at the same time.

"Angel. It's Eric. Say something. Please."

She tried to speak but couldn't.

Eric sighed, long and deep. "All right, I'll get on with it then. I know this is a breach of our agreement, but I had to—"

"How did you get this number?" She stuttered on the words, barely managed to get them out.

"From your cell phone when you were taking a shower."

But how...? And then she remembered that the number flashed on the screen when the phone was first turned on. Something she hadn't considered when they'd decided not to contact each other. But then she hadn't—

"It was dishonest of me, I admit. But I'm not sorry. I—"

Her knees had begun to wobble so she moved back to the chair, sank down on it. "Wh—what do you want?"

"I want to see you again before I leave. I don't have to be at the airport until this afternoon. I thought we could—"

See him again? No, she couldn't. "We agreed it was only for a weekend." Where had this bravado come from? When had her tongue and her mind formed such a partnership that she could talk without trembling, say such ordinary words when her head was spinning? When her heart was splitting in two.

"Angel, there are so many things I never told you. Things I want you to know before I fly across the ocean and out of your life."

How could he know that he had never really been in her life? That she really wasn't sure she had a life left at all?

"The only thing either of us needs to know is that we were weekend lovers. And it was wonderful. But it's over."

"Angel, please—"

She whispered good-bye to him in her heart, turned the cell phone off and dropped it back in her purse. Bypassing the chair that had cradled her all night, she threw herself across the bed and cried until her eyes were dry and her throat was raw.

At nine o'clock she put the bedside phone back on its cradle and waited.

* * * *

It was just a damn good scare. You're fine, Angel. They ran the new test twice. I'll prescribe something for the anemia and...

For two hours she had sat by the phone this morning waiting for the dreaded call that would confirm her worst fears. And when it came the good news had knocked her for a loop.

Relief washed over her like a tidal wave and beached her, alive and well in the world of the living again. But it was now a world without Eric.

Recrimination came fast and hard. *If only she had never spent this weekend with Eric. If only she hadn't fallen in love with him. If only she had agreed to see him one more time.*

Frantically, she dug the cell phone out of her purse and turned it on, hoping for a message. Hoping for a miracle. But two miracles in one day were more than anyone deserved.

He said he wanted to see her again. To tell her things.

Maybe now that it was over he realized he wanted more than just one weekend. Could that mean...?

But what if she'd misread him? What if his only reason for calling was exactly what he'd said? To tell her things he wanted her to know.

Maybe he wanted to tell her that he hadn't been honest with her—that he was married. But why would he want to see her to tell her that? No. There was something more. Something she'd felt between them from the first time they met and had refused to acknowledge because she wasn't looking for a relationship, even before she received the scare from Dr. Frazier.

And after the scare about her health, it wouldn't have been fair to Eric. But now things had changed. For her, anyway. But had they changed for Eric? Dare she hope?

Struck by a new thought, she glanced at her watch, checked the list of recent calls to her cell phone. Looked for the last number recorded. *Unavailable.* Her heart fell to her knees.

She began to pace. Pacing always made it easier for her to think. To work out problems. But when had she ever had a problem this big to deal with? A problem that spanned an ocean. And a lifetime of loving a man whose heart, whose life, was still unknown to her.

Maybe she should be satisfied to wrap it all up now. Cloak herself in the memories she had of Eric. Carry them forward with her, content to know that now she could love deeply, completely, eternally. That she'd even take a chance on marriage with someone like Eric. She shook away the thought. She didn't want someone *like* Eric. She wanted the real thing. She wanted Eric.

She stopped pacing as a decision came to her as swiftly as falling in love with Eric had.

She had one week left before she had to be in Milan for her next job. If she was lucky and could change her flight plans now, she could be in London day after tomorrow. She had no idea how she would find one lone jazz piano player in a city of twelve million people. But she was going to give it one hell of a try.

She started packing as soon as she got off the phone with the airline and didn't stop once to reconsider her decision. She didn't even give herself time to breathe until she was in the air and on her way to London. Then it hit her. Suppose she found Eric and he wasn't happy to see her. What would she do then?

Eight

It was approaching noon when Angel collected her baggage at London's Heathrow Airport. She'd slept fitfully on the flight over. Her dreams had been so filled with Eric and her imagined meeting with him that she was surprised she'd slept at all.

Now that she had landed she wanted to get to the hotel as quickly as possible, freshen up, get a bite to eat and get started calling every club in London that had a piano. And if that didn't turn up anything, then she'd just have to contact every government agency in the whole damn city that had anything at all to do with nightclubs, jazz, and piano music.

She loaded her three pieces of luggage onto a self-service cart and headed toward the terminal exit, already working out Plan B in the event Plan A fell through.

Her stomach felt as if it was on fire, and she realized it wouldn't be wise to wait until she got to the hotel to eat. She decided on a quick snack of milk and a biscuit and headed for the nearest food kiosk, thoughts of Eric relegated to second place for the moment.

Until the photograph on the front page of the Daily Telegraph jumped out at her.

Right there in front of her was a picture of Eric seated at a Grand piano. She closed her eyes and then opened them. It wasn't a mirage. It really was a picture of Eric. She read the newspaper caption in a blur.

World Famous Pianist Back Home. Her gaze lowered to the next line. *Eric Swensen...*She blinked a couple of times, swallowed. Eric Swensen...*joins the London Philharmonic tonight for his first appearance in over six months.*

Eric Sweeney, *her* Eric Sweeney, was none other than Eric Swensen, the noted classical pianist known all over the continent.

Never having seen a picture of Eric Swensen, she hadn't had a clue to Eric's real identity. Now she understood his ability to pay for a penthouse suite and the expensive outfit he'd insisted on buying for her.

Her hands shook so badly she had difficulty lifting the paper. She somehow managed to find enough money in her jacket pocket to pay for the purchase before a wave of dizziness washed over her. Perspiration slid from her temple and inched down her cheek. She looked around desperately for a place to sit and made it to an empty bench before her legs buckled.

"Are you ill, dear?"

Angel looked up. An elderly woman, a brightly colored knit cap pulled down to her ears, stood in front of her. Resentment at the unwanted intrusion flared up inside her, but it quickly abated when her conscience scolded her. "I'm just a little woozy, is all. Hungry, I think."

The woman sat down beside her. "It's a might warm in here, too. Can I get you something? A bottle of water?"

Touched by the stranger's concern, Angel offered a weak but genuine smile. "No, thank you. I'll be fine in a minute."

The woman leaned over and tapped the picture of Eric with her finger. "The whole city is celebrating today. Salt of the earth that Swensen lad. We couldn't love him more if he were one of our own. He's Swedish, you know." She leaned back and crossed her arms over her ample breasts.

No, Angel thought, she didn't know Eric was Swedish, hadn't given his ethnicity much thought. And she didn't really care now. All she cared about was Eric, regardless of his background.

As if Angel were thinking out loud, the woman picked up the thread of her thoughts. "Don't know how he managed to get through it all and come out as fine and talented as he is. His mum and dad fighting all the time, pulling him this way and that. One wanting to keep him chained to the piano, the other wanting him to lead a normal life."

Remembering what Eric had told her about his parents' unhappy marriage, how he'd never even read a comic strip before he met her, her eyes filled with tears and a painful lump rose to her throat.

"Have you...have you ever heard him play?"

"More than I can count on one hand. I'd be going tonight if I didn't have to be at work over there." She pointed to one of the food establishments across the terminal.

"Do you...do you think there are any tickets left for tonight's performance? And where I might get one?"

"Might be. Where are you heading now?"

Angel gave her the name of the hotel the travel agent had booked.

The woman hauled herself up. "Seems I remember reading once there's always some extras kept for tourists and last minute

VIPs who come to town. If I were you I'd ask as soon as I got to the hotel." She turned to leave. "Good luck."

Luck. She needed more than luck. She needed another miracle. She was about to go out on a limb, and she had no idea whether it was strong enough to hold her. Or if she fell, how she'd manage to put her heart back together when it broke into a million pieces.

She was going to see Eric play tonight if she had to beg on the street corner for a ticket. Afterwards she would seek him out and find out if she had only imagined she'd heard more in his voice than just the need to talk when he'd called her.

* * * *

At seven thirty-five, dressed in the same outfit she'd worn when she dined and danced with Eric just a few nights earlier, Angel slipped into her balcony seat at the Royal Festival Hall. She clutched the evening's program with Eric's picture on the cover to her chest, as if it were a rare antiquity.

Below, the orchestra was warming up. There was the sound of violins here, a flute there, and then an intermittent tinkle of percussions or a horn thrown in the middle of the mix. The excitement in the air was contagious and had she not been floating on her own personal high she would have been lifted up by the enthusiasm around her

Out of bits and pieces of conversation, Eric's name drifted to her and she felt both a sense of pride and awe. But most of all she felt fear. She was here to see their idol, and she had no guarantee he would welcome her presence.

When the curtain finally lifted to the full orchestra and Eric walked onto the stage to the thundering welcome of a standing ovation, Angel rose with them. Her breathing was fast and shallow, her head light and giddy. Her heart was ready to burst at the mere sight of him.

The first thing that struck her was his hair, loose and tumbling about his head like a wild, proud stallion. Her hands ached to touch it, to touch him, to hold him in her arms again. And in that moment, she never doubted that what had existed between them had been as powerful and as brilliant as the music he made.

Somehow she sat through the next two hours, numb at times, at others caught up in the euphoria of the crowd and the heartbreakingly beautiful music that filled the Hall. Once, when Eric performed a solo, she nearly jumped over the balcony and ran to him. Probably would have if she hadn't been certain she'd break both her legs and wind up lying in the center aisle, embarrassing them both.

And then the concert was over. The moment of truth was upon her. She let herself be swept with the crowd to the lobby, where an usher had told her Eric always came after a performance to greet his fans and generously hand out autographs.

She stood far enough away from him, shielded by the crowd so she could watch him without being discovered until the moment of her choosing. But she was close enough to run to him the moment he was free.

A slim, elegantly dressed blonde approached Eric at the same moment Angel saw the television camera and the reporters descend on him.

A reporter stepped up, and Eric nodded, smiled, as he put his arm around the woman's shoulder and drew her close to his side.

Angel was too far away to hear what Eric was saying, but bits and pieces from the crowd drifted over to her. *Been going together. Lovely woman. Announcing their engagement tonight, I heard...*

Angel's ears started to ring, the noise from the crowd melding into one huge roar. She looked for an opening, the crowd shifted, and she came face to face with the man who had just broken her heart.

The look of astonishment on Eric's face told Angel everything she needed to know. She was the last person on Earth he was expecting to see. Without thinking, she spun around and dashed through the first opening in the crowd. When she caught sight of the entrance, she ran outside. Taxi's lined the street, waiting for fares. She hailed the closest one and dashed toward it.

"Angel, wait!"

She didn't turn around. She had only imagined it was Eric calling to her. She had to keep going forward, get in the taxi and get away as fast as she could.

In the back seat of the taxi, Angel gave the driver the name of her hotel and instructed him to take her there as quickly as the law allowed.

* * * *

Eric sat hunched forward in the back of the taxi, his hands

clasping his knees and his eyes full front. "Don't lose them," he shouted to the driver.

"I'm doing the best I can, bloke."

"Do better than that. There's two hundred pounds in it for you if we keep up with them."

He would give two thousand pounds, if need be. He couldn't believe she'd found out who he really was. That she'd come after him. It must mean she loved him, right? Oh god, he hoped so.

Eric pointed straight ahead. "There. They've stopped. Pull in behind them."

But even as he shouted instructions, the driver had already slid behind the other taxi. Eric slapped the promised currency in the driver's outstretched palm, lunged from the cab and sprinted across the pavement and into the lobby of the hotel. He managed to slip into the elevator one second before the door slid closed. Angel was huddled in the corner of the elevator, her face in her hands.

He pulled her into his arms, but she shoved him back, beating her fists against his chest. "Leave me alone, Eric. Please."

After a short ascent, the elevator door opened and Eric stepped outside, taking Angel with him. "Leave you alone? You find me on another continent and ask me to leave you alone? Never. I love you, Angel, and you must feel the same about me if you went to all this trouble to find me. Which way to your room?"

Angel's chin bobbed up. Tears welled up in her eyes, spilled over. "You love me? *You love me?*"

"My God, Angel, if you only knew how much I love you."

It was crazy, unbelievable, a fantasy come true, and she still couldn't accept that it was real. Couldn't stop the tears. Tears of joy, now.

She still couldn't speak, wasn't sure she could walk. But she tested her legs. Miracle of miracles they worked, carried her to the door and kept her upright while she swiped the key card. She was still standing, but barely, when the door closed behind them and Eric dragged her up against him.

He felt so good, so strong, and so sexy. She shifted against the long, hard length of him, and it was as if they had never been apart, like they had always been together.

Eric's mouth came down hard over hers, his hands sliding every which way over her body.

She ran her fingers through the golden thickness of his hair. "You left it down."

"You said you loved it this way."

"I do. And I love you. I love you so very much."

He pulled her down with him to the carpet, his hands pillaging beneath her skirt, her fingers unzipping him, catching his thick, hot erection in her hand.

He pulled in a sharp breath. "You've no underwear on."

"I was hoping."

He groaned, pulled her on top of him.

After she fisted herself around him, the heat built fast, carrying them to the top of the cliff, tumbling them over the edge, and leaving them sated and spent, clinging to each other.

After a time, Eric rolled them to their sides, keeping her close to him with one arm under her shoulder, the other around her waist. "How did you find me?"

She told him about the newspaper in the airport terminal. "But I was prepared to call every night club in London looking for a jazz pianist, if I had to." She grabbed a hank of hair and ran her fingers through the strands. "I had no idea who you were. I'm still in shock."

"Does it matter that much to you?"

"Nothing matters now that I've found you." She lifted up on an elbow and looked at him intently. "Except I need to know about the woman I saw you with. People in the crowd were saying you were getting ready to announce your engagement."

"It seems everyone but the two of us were certain of that." He explained to her how he and Joan had voiced their uncertainties about a future together before he left for the States. That they'd mutually agreed to see other people during the six months they were separated before they considered whether or not they wanted to take their relationship to the next level.

"Joan is already seeing someone, rather seriously, from what she told me." He planted a couple of quick, light kisses on Angel's cheeks and the tip of her nose. "We had just made the announcement that we were not planning to marry but would remain good friends when I spied you in the crowd. I'll have to call Joan tomorrow and apologize for running out on her the way I did."

Angel threaded her fingers through the mat of curls on his chest and nuzzled the base of his throat. "Did you love her?"

He tugged her closer. "Yes, but not the way I love you. There was never the passion between us that you and I have. It was one of the things that made us both wonder if we were incapable of enjoying that kind of physical pleasure, or if we just didn't click together. During this last separation, we both found out we clicked pretty well with the right person."

She dropped a kiss where the pulse at his throat had suddenly quickened its beat.

"I am quite fond of Joan, however, so please tell me you're not one of those jealous females who'll throw a fit if I so much as talk to an old flame."

She reached up and touched his lips with hers. "Not as long as she's out and I'm in."

Eric touched the corner of her mouth with his tongue and ran it along the seam of her lips. "You're in, Angel. You're in for life." He passed his hand over the nest of curls between her thighs, found the delicate folds still swollen and wet, slipped a finger deep within. "Talking about ins and outs. I'm ready to see you naked again and begin a slow excursion of the ins and outs of your body."

"Can I coax you into the bed this time?"

He sprang to his feet, helped her up and carried her to bed.

He took his time loving her, pleasuring her until she thought if she had one more orgasm she would fly apart and never find the pieces. And then he took a nipple in his mouth, put a finger inside her, his thumb teasing her clitoris until it burned from the heat. He entered her, hard and hot, stroked her until they both almost lost their minds from the bliss of it.

Later, as they lay in each other's arms, Eric asked her, his voice thick with emotion, "Why wouldn't you talk to me before I left? Were you really angry that I called?" He lowered his voice to a whisper. "I almost went crazy when you cut me off, and I thought that was truly the end. That I'd never see you again."

She told him then about finding out that she may have had a rare, incurable disease. How she'd started out just wanting a weekend of sex with him, and how, after she realized she was falling in love with him, she couldn't bear the thought he might have come to care for her, too. That if he had, he would be doomed to carry the burden of her illness along with her.

"I didn't find out until two hours after you called that the second test gave me a new lease on life."

Eric clasped her so tightly to his chest that she couldn't breathe. "Promise me you'll never keep something like that from me again. Where you walk, I walk."

Tears leaked from the corners of her eyes and slid onto his shoulder.

Eric cupped her chin and lifted it so he could look into her eyes. "Tell me those are tears of happiness."

"They are, but I can't help wondering..."

"Wondering about what?"

"About what comes next. What—"

"How long do you have before you need to be in Milan?"

"A week. I could stretch it to ten days if I had to."

"That should be enough time to fly your parents here for a wedding. I can't guarantee mine will come. I don't know if they've even been in the same room with each other since their divorce. My father's back home in Sweden. Mother's in Holland."

"Both my parents are in California."

"We can do this, Angel. We can be married before you have to leave. Unless, of course, you need a year to plan one of those extravaganzas I've heard about."

The tears were still flowing, and she grabbed the edge of the sheet to dab at her eyes. "I love small weddings, but..."

"But, what?"

"You'll be here, and I'll be in Milan." She was all choked up with tears again. "I don't want to be away from you."

Eric hiked up on his elbow and brushed another tear from the corner of her eye with his thumb. "Only for three more months, sweetheart, until my contract ends. We'll have to be content with weekly visits until then. I won't like it any more than you, but we'll have that to keep us going. Can you live with that?"

"I won't like being separated from you for one day, much less one week. But if I know that one day we'll be together forever, then I'll live through it." She didn't want to press any further. She was truly ready to follow him wherever his career took him since she could always find work wherever they lived. But she needed to get it out in the open. "But what happens after that? After you've fulfilled your obligations here?"

Eric gave her a cat-that-ate-the-canary grin. "There's something else I haven't told you."

She popped up on an elbow and brought her face level with his. "Oh?"

"I'm leaving the concert stage and devoting the remainder of my career years to jazz. That's what my gig in Manhattan was all about. Mike, the club's owner, has been a long time friend, and he gave me the opportunity to find out firsthand if that's what I really wanted. It is. Think you can live with a no-name jazz man instead of a world renowned classical pianist?"

"I can live with you any which way you are."

Eric bent down and brushed her lips with his. He started to deepen the kiss, but he pulled back. "Think you're ready to open that business you talked about?"

"What do you have in mind?"

"A jazz club of my own. I was thinking of Manhattan. What better place for you to drum up clients?"

It was too good to be true. "You're not doing this because of me, are you? Are you sure you won't miss the concert stage? The excitement and glamour? Your name is a household word all over Europe."

"I'm doing this for me, first and foremost. It's something I've thought long and hard about for years, and I'm only giving up the stage, not music. And woman, believe me, you bring me all the excitement I can handle in my life."

What a turn on that was, she thought, and pulled him on top of her. As usual he was splendidly aroused. She wrapped her legs around his back and lifted her hips. Like always, his first penetration sent sparks through her system. She cradled his head in her hands and brought his ear to her lips. *"Lo riempite splendido."*

"I don't speak Italian," he said at the end of a heavy breath.

"I said, 'You fill me splendidly.'"

He rested his forehead on hers. *"Ik ben gelukkig to verplichten."*

"I never studied Dutch."

He withdrew as far as he could without leaving her completely before he thrust deep inside her again. He fought for a steady breath. "I said 'I'm happy to oblige'."

And oblige her he did. Very well, indeed.

* * * *

Angel let out a long sigh as she turned from her stomach to her back. Thirty minutes ago, Eric had left for a trip home to get a change of clothes. "I live in Kensington. It's only about ten minutes from here," he'd told her. "I'll be back before you know it." His last words, instructions really, had been for her to remain exactly as she was. Naked and waiting for him.

The door opened just then and Eric walked in dressed in navy slacks, a blue and white striped dress shirt and a navy blazer. He might have been a businessman returning home from a day at the office. Except, instead of a briefcase in his hand, he was carrying a shopping bag.

Angel sat up, pulling the sheet up with her. "Breakfast, I hope."

Eric grinned, set the bag on the writing desk under the window and reached inside. "You could say that."

The edginess in his voice excited her. "You have something devious on your mind. I can tell."

His grin broadened as he took a familiar jar of peanut butter from the bag, set it on the table, dug back in the bag, came up with the not quite full jar of honey.

Her jaw went south. "You didn't."

"Yes, I did."

"You kept everything?"

"Everything."

"But suppose I hadn't found you?"

He shook his head in disbelief. "You don't think I was going to give up that easily, do you? I was prepared to track you down, even if I had to call every language service in New York City to find out exactly where you were. I would have put an ad on the front page of every newspaper in Italy to find you."

He dug back in the bag for one more item. Brought out the comics section of the Washington Post.

Angel gasped. "I don't believe it."

"Believe it."

"*Ti amo,* Eric Swensen. In Italian that means 'I love you'."

"I love you too, Angel. And by the way, I think its time I knew the full name of the woman I'm about to marry."

"Angelique Duvernay."

"Very well, Angelique Duvernay," he said, walking toward her, a jar in each hand and the paper tucked under his arm. "First we'll have my idea of breakfast. And then we'll have a read-through of the funnies. We'll pick up where we left off on Sunday."

Happiness bubbled out of her in an explosive chuckle. "I

really, really love you, Eric Sweeney Swensen."

"And I really, really love you, Angelique Angel Duvernay."

He opened the jar of honey, dipped his finger inside and dove under the sheet.

Angel couldn't hold back the laughter.

She had a feeling Eric—her Eric—would never prefer the *Times* to the *Post* again.

"Toil and Trouble"
by
M. A. duBarry

Prologue

1558 Cork, Ireland

Mage Trevor McGovern eyed the seething mob of women gathered outside his castle. A rainbow of fiery reds, deep, earthy tones, and golden ash flashed beneath the window. Oh, how he could lose himself in such a sea of rich, silky hair. Visions of long locks spread out over the pillows on his bed and draping over the skin of his bare chest filled his mind on the instant. If only he could convince even just one of the lasses to come inside...

A stone hurled toward the window missed its target, but it quickly brought him back to reality.

A fortnight ago, the luscious lasses had managed to climb the stone wall surrounding his lands and set out to take over the courtyard, forcing him to become a prisoner in his own home. While he had always admired a woman with a bit of sprite in her soul, surely he couldn't have bed them all. But what other reason would a lass have to be angry at the mighty, magickal McGovern? Women usually fawned over him, racing even their own sisters to be first to tumble with him. But for the life of him, he had no idea why the fairer sex had decided to turn on him. And they apparently had done the same upon his best friend and partner in bed-crimes, Brennan O'Brady.

"I've ne'r known so many lasses to agree on a single cause in all me life," Trevor said. He turned away from the window and shut the glass pane, locking out the women's ranting voices. "We're in over our heads this time, doomed to say the least."

Brennan shrugged his shoulders. "They'll quiet down in due time. If not, I'm sure you can weave a charming spell to settle the matter."

"Spells and affairs of the heart never go hand in hand," Trevor said. "Bending a person to one's own will never works. I say we have a better chance at the women eventually coming to their senses. They can't last long without us." He paused. No woman had ever turned against him, or Brennan, for that matter. "You don't suppose this has anything to do with Molly Claire?"

"What?"

"You remember. The redheaded spitfire we met in Dublin."

Brennan rose from the bench. "She wouldn't dare venture this far for revenge...or would she?"

"I'd never seen a woman angrier than Molly."

"Nor have I, not even to this day. I also remember her spitting out words of a hex at our backs. Lucky for me, I was still in the gods' good graces at the time and immune to the lass's curse. You, on the other hand, will not fair as well if her magic is indeed what the Dublin witches claim it to be."

Trevor plucked an apple from a half-empty bowl sitting in the center of the table. If the women remained in the courtyard for much longer, he'd starve. "This is all your fault." He bit into the shiny red piece of fruit and lowered his body onto the bench.

"My fault?" Brennan shot him an angry glare. "You tumbled her first."

"And you insisted on having her next. If only one of us had loved her and then left her, it wouldn't have been half as bad."

"You owed me," Brennan said.

Trevor took another bite of the apple. "Still sore about Elizabeth?"

"If she was your woman, you'd be just as angered."

"You can't blame me for that incident," Trevor said. "I had no idea. How was I to know you had finally found the one? We both agreed neither of us would be saddled with a wife until our estates could no longer survive without heirs." He tossed the well-chewed apple core into the burning hearth.

Brennan offered him a sly smirk. "You broke that oath several times over."

"My sons with Catherine don't count. Estates can only pass to legitimate heirs."

A rock hurled through the window, this time making its mark and shattering the glass pane into tiny shards.

"Sweet mother of God." Trevor rose from the table and ventured back toward the window. He ducked as a second rock flew past his head. "I do believe they mean to kill us, Brennan."

"I suppose they have every right."

Trevor reached for the first stone, grabbing it with his right hand. He inspected the gray rock and then tossed it to Brennan. "They've marked it with Esmerelda's circle."

A pale look crossed Brennan's face. "If old Esme is involved in this, neither of us will ever lay between a woman's thighs again. Do you remember what happened to Tom Cooke?"

"Aye," Trevor said. "The Lady Sarah has a new pup. She keeps him tied up at the foot of the tree in her husband's old yard. The poor dog is fed nothing but scraps and water. If he's fed at all."

Brennan turned to Trevor. "Do you really think old Esme has the power to turn a man into a dog?"

"I don't know, and I have no desire to seek the truth."

Brennan sneezed. He rubbed his nose and took a deep breath. "Tell me you haven't brought Catherine's dratted cat back here again."

Trevor shook his head. "I hate cats. Catherine knows to keep that wild beast as far away from here as possible."

Brennan sneezed a second time. "That was definitely a cat sneeze."

A sudden realization struck Trevor's soul. "You don't suppose…"

"She wouldn't…" Brennan said. "Old Esme couldn't…"

"If Tom is now a dog…"

"Sweet Jesus," Brennan said. "The old hag is going to turn you into a cat."

A loud rumble shook the castle. Pebbles popped out from the mortared walls and danced onto the floor. Trevor felt his body shrink and then suddenly change shape. He turned to search for Brennan amid the falling walls, but froze when he saw two black paws in place of his arms.

The rumbling stopped.

"She's turned you into a cat, Trevor," Brennan said. "A black and white cat."

"Must be from that streak of white in my black hair. Devil be damned. The old hag does indeed have the power to make a changeling."

"What now?"

"How am I supposed to know? In all my years, I've never been a cat."

"Can't you change back with your magickal know how?

Isn't that what a supreme mage is supposed to do?"

"I have no control over other people's spells," Trevor said. "Real magick doesn't work that way."

A pair of large, purple boots with turned up toes stomped across the room. "Do you believe in me now, me lords?"

Trevor looked up at the old hag. "Change me back, Esmerelda. Now!"

"Not until you've learned a lesson."

Trevor leaped for the table, springing from the floor on his hind legs. "Tell me what to do to break this hex and I'll do it. I have sons to care for."

Esmerelda leaned across the table and picked up Trevor. "You're such a cute, cuddly, little thing, my lord." She rubbed him behind his ears. "I do say you fair better as a cat than a man."

"Stop that." He swatted her with his paw. "Cut it out."

"You never cared much for your sons in the past, my lord. And as for Catherine..."

"That's not true," Trevor said. "My sons mean the world to me. I'll make amends. Anything. Just change me back."

Esmerelda shook her head. "I'm afraid I can't."

Trevor meowed. "Why not?"

"It's Molly Claire's hex. She asked for my help in placing a hex against you. Combined with my powers, the curse is very strong. There's only one way you can revert to being a man again."

Brennan looked over to Esme. An angered glare crossed his face. "I have the power to summon your master Esme. If you want to keep him out of this, you better tell us how to break Trevor's curse."

Esme frowned, but relented. "You must find true love on your own, and have true love returned to you. Only then will you be able to break Molly's hex."

"An easy pittance," Brennan said. "Is that all?"

Trevor jumped out of Esme's arms. "There must be more, Esmerelda. I know you all too well. Poor Tom Cooke fell in love many times. I've seen him eyeing Lord Stoke's bitch. He's like a love sick puppy around that dog."

Esme smiled a wicked witch's grin. "You must commit to the love you give and get back."

"Commit? As in...marriage commitment?"

"Aye," Esmerelda said. "And until you do, you'll remain

as a cat. Even if it takes centuries."

Trevor pawed at Esme's skirts. "And what about my sons and Catherine?

"I'll see to it they are cared for properly."

"And my magickal powers?"

"They'll return once the curse is lifted. Until then, you will be nothing more than a man trapped in a feline body."

Trevor didn't like the idea of living without magick, but he didn't see that he had any other choice in the matter.

Trevor jumped up to the windowpane. He stared down at the crowd of women below. "Then it's settled. I'll find true love."

"You're a cat, Trevor," Brennan said, joining his friend at the window. "How can you find women while you're in feline form?"

"How hard of a task can that be? Women *love* cats."

Brennan shook his head. "I'm not all too certain about this, Trevor. Women are mortals, humans, and you're not either of those anymore."

Trevor didn't answer. If truth be told, he couldn't agree with Brennan more. But he had no choice. He'd watched Catherine's cat often enough, and getting friendly with the ladies was something any feline could easily do. Besides, they didn't call it animal instincts for nothing.

One

"Beware of the mage." Madame Borghini leaned over the wildly decorated table and stared into a smoky crystal orb sitting on a cat-shaped stand. A frown crossed the aging gypsy's face.

Tabitha Cole watched the woman's every move, a familiar sense of dread filling her soul. "The image faded again, didn't it?"

"I can't force Fate to see what it deems only for your eyes." The old gypsy glanced across the table, a frustrated look veiling her face.

Tabitha tossed back her head and slouched in the chair. For more than a month now, she'd been using Lady Borghini's help to decipher the words of a haunting voice heard only in her dreams. But apparently there was no hope for the matter. "He's trying to warn me," she said. "Peter is warning me of something I can't see, and I'm at my wit's end trying to figure out exactly what the hell he means."

"The dead communicate on a different level than the living, Tabitha," Borghini said. "You have to remember that fact if you want to ever find out what your late mentor is trying to tell you." Madame Borghini pushed aside the crystal ball and leaned forward. "As a friend," she said, "I advise you to stop thinking magickally and start thinking in reality."

Tabitha shook her head. "No, I knew Peter better than anyone else knew him. This message has to do with magick. I just know it does. I can feel it in my soul. It's a gut-wrenching sensation that reaches beyond this plane."

Borghini packed up her Tarot cards. "Have you gone to the police?"

"And tell them what? My dead mentor is talking to me in dreams? I doubt that's a precedent to reopen the case."

"Peter was murdered," Borghini said. "And his killer is still on the loose." She shoved her magical paraphernalia into a large, handwoven shoulder bag resting on the floor, taking extra care with the crystal orb.

"Peter's death was ruled an accident," Tabitha said.

Borghini peered up at her from the edge of the table. "Do you really believe that?"

"Do I have a choice? According to reports, Peter used a deadly concoction of herbs in his flying ointment that night. Apparently he was too dazed to realize where his property ended and the Long Island sound began. There appears to have been no foul play in his drowning, and Peter wasn't suicidal..."

A cold breeze filtered into the room, wrapping its way around Tabitha's legs and slowly venturing away toward the table and Madame Borghini.

Tabitha froze. If she'd learned anything in her years of magickal studies, it was to immediately silence spoken words if ever they might be heard by unscrupulous forces. She raised an eyebrow in question, only to find her hired psychic being as cautious as herself.

Borghini raised a finger to her lips.

The cold air sauntered away, dissipating into nothingness.

"Do you see now why I don't question Peter's death? Everything points toward an accident, so no one is going to listen to me."

Madame Borghini rose from her chair. "I knew Peter from when he was a child. I watched him grow up, take on his mother's successful business and turn it into the empire it is today. If it weren't for Peter Morghan, Morghanna's Maze wouldn't be one of the world's largest purveyors of magickal goods. And all the while he never forgot his humble beginnings or the agony his ancestors suffered for being witches. He worked hard at educating people about all aspects of the Craft, and he donated an unbelievable amount of monies to charities and the needy. The man did nothing but good for the world, and somehow I believe Morghanna's Maze is at the heart of his murder."

Tabitha agreed with Madame Borghini, but for the life of her, she hadn't been able to find out who or what wanted Peter dead. "I've gone over things so many times that whatever I am missing has to be so minute or so well hidden, it will continue to remain in the dark until Peter's enemy is ready to reveal himself."

"Just be careful, Tabitha," Borghini said, picking up her straw tote. "This isn't something you should take on alone. Morghanna's Maze is all yours now and if five generations of witches' souls couldn't protect their own blood, they certainly won't be able to protect an outsider."

The door to her office opened with a bit of a thrust, revealing a tall, blond-haired gentleman standing on the other side.

Tabitha jumped.

"Oh, I didn't realize you were busy, Tab."

"That's okay, Baxter. I was just finishing up here." Tabitha rose from her chair and scooted around the table to where Madame Borghini stood ready to leave the office. "This is Baxter Flint, Madame Borghini, my head advisor at Morghanna's Maze."

"A pleasure to meet you, Madame." Baxter extended his hand.

The gypsy didn't budge.

Tabitha didn't like the coldness developing between her trusted friend and her advisor. "Madame Borghini works as a psychic reader during the day," she said, hoping to ease the tension. "She'd prefer not to pick up other people's energies."

Baxter retracted his hand and placed it back upon the doorknob. "I fully understand. I do readings myself from time to time."

"And I'm sure you're very good," Borghini commented. "I can sense your strong aura."

Baxter turned his attention to Tabitha, his bright blue eyes suddenly seeming as icy cold as a winter's storm. "I just wanted to know if there was anything I could do for you before heading out for the weekend."

"As a matter of fact, there is something you can take care of," Tabitha said. She left Madame Borghini's side and ventured to a small table in the corner of the office. She picked up a brown paper-wrapped package tied with string and walked back toward the door. "Can you take this down to the museum for the exhibit? It's a small portrait the McGovern family donated to our collection. I thought it would be a nice addition to the exhibit showing next week." She handed the package to Baxter.

"Great. I'll run it over to the museum on my way home. Shall I pick you up Monday night, say sevenish?"

Tabitha smiled. Since Peter's death, Baxter was her pillar of strength, helping her ease her way into taking over Morghanna's Maze without incident. "Seven sounds fine."

Baxter nodded to her and Madame Borghini, and then closed the door behind him.

Tabitha noted the cautious stare glazing the gypsy's large brown eyes. "Ease your mind, Madame Borghini," she said, gently patting the woman on the shoulder. "Baxter believes Peter was murdered, too. In fact, he's the one who first expressed the notion to the police, even before I thought of it."

"Just heed Peter's words. I'm sure in time you'll come to learn the meaning of them."

"Yeah, I'm sure of that, too," Tabitha said. "I just hope when that time comes, it's not too late."

Two

The ride home from Manhattan had been anything but pleasant. Between rush hour traffic and the constant thought of Madame Borghini's ill-fated reading, Tabitha couldn't help thinking now was the perfect time for her to perform her own flying ritual. With the help of the powers that be, she hoped using an altered state of mind would allow her to see things more clearly, and in the process decipher her haunting dreams.

Following the bend in the road leading to her house, Tabitha hit the button on the remote sitting on her dashboard and waited for the driveway gates to open. The large, black, wrought-iron fretwork parted ways, leaving a space for her to pull up into the drive. Clearing the gates, she drove up the winding, blacktopped pavement, twisting around a path lined with gnarly trees and several statues, including those in the likeness of Diana, Queen of the Witches, and the god Cernunnous.

Tabitha pulled her car up under the porte-cochère and turned off the ignition. She checked the rearview mirror to make sure the gates had closed securely after she drove past them. Seeing them in a locked position eased her mind a bit. The thought of a possible prowler on the house's grounds the night Peter had died made her more than a little uneasy these days.

As she got out of her car, a slight breeze whisked away the orange and brown leaves lining the pavement at her feet. She wrapped her long sweater coat closer to her body as the crisp fall air chilled her to the bone. She didn't like it when the weather turned cold sooner than expected. Another week of Indian summer would have suited her just fine, especially since she planned to do her flying ritual this weekend. The thought of going naked outside in the cold didn't please her in the least.

Tabitha leaned back into the car and grabbed her pocketbook from the floor on the passenger's side and the small bag of groceries she'd picked up from the local supermarket on the way home. A can of cat food rolled free, sliding under the seat. She huffed and decided to let the darned thing stay put. There were more than enough cans still in the bag. Reaching for her house keys, she nudged the car door shut with a slight tap from her hip and headed up the stone walkway to the house.

A faint meow echoed from behind the large bow window where her new pet Toil sat perched, watching her every move from the car to the door. The cat meowed a second time and then jumped off the sill, fading away behind the curtain. Inside, scurrying sounds of cat paws dancing over the foyer's tile floor reached her ears.

"I'm coming, Toil," she said, rattling her keys as she worked the lock. Her sister Maura had thought it a good idea that she get a pet to keep her company after Peter died. But a pet meant another living being to worry about and she hadn't been sure she was up to the task just yet. For more than a year she'd managed to fend off her sister's idea, but last weekend, after seeing the black cat with the white stripe in his hair at the local shelter, her heart melted. And now she was the proud owner of Toil the Cat.

Tabitha undid the door latch and pushed the wood portal open a smidgen, fearful of her new cat escaping. But the instant she made eye contact with the cat her worries vanished, for no sooner did she open the door than Toil reached up and aimed for her knee with his shiny black paws.

Tabitha dropped the grocery bag and bent down to pick up the furry tike. A loud purring greeted her ears. "There, there, my little guy. No need to worry about being alone for the next couple of days. Tabby's off on weekends and, as usual, has no place to go." The cat rubbed his head against her chin, falling further into the hands that petted his ears in a soothing manner.

**

God, but he hadn't felt hands like hers against his skin in years, thought Trevor. And the scent of her rose perfume, a fragrance mixed with what he deciphered to be peaches and berries, wafted to his nostrils. The woman even smelled good. Now he knew what it must feel like to have died and gone to heaven. He squirmed in the woman's arms, twisting his feline body so that his back faced her chest.

"Want your back scratched, little guy?"

She raked her red-polished, manicured nails over his spine, scrunching his fur as she massaged her fingers into his skin.

Yes, this was an owner he could live with, although he didn't like the fact that this Tabitha kept calling him a little guy. If only she had known him when he was still human, he was certain she wouldn't call him little, by any means.

The phone rang, interrupting his wonderful massage.

Tabitha put him down and headed over to the answering machine, which sat on a table near the main stairs.

He followed her, a close step behind, the scent of her unique fragrance never getting too far away from him. Trevor, as he preferred to be called, jumped onto the table and perched himself off to the side. The cold marble top froze his feline butt the second his bottom made contact with the shiny slab. He flipped his tail and fixed his hind legs, settling into a semi-comfortable position. The view down Tabitha's blouse made it a tad bit easier to accept the numbness enveloping the bottom half of his body. He could freeze to death for all he cared, as long as his new owner kept bending over like she was, listening to the annoying male voice being played back over the recorder tape. Who the hell was this guy anyway? Trevor nudged a bit closer to the machine, rubbing his head up against Tabitha's exposed bosom as he passed by.

"Tab, just me, Baxter. I wanted to see that you made it home safe. I was worried about you after meeting that Borghini woman in your office today. She gave me the creeps. If you need anything, call me later."

A loud buzz followed the man's message.

Baxter... Trevor didn't like the sound of this guy. And what about this Borghini woman? If memory served him right, Borghini was the name of a long-standing gypsy family famed for their psychic abilities. The thought that his new owner was familiar with magickal things pleased him. Maybe she even had a spell book lying around that could help him undo the curse Old Esme had placed on him. Yeah, right. After all these years, there was little chance of that happening.

Tabitha backed away from the table.

Her bosom went with her.

Damn, just when he thought he was getting lucky. Trevor jumped off the table and followed Tabitha into the kitchen. This was a big house, and he'd spent the last few days scouting out all the rooms. The woman had taste and money from the looks of things, but there was too much guy stuff in the house to have been all her style. He wondered where her Mister Right had gone off to. Tabitha Cole didn't seem the type of woman who should be alone. She was beautiful, from her long black hair to her high cheekbones, even down to her small feet. She wasn't skinny, but he'd never preferred the stick-thin type anyhow. He saw beauty in other assets. Visions of his former love, Catherine, came flooding back to him. He wondered what had happened to her and the boys. Mayhap the McGovern line he had sired didn't even exist anymore. If only he could learn his bloodline had been cared for, that Old Esme kept her promise. If only... There were too many painful memories in the past. He had to find a way to make the best of the present.

Tabitha placed a bowl full of dry cat food on the floor near the sliding glass doors that went outside to a wood deck.

Trevor sauntered over to the white ceramic dish and sniffed the food inside. A second serving of dinner was placed down next to the first, this time in the form of diced chicken on a paper plate.

He looked up at Tabitha, who now made her way to the table, her own dish of chicken waiting for her on a black place mat. A thick book sat next to the dish.

She looked so lonely eating by herself.

A knot twisted in his soul.

The phone rang again.

Tabitha got up from her chair and picked up the receiver. "Oh, hi, Baxter."

It was *him* again. The guy with the annoying, nasally voice.

"Ha? No, really, I'm fine. I have company coming over tonight."

Company? That was news to him. Trevor jumped up on the table and sat on the book.

Tabitha swooshed him away and reached for the heavy volume, the phone receiver never leaving her ear.

"Who? Um..." She thumbed through the pages. "Trevor. Trevor McGovern, an old school friend. He's coming over for a visit."

Trevor's ears went up. What was his new mistress up to? Apparently she didn't fancy this Baxter guy. That pleased him, but he had no idea why it did. He jumped off the table and took a leap for the counter. He butted his head up against Tabitha's arm, pushing the book in her hands closed. The site of the cover stunned him.

In the centuries since he'd been turned into a cat, he hadn't seen his own face—his own *mortal* face. Whenever he looked in a mirror all he saw were white wispy whiskers and wild strands of long black cat hair, save for the white patch running through the top of his head. But the book Tabitha had in her hands had his face on the cover. He leaned in closer.

The Legend of Trevor McGovern and the Bloodline He Left Behind - Generations of the Magickal Mages.

His new mistress did indeed know about magick, and mayhap, she even fancied it.

Tabitha hung up the phone and returned to her dinner.

Trevor followed her back to the table. He was dying to know about his family and what had happened to them. But he couldn't sit down, open the book and start reading right in front of his new owner. No, that would look a tad bit odd to the woman. He'd have to settle for waiting until she'd fallen asleep or gone out again. And judging by the heavy look in her eyes, he'd bet his next best chance would be Tabitha going to sleep.

Trevor jumped off the table and went back to the bowl of cat food. He ate the chicken without stopping and forced himself to down a bit of the dry food, figuring it was the best thing for brushing his feline teeth.

The sound of a shoe hitting the tile floor caught his attention. Trevor turned around and found Tabitha kicking off the other shoe, then rising from her chair and placing her dish in the sink. She washed the silverware and the dish in a matter of seconds and dried her long, slim fingers on the dishcloth hanging from one of the handles on the bottom row of kitchen cabinets.

He liked the way Tabitha moved—slow, deliberate, and much like a cat. While he hated being in feline form, he had to admit he'd finally grown fond of the creature he'd become. Should he ever return to a mortal state, he'd have to get a cat as a pet.

Tabitha rubbed her neck and released a slight sigh.

Oh, how he wished he could be the one touching her soft, silky skin.

She flipped the light switch and headed out of the kitchen.

Trevor walked in her shadow, his four paws silently skimming the marble tiles in the hall and softly patting the carpet covering the stairs leading up to the second story of the house.

He watched her small feet glide over each step.

Tabitha turned into the room at the end of the hall. With a flick of her wrist, a crystal-laden chandelier illuminated the bedroom suite.

Trevor marveled at the soft lighting and how it danced over Tabitha's alabaster skin, giving off a shimmery effect.

She undid the buttons of her blouse and removed the white

garment in a nonchalant way, tossing it onto the floor.

Trevor watched her every move.

As Tabitha undressed, she made her way toward the closet and retrieved a long, thin robe.

The sheer garment reminded Trevor of a gown worn by the ancient Greek goddesses. The faint smell of clove and poplar brushed the air, teasing his highly sensitive cat nose. He ran across the room to where Tabitha now stood naked, and he reached his front paws up to get a firm grasp on the robe. The edge of the hem tickled his face, the light, yet exotic scent of poplar cocooned his nose.

Green ointment... He'd recognize the fragrance of a flying ointment from a thousand miles away. But surely witches today didn't use the same deadly concoctions a few had used eons ago? The thought of something happening to his new owner worried him.

Tabitha tugged the robe free from Trevor's grasp and slipped her arms inside the sleeves. She tied the gold-tasseled belt tight about her waist. "Care to come outside, little guy?"

There she went, calling him little again. If the woman had any idea who she was truly addressing, she'd know better than to call him little.

She scratched his head and that sensitive area between his ears. God, the woman was good with her hands. He imagined those same digits would feel quite nice wrapped about his cock. If only he could be a man once again, he'd tumble his Tabitha like he had never tumbled any woman before. A slight jar of his memory brought him back to reality. No sooner did such wicked thoughts taunt his brain, so did visions of old Esme come back to haunt him, reminding him exactly why he had been turned into a cat. He offered a slight cat howl and brushed up against Tabitha's bare ankle.

"Come on, Toil, let's get you some fresh air." Tabitha scooped him up and carried him to the French doors leading from her bedroom onto a spacious balcony. She set him down on the brick floor, scratching his head once more.

He purred and curled up in the corner. He wondered what the woman was up to out on the balcony in nothing but a sheer robe, her skin dotted with goose bumps from the chilly night air.

Tabitha pulled out a small table on wheels and lifted the top. She leaned in and huddled over the opened space.

From his corner, Trevor could hear what sounded like glass bottles being clinked around. Then the heady aroma of poplar and clove came back to tease his senses.

Green oils... Now he knew his mistress was indeed a witch, but this witch was different than Old Esme or Molly Claire. Tabitha had a kind heart, a good soul. He thanked the gods for the feline ability to sense such things in mortals. Being a cat had some advantages, he supposed.

Tabitha gathered some stray twigs and placed them in the patio Chiminea. She lit a fire, illuminating the otherwise dark area, and then stood back.

A slight breeze carried a second round of potent smelling herbs to his nose. Trevor's senses went on full alert. He sat up on his back paws and watched in silence as his mistress removed her robe.

Tabitha's ample breasts were now fully in view, no clothes marring his vision. Trevor enjoyed the sight, his own body reacting almost instantly. He eyed her from head to toe, his roving glance doing several ups and downs, finally settling on her erect nipples. The firm tips reminded him of succulent berries. He wondered what the woman would taste like. *Damn Old Esme for her dratted curse.*

Tabitha dipped her fingers into an open, blue, glass jar. With a fair amount of balm piled high upon the pads of her fingers, she began slathering on the fragrant mixture. She applied the ointment first to her wrists, using slow, steady circles, then to her forehead and finally over the soles of her feet.

Trevor wished he could apply the ointment to her body himself. He was certain had he the chance, he'd make Tabitha feel very good with his own circular motions. Thoughts of her lying naked in his arms, his fingers circling her breasts, enticed him.

"To the powers that be," Tabitha whispered, "protect me from misjudgment and show me what is meant for my eyes to see. Reveal to me my guide, my protector, my fate."

A slight breeze rattled the few remaining leaves on the trees in the area.

Trevor's cat fur stood on end. As a feline he'd had several witches as owners over the years, but none had ever managed to emit the aura his Tabitha had. He sucked in a deep breath, his head spinning.

Tabitha's whispered voice echoed in the distance.

"...My guide, my protector..."

He watched her in silence, his body unable to move, intoxicated by the heady aromas of the flying ointment. His vision faded in and out.

A thump resonated from the area where Tabitha had been standing.

Trevor sensed in his soul that Tabitha was no longer conscious, yet he couldn't move to help her.

A sudden pain struck his spine. His bones stretched, his fur felt as if it were being plucked from his skin. He hadn't felt a change in his body like this since the day Old Esme turned him into a cat, a day he tried so desperately to forget. If only he could go back in time. He tried to growl and screech, but no sound fell from his lips. His heightened feline vision grew dim, shadows taking form where clearly defined shapes previously existed. In a matter of moments, everything in Trevor McGovern's world faded to black.

Three

Trevor woke with a start, his heart racing, beating as if to escape his chest. His limbs ached and his head pounded. In all his years as a cat, he'd never had an owner as powerful a witch as Tabitha Cole. The woman had surely cursed him worse than Old Esme.

Trevor shrugged his stiff shoulders and let out a deep breath. The cold, stone pavement of the patio iced his back. He rolled slightly onto his side, but something warm and soft blocked his body from going any further than the mere inch he had just turned, something the same size as his own body. He froze.

Trevor didn't recall another cat being in the house. This was his territory and his alone.

A soft moan vibrated at his ear.

Trevor refused to remain still any longer. Giving in to curiosity, he opened first one eye, then the other and found, much to his shock, a very naked Tabitha curled up against his body. The soft curves of her ample bosom rested at the crook of his arm and strands of the woman's long, shiny locks draped his bare chest. Trevor lifted his head and peered downward. He was as naked as Tabitha—naked without any feline fur covering his skin.

Sweet mother of God! He was mortal again—mortal and very much aware of the fact. For the first time since being hexed by Old Esme, his senses suddenly felt less perceptive than a cat's. While his vision, sense of smell and intuition seemed only slightly changed, his tongue didn't feel anywhere near as rough against the top of his mouth. Shock washed through him like a raging sea.

Tabitha stirred. She moved her left hand down a bit from where it had been resting near his navel and settled her fingers naturally around his cock.

Trevor didn't know what to do. He felt as if he'd died and gone to both heaven and hell at the same moment. His body reacted to Tabitha's warm touch almost instantly.

Tabitha let out a soft sigh. She lifted her head and opened her eyes.

Not knowing what to say, Trevor waited in silence as he watched a veil of sheer terror cross her face.

Her scream shattered the night air. She rose from the patio

floor and moved away from him in a matter of mere seconds.

A flash of shiny metal blinded his vision. Trevor instinctively reached his hands upwards, grasping Tabitha's right wrist. "Don't!" He yelled as his vision cleared and he found himself staring at a very sharp dagger.

***

"Who the hell are you?" Tabitha's heart pounded like a wild beast racing in her chest. "How did you get in here?" She really didn't care if the man answered. She just wanted to shock him, confuse him, and keep him from gaining the upper hand until she could think of something better. "What did you do to my cat?"

"I am your cat!"

The man was insane to boot.

"Really, I am," he said.

She pulled her wrist free from his grasp and aimed the sharp-edged boleen knife at his throat. "I may believe in the power of flying ointments, but do you really think I would believe something as ridiculous as a shapeshifter?"

"Haven't you ever heard of familiars, woman?"

"Not in mortal form," she answered.

"If I were an intruder, I would not have taken a catnap at your side while you were lost to the world of dreams. You mixed too strong a concoction in your green oils and passed out."

The man had a point, thought Tabitha. She knew almost immediately following her application of the flying ointment that the mixture was too strong, but her body had already succumbed to the effects. "Fine, I'll give you that one. But what the hell did you do to my cat?"

"For the last time, I am your bloody cat!"

She bit her bottom lip. Did the man really think she was that dumb to believe such an outrageous lie? Besides, with the amount of cat hairs flung about the patio floor, the evidence mounting against this guy was growing by the second. "Prove to me you're my cat."

"I'm afraid I can't do that. I have nothing to verify who I am other than to tell you my name and how I came to be in this bloody predicament."

"Start talking." She kept the boleen aimed at his throat.

"My name is Trevor McGovern, mage and lord of Castle McGovern. I was born in Dublin, but I spent a good part of my life in Cork. In 1558 a witch by the name of Old Esme turned me into a cat as punishment for the sins I had committed."

"And what exactly were those sins?" She actually found his story interesting—bizarre, but interesting. *God, she really did need to get out more.*

"I was what you would call today a love 'em and leave 'em rogue."

She eyed him from head to foot and back up again. The man certainly had the looks a woman could swoon over. From his dark black hair, all the way down his tall, muscled body, this was certainly one man she could understand women falling for, especially if they managed to get him in the buff. "And you've been a cat since 1559?"

"'58," he corrected, his wonderfully handsome head nodding in agreement.

"And I suppose no one ever went looking for you?"

"Mayhap they did," he said. "Mayhap they didn't. All I know is that since that night, I haven't been in mortal form until this moment. And even if my family did look for me, what could I do as a cat? I certainly couldn't sit up and talk to them. Do you know what they did to cats suspected of magick back then?"

"Yes, they met similar fates as bad as mortals accused of being witches."

He frowned. "And you wonder why I haven't come forward until tonight?"

"Why did you change with me?"

"If I knew, I'd be more than happy to tell you. Now, I suggest you put on that robe you wore earlier, or I might be accused once more of my old tricks."

She was naked. Damn, she had forgotten that fact in all this commotion. But if she reached for the gown, she'd have to pull the boleen away from McGovern's neck. "How do I know I can trust you?"

"You don't."

"Then I don't think I'll put the robe back on." *Now that was being smart*, she thought to herself. *Keep yourself naked in the presence of a strange man.*

"Suit yourself," McGovern said, as he gave her a once-over glance.

Tabitha cursed to herself. The heat of the man's gaze sent a spark of desire zapping through her body, making her crave things she knew better than to satisfy with a stranger. The glint of mischief, aided by moonlight, twinkling in his eyes didn't help her any either.

"We can stay like this all night, if it pleases you, he said.

"I didn't say that."

"No, but if you keep that knife at my throat and refuse to move, we aren't going to get anything accomplished."

She let out a deep breath. *Trevor McGovern...* The name sounded too familiar. "You saw the book, didn't you?"

"What book?"

"The one I had in the kitchen. The one on Trevor McGovern and the Magickal Mages of Dublin."

"Well, I did see the book. If truth be known, I was hoping to read it after you had fallen asleep. But fate changed that plan."

"Did you really think I would believe you? Stealing McGovern's name?"

"Woman, do you think I died my hair just for you as well?"

Tabitha took a good look at the man's head. He had the same white streak that Trevor McGovern had been known to have back in 1558. "Coincidence, nothing more."

"Bloody hell, woman. What can I do to make you believe me?"

"Tell me something no one else knows about Lord McGovern."

He let out a deep sigh and rolled his eyes. "Let's see now. An old witch named Esmerelda turned me into a cat. I had a mistress and fathered several bastard sons. I hated cats—until I became one, of course. I was rescued from the local animal shelter by you and your sister Maura, and I was doomed to remain in feline form until I found the one woman I truly loved and who loved me back."

"Not good enough," Tabitha said. "A good try, but not even close."

"Fine," he said, annoyance icing his voice. "If nothing else comes of this strange meeting, at least you will know Toil is far from being a 'little' guy. As you can see I am quite big in all the right places. So, should this mortal existence of mine not last, please do one thing and refrain from calling me little guy."

Well, she had to give him that. The man was indeed big in all the right places, not just in his muscled torso and abs. Tabitha shifted slightly to one side. Her inner thigh brushed against

Trevor's large cock which was presently inching its way up toward her pussy. *Damn...* She really didn't need to be outside, buck-naked and with a handsome devil lying between her legs. She took a deep breath and turned her thoughts back to her missing feline. No one knew she called Toil "little" except the cat. Of course, Morghanna manor was filled with secret hiding places and nifty crevices. Any intruder could have overheard her call the cat little.

A breeze swept across the patio, and a cold chill ran down Tabitha's back. Goose bumps dotted her flesh and her skin tingled.

Trevor looked up at her, his bright baby blue eyes seeming to stare right through her. "I really think it would be in both our best interests if you put the robe back on and we go inside."

The man had a point, she thought. If he was some kind of stalker or intruder, he certainly could have attacked her by now, and he certainly wouldn't want her to put her clothes back on. But she wasn't going to give into him totally. Putting the robe back on was one thing, retracting the boleen another. "Get up slowly and don't try any tricks. If you do, I promise you'll be neutered and the job won't be as neat as a vet's."

"Tabitha Cole, you're a wicked woman."

"I've been called worse. Now get moving."

Trevor rose from the floor and turned his back to her. He moved with the graceful air of a typical cat, his sinewy muscles flexing with every step.

Tabitha caught her breath as she watched him head into the bedroom. The man had the most perfect ass she'd ever seen. She could easily envision herself reaching out and pinching him on the butt. The thought shook her brain, knocking all sense from her usual feet–firmly-planted–on-the-ground morals. What was she going to do with this guy once she got him into the house? Tie him up? The idea of him bound and at her mercy tantalized her wicked mind. *Not a good thing.* She quickly erased those thoughts. She could call the police, but she didn't know exactly what to say. She doubted they'd believe a woman who had just used an intoxicating mixture of herbs to perform a flying ritual and then woke up with a naked man next to her. No, thought Tabitha, that story would only land her in more trouble than she was in at the moment.

As much as she hated to admit it, her best option at present was to find this guy something to cover up his sinfully gorgeous body and then try to sort out their mess. If her odd predicament really was the result of magick, then she was in more danger than Madame Borghini had thought. Peter said to beware of the mage, and Trevor McGovern was the most famous mage ever to hail from all of Dublin. And who but a dangerous, magickal mage had the power to transform himself from a cat into mortal form?

Four

Trevor made his way back into the bedroom and then to the bathroom. Apparently Tabitha had a habit of not shutting doors all the way, because he remembered the linen closet door being slightly open when he explored a good portion of the house earlier in the day. Grabbing a towel off the second shelf, he wrapped it around his waist and went back into the bedroom.

Tabitha sat waiting on the four-poster bed, the sheer robe doing very little to cover up her curvy body. "So, Lord McGovern, what do we do now?"

He dropped down on the bed next to her and propped his elbow up on the pillow, resting his head in his hand. "For starters, I could give you a sampling of why Old Esme turned me into a cat."

"I don't think so," said Tabitha, her words hesitant.

Trevor smiled to himself. Even after all these years, he hadn't lost his potency. Yet, as much as his feline abilities allowed him to sense desire stirring in Tabitha's soul, it also allowed him to sense her uncertainty, mixed with a touch of fear. For some strange reason, he didn't like the idea of his new owner being scared of anything. He rolled onto his back and turned his face toward Tabitha. "Something in your flying ritual brought me back to a mortal state. What curse did you use?"

"Curse? Are you crazy?" A look of shock washed over her face. "I know better than to play with fire. The last thing I need is to use dark magic while performing a flying ritual." She toyed with the end of the gold tasseled belt draped around her waist. "I sought guidance on a personal matter, nothing more."

Trevor knew better than to ask Tabitha about something she considered personal, but without that knowledge, he couldn't make heads or tail of the situation at hand. "I need to know what you're concerned about."

She gave him a blank stare. "That's none of your business."

He sat up and ran a hand through his hair. This was going to be more difficult than he'd thought. "I have no idea why I've been returned to mortal form. Without knowing exactly what you said in your ritual, I have no idea how to proceed.

Maybe I will remain this way, and maybe I won't. But I need to know."

She worried her bottom lip and tossed back her hair.

Trevor noted the sharp boleen still rested in her right hand. Her fear was apparently greater than he had originally sensed and that bothered him. He gave Tabitha his best feline stare, concentrating on her eyes and trying desperately to search out her inner soul. Suddenly, a calm settled over him. The cat still inside his soul sensed that Tabitha's fear wasn't directly aimed at him, nor was he the total reason for her angst.

"Five years ago, my mentor in magick was murdered, Tabitha said. His name was Peter Morghan, owner of Morghanna's Maze, the largest purveyor of magickal goods in the world. His killer was never caught."

Trevor rubbed his chin. "I remember the name from the news."

"You watch TV?"

"I can even access the Internet. Is that such a shock?"

"For a cat, yes."

"I'm not a cat," he said. "I'm a man who was trapped in a cat's body. And after living for almost 500 years, I have learned a lot of things. Why don't you believe me?"

She gave him an uncertain look, but said nothing.

Trevor sensed Tabitha's fear again, and he really didn't blame her for keeping silent on the matter. Even to him, his absurd story sounded a tad unbelievable. Yet something in the pit of his stomach told him Tabitha believed at least part of his tale. The woman was a witch and therefore had to somewhat accept the idea of shapeshifters and familiars, even if she didn't admit it verbally.

"I'm not sure what I think at the moment," she said. "Besides, I don't have time to waste discussing what I do and don't believe in."

"I thought Morghan's death was ruled an accident," Trevor said, turning the conversation.

"It was," she said, "but knowing Peter, and knowing magick as I do, I saw the hidden signs. Peter's death was caused by the misuse of magick."

"And this frightens you?"

Tabitha let out an annoyed laugh. "Damn right it does. Especially since I believe his murderer has resurfaced."

He didn't like the thought of someone frightening his

Tabitha. *His?* The notion of considering her "his woman" struck him with a sudden sense of concern. He hadn't felt responsible or protective of anyone in years. Even his prearranged relationship with Lady Catherine hadn't provoked such feelings in him. The notion perplexed Trevor, and he didn't like it one bit. "Why would anyone harm you?"

"I believe Peter's death was somehow tied to Morghanna's Maze. When he died, he left everything to me—the business, this house, the ancient spell books, even his collection of magickal antiquities. His most prized possession was the Merlin Crystal, a magickal prop he wanted to donate to the Museum of Gemology. He died the day before the crystal was to be turned over to the museum." Tabitha let out a deep breath and tightened her fingers around the boleen. Trevor noted her knuckles turning white, but he refrained from commenting.

She looked him in the eye and continued. "Lately I've been having dreams of Peter. He calls out to me, warns me, and then he fades away before he can show me something behind a closed door. I had hoped the ritual would give me guidance in deciphering the dreams."

Trevor scratched his chin. "None of those things are reason enough for me to turn back into mortal form. The answer has to lie in your flying ritual."

She shook her head. "I told you, I was looking for guidance in deciphering Peter's dream. I didn't do or say anything else. Especially nothing that related to a cat."

A loud, tinny sound echoed from outside.

Tabitha jumped. She stuck out the boleen defensively, aiming at the air, but still prepared to fight whatever it was that had made the noise.

Trevor ran to the patio doors.

Tabitha followed close behind.

"Stay here," he whispered.

"I don't think so. I refuse to leave my safety up to a cat."

He frowned, but he didn't have time to argue with the woman. Trevor reached his arm behind his back and held on to Tabitha, keeping her safe from whatever or whoever had invaded her yard below.

He leaned over the wrought iron rail and peered over the metal fencing. In the distance he thought he saw the figure of a man running into the wooded area. He squinted and searched the grounds below with his still acute feline vision. The humanlike shadow leaped over the tall stone wall lining the property and vanished. "I think whoever it was has gotten away," he said. "I saw a shadow, but it's gone now."

Tabitha didn't move.

Trevor felt her tremble, felt her body go cold. "Mayhap you should call the authorities."

"And tell them what? A shadow trespassed on my property?"

He turned around and headed back inside, pulling the French doors closed behind him. He secured the top and bottom locks. "Do you have a light for the patio?"

"Yeah, over in the corner." Tabitha gave a nod with her chin.

Trevor flicked the switch. "Leaving the lights on might keep the intruder away." He reached out and drew her close. "I won't let anything happen to you."

"I still haven't decided what to think of you, yet."

He pulled back a step. "You rescued me from the shelter and took me in. It's the least I can do to repay you."

Tabitha had witnessed a lot of things in her days as a witch, especially with the magick Peter had exposed her to. The man had been one of the most gifted witches of modern times. She wondered what he would have thought of Trevor, a man turned into a cat and then back into a man.

Trevor pulled her close again. He wrapped his strong, muscular arms about her body and slowly rubbed the spot at the small of her back. He had a wicked touch, and she wasn't in the mood to protest. A sudden calm descended upon her soul. She hadn't felt this at ease in years.

God, what was wrong with her? She was in the arms of a cat!

She pulled away a bit.

Trevor tightened his hold on her.

"Relax, Tabitha. I can sense you haven't slept in days. At least not a good sleep."

She looked up and met his wild blue eyes. "And I don't think tonight will be any different."

"Come," he said, pulling her toward the bed. "As long as I am in mortal form, you have nothing to worry about. I may not have been able to fight off Old Esme's curse, but I'm deadly with a sword." He eyed the boleen. "Or a dagger."

"I don't turn my knife over to anybody, thank you. Now, if

you want a place to sleep, fine. You can have half the bed, but the boleen stays in my hand."

"Fine." Trevor pulled back the comforter and dropped his towel.

"What do you think you're doing?"

"Getting into bed."

"Like that?"

He looked down at his naked body. "If you'd rather have me in a different state, I am sure that can be arranged."

She rolled her eyes, but she said nothing. Getting into her side of the bed, Tabitha wrapped the covers tightly about her body and turned her back to Trevor. She felt the bed dip as he got in. "I can't believe I'm doing this."

"Neither can I."

She turned around and offered him a glare. "Insult me again, and you'll find yourself sleeping in that chair over in the corner." She nudged her chin at a white and pink antique chair next to her dresser.

"I wasn't referring to your reputation. Quite the contrary, to be exact." He inched closer to her. "I was referring to my own sins. I can't remember a time when I shared a bed with a woman solely for the purpose of sleeping." He wrapped his arm around her waist.

Tabitha didn't move. She couldn't help herself. Something about having a sixteenth-century lord snuggled up to her felt romantic, even if it did seem more than mere fantasy. If only she knew what the hell she had gotten herself into. And it had all started with her sister Maura insisting she take home a stray cat. If she knew then what she knew now...

She stopped the thought in mid-process. What woman would pass up the chance to have a real knight in her bed, and one that would want to save her from danger, at that? The thought unnerved her, yet tantalized her. She'd read quite a bit about Trevor McGovern and his heroic deeds back in the sixteenth-century. She'd also read about his sins. Yet, somehow, the whole package attracted her. And that made her more worried than anything else in the world. Mage or no mage, her biggest worry about Trevor McGovern was his charm— and how she could easily fall for it.

Five

The soft, morning sunshine filtered through the slightly parted curtains draping the patio doors. Tabitha let out a soft sigh and stretched. She'd slept better last night than she had in ages, and she had to admit to herself, it felt good to finally get some rest. She adjusted her shoulders against the pillow and froze. The tantalizing touch of Trevor's warm fingers trailing a circle around her nipple sent a zing straight to her clit.

"Only one night and you've forgotten about me already?"

She shook her head and bent her chin downward. "Hardly," she said, watching his hand slowly caressing her breast.

He grinned devilishly. "Let me guess, you still haven't made up your mind about me."

Oh, she'd made up her mind all right. She just wasn't sure she should share that information with the rogue.

He drew his finger up over her taut peak and then gently rolled her nipple between his thumb and forefinger. "You have beautiful breasts, Lady Tabitha."

"I'm not a lady."

He offered a sly smile.

"I didn't mean it that way," she said, rolling her eyes.

"Of course not," he replied. "But being the rogue that I am, I think I'll choose to ignore your protest." Trevor dipped his head to her breast and gently kissed her nipple. Then he nipped and suckled and teased.

A warm sensation radiated throughout her body. As a mounting pressure built at the apex of her thighs, Tabitha squeezed her legs together. She had to be crazy. This just wasn't like her. In the past she'd never entertained the idea of having a complete stranger in her bed. And yet, she didn't push Trevor away or even want him to stop.

Trevor shifted his body and leaned in closer. He ran his left hand down the side of her arm, his fingers lightly teasing her bare skin.

Tabitha instinctively reached out and intertwined her fingers with his. For the first time since she'd discovered her handsome Lord McGovern, she realized her boleen was gone. Her hand was empty. She undid her fingers from his. He didn't let go.

"My knife."

"It's in a safe place," he said as he trailed kisses from her breast to her neck. "Between the mattress and the box spring."

She wanted to believe him, but her heart and her head were telling her two different things.

"I took it out of your hand after you fell asleep," Trevor said. "I didn't want you to hurt yourself."

He placed his lips upon hers. The heat of his touch scorched her soul. A zing zapped through her body and made her suddenly more aware of her own desires than she'd ever been before.

She wanted desperately to believe him, but her head insisted that she check under the mattress.

"Go ahead," he said, lifting his lips from hers.

Tabitha dropped her hand to the side of the bed and stretched her arm over the edge of the mattress. Guilt wracked her, but she had to be sure.

Her hand slid over the mattress quilting. Slipping her fingers inside the crack between the box spring and the mattress, Tabitha found the cold, round nub of the boleen's white marble hilt wedged firmly in place. The knife rested exactly where Trevor said he'd placed it. She didn't know what to say to him. She opened her mouth, but no words came out.

Trevor placed his forefinger over her lips. "Now you know you can trust me. There's nothing more to say." He lowered his head once again and picked up right where he'd left off.

She swallowed hard and tried to make sense of her situation. But nothing made sense to her at this moment.

Trevor moved his hand downward and sought the sensitive area at the top of her inner right thigh. He brushed his knee against hers and gently parted her legs, settling his body in between. The moist tip of his hard cock rubbed her clit.

Tabitha gasped.

Trevor's hand wandered further downward. At the opening where her nether lips parted, he slipped his forefinger between the folds and gently massaged her clitoris in circular motions, flicking back and forth over the sensitive bud.

"Relax, my lady. Give in to your own desire."

He even sounded like a sixteenth-century lord. God, she didn't think she'd survive this magickal fiasco. Every muscle in her body tightened, every nerve heightened. Tabitha pushed herself closer to Trevor's working fingers. She grabbed the sheet with her fists and cried out. Spasms wracked her vagina and shot an explosive quake through her body. Yet, she couldn't help feeling as if she were missing something.

Trevor leaned forward and kissed her on the lips. He placed a firm hand upon her buttocks and pulled her toward him. His large, hard cock teased her hole.

She wanted him. And she wanted him hard and fast.

Trevor nuzzled her neck.

She reached her hand for his jutting cock.

Trevor brushed her hand away and slid inside her with a slow, yet full, thrust.

The feel of him filling her felt exquisite. The walls of her vagina stretched to accommodate him, wrapping around his cock like a hungry beast. She squeezed her muscles.

Trevor let out a groan and started moving with a faster rhythm. Tabitha matched his every thrust. The mounting pressure building in her pussy brought her to the edge. She reached her hand to her breast and gave her nipple a light pinch.

Trevor stared down at her. His blue eyes turning wild, like a brewing storm whirling on the horizon. Tabitha let out a soft moan and wrapped her legs around his body as her pussy exploded for a second time.

Trevor let out a groan and gave one final thrust. Then he collapsed on top of her and nuzzled her neck.

She enjoyed the feel of him still inside her.

"You've bewitched me, Lady Tabitha."

"Is that a good thing or a bad thing?"

Before he could answer, the sound of shattering glass echoed through the air.

Trevor rolled off the bed instantly, pulling Tabitha with him. "Stay here." He grabbed the towel he'd tossed on the floor the night before, wrapped it around his waist and crawled to the window.

Tabitha peeked out from behind the side of the bed, her heart racing frenziedly.

Trevor inched his way closer toward the window. He tossed aside shards of broken glass as he moved. She watched him hunch beneath the window and slowly raise his head just above the sill.

The sound of a car screeching on the pavement sliced through the morning air.

Trevor spent several seconds at the window, and then he turned around. "They're gone, whoever it was."

"Do you think it was the same guy from last night?"

"Possibly. We didn't hear any cars last night. Maybe they didn't have a way back. It is a bit desolate around here, save for your few neighbors." He rose to his feet, bent down and retrieved a fairly large rock sitting on the carpet amid the broken pieces of glass.

"What is it?"

"A rock with a note," Trevor said. "They had to be pretty close to toss it through the window."

"Who's it from?"

"There's no name. Only a message saying, '*The Time of The Mage has come.*'" He walked back to Tabitha's side of the bed and handed her the gray stone tied with cord. A piece of jagged edged paper dangled from the frayed material.

Tabitha studied the note. A sense of dread filled her soul. "Peter warned me of the mage in my dreams."

"Do you have any idea of this man's identity?"

She shook her head. For all the years she had studied under Peter Morghan, she never knew him to have an enemy. Nor did she know him to have any true friends. "Magick was Peter's life. He had a great responsibility in protecting many ancient secrets, and he never let his guard down."

"Until the night he died," Trevor said.

The notion perplexed her. "Peter rarely had guests here at the house and no one ever used his private apothecary. That's where the flying ointment he used the night he died was made. I found herbs and several other magickal components, as well as a list stating he had to order more clove, left on the main work table. It's also where he kept the Merlin Crystal. No one knew about his secret workroom, not even me until the reading of his will. I found out about the apothecary in a sealed letter his lawyer gave me after he died."

Trevor stared at her inquisitively. "Where's this apothecary? And who else knows about it now?"

"It's in a secret room behind my office. The building was built by Peter's grandfather and only the present owner of Morghanna's Maze, namely me, is privy to the apothecary's location."

"If Peter was murdered," Trevor said, "then someone besides yourself has to know about it."

Tabitha leaned back against the side of the bed, her shaken nerves starting to calm. "There were no witnesses to Peter's death, and everyone who could have had access to him had solid alibis. I'm convinced magick played a part in his death, but I obviously can't prove that."

"And what about the Merlin Crystal? If memory serves me right, isn't that the powerful prop supposedly made by Morgaine and the evil entity who sired Merlin?"

"There's a long story to the legend," Tabitha said. "But to make it short, only a direct descendant of the Goddess Morrigu or Morgaine, can access the crystal's powers. And Peter was the last of his bloodline."

Trevor gasped. A strange, wide-eyed look crossed his face.

"What's wrong?"

"I'm not sure, but I think I'm changing back into feline form."

"No," Tabitha screamed. "You can't! Not now. I need you."

"Who...ever...threw the...rock...is now...gone." Trevor sucked in a deep breath and froze. His body shrank to the size of a small cat, his hands and legs turning back into paws covered with long, shiny black fur.

Tabitha stared at him helplessly. She wanted to reach out and lift him into her arms, but she feared she'd injure him if she touched him during his transformation. She waited in silence, her heart wrenching.

"I think it's completed," Trevor said after several seconds, staring up at her from behind bright blue cat eyes.

"You can still talk?"

"Talking is about the only human ability I never lost. I just made sure never to talk in front of people for fear of being tortured. Back in our time, cats with any kind of gift were often considered evil, and I certainly had no plans of going to an early grave."

She reached out and picked him up. "Are you in any pain?"

"No," Trevor said. "Not anymore. The transformation is horrific, but once it's finished, the pain disappears." He nuzzled her neck.

"You're a rogue, even in cat form."

He purred and gave her a soft lick. "I am what I am," he said.

"I have to find a way to change you back. I don't feel safe without you."

He rubbed his head against her chin. "Think back to last night. Something you said or did caused me to change. If you can remember it, and then repeat it, maybe I will take human form again."

She wracked her brain, thinking of the ritual. But nothing specific came to mind. "All I did was ask for guidance, for the powers that be to show me my fate and send me my protector. I was hoping for an animal spirit to reveal itself, and then I was going to interpret its meaning."

"None of that applies to me," Trevor said. "If I were your guide or your protector why would I change back to feline form? What good can I do you like this?"

He had a point, thought Tabitha, but magick didn't always work the way mortals thought it should work. "Maybe you are my protector, just only in the worst of times."

"Oh, and so now is a better time?"

She scratched him on the head between his ears. "Don't get pigheaded just because you've turned back to cat form. The gods can always hear you."

He rolled his eyes and meowed. "Whatever." He jumped out of her arms and back up onto the bed. "I guess we'll just have to wait and see if I turn back again. Why don't you call your sister and see if she has any ideas on how to break the spell?"

"No," Tabitha said, rising from the floor. "I can't tell Maura any of this right now."

He sauntered over to her side of the bed. "Why not? Isn't she a witch, too?"

"Yes, but I know my sister. She'd panic and race out to the Island and then she'd be in danger. And I won't ever put Maura in danger. I haven't even told her everything about Peter, for fear if she learned the truth, whoever was stalking me would also stalk her."

Trevor slammed his right paw down upon the bed. "But I need to know how I changed form and how I can do it again. Maybe last night had nothing to do with magick. Maybe it had to do with some other great cosmic event or something. Aren't two heads always better than one?"

"Don't get huffy, little guy."

"Little? I thought after seeing me in the buff, you'd never call me little again."

She shot him a flirty grin. "Well, as a man, you certainly aren't little by any means, especially where it counts. But as a cat..."

"Oh, all right, I get the picture." He curled up on the bed and wrapped his tail around him, the tip touching his nose.

"Is that how a cat sulks?"

"I'm not sulking, I'm thinking."

"Fine, you think, and I'll take a shower." Tabitha headed toward the bathroom.

Trevor meowed and hopped off the bed. "I may be in cat form, but I refuse to leave you alone. Not even for a split second." He jumped up on to the toilet seat and perched himself on his hind paws, sitting upright.

Tabitha turned on the shower and stepped inside.

Trevor jumped down from the toilet lid and scratched at the shower door, his black paws working frantically at the glass.

Tabitha opened the glass panel and poked her head out. "I thought cats didn't like water"

"Don't believe everything you hear," Trevor said. "They just pretend that to avoid baths, like kids do."

She shook her hand at his face, spraying him with droplets of water.

He blinked. "Hey, cut that out. I'm just trying to keep an eye on you."

"Ah ha."

He flicked his tail at her and then turned around, prancing back to perch upon the toilet seat.

Tabitha left the shower door open a smidgen. The warm, pulsing water felt good gliding down her back, if only her problems could wash away as easily, she'd be okay. But considering what she knew about magick and Morghanna's Maze, washing away her problems wasn't going to be that easy.

Six

After her shower, Tabitha headed back downstairs and hoped, with Trevor's help, she'd manage to find her way out of this magickal mess. She leaned over the kitchen table and thumbed through the stack of ledgers and folders she had pulled out from the file cabinets in her home office. Trevor sat next to her on a chair of his own. She wished he hadn't changed back to feline form. The thought of him basking naked in her bed this morning still tantalized her. If she didn't know better, she'd swear she was falling for her cat and that had to mean only one thing—she was insane. What kind of woman would fall for her cat?

"Do you really think you're going to find what you're looking for in those papers?" Trevor asked, his voice interrupting her thoughts. "I have no other choice," she said. "Merlin's Crystal was to be donated to the Museum of Gemology the day after Peter died. His death halted the donation, and now that it's back on again, I'm being stalked. Something tells me that's not a coincidence."

Trevor jumped onto the table. "Why would someone want to keep you from giving the crystal to the museum? We don't even know if Merlin really existed, so why is it so important to someone that they'd kill for it?"

"I don't know. Peter said he never used the crystal in any magick, but that it had been in his family for generations. According to legend, its magickal properties only worked for its rightful owner, a powerful witch or mage descended of the Morrigu." She froze.

Trevor gave her a strange stare. "What is it?"

She didn't answer him.

"Tab?" He swatted her arm with his right paw and wrapped the left one around her elbow.

"In my dreams, Peter said to beware of the mage."

Trevor let go of her arm and sat back down on the table, causing several pieces of paper to fall to the floor.

"I need to know who the mage is."

"And what makes you think you'll find that information in these papers?"

She pulled out a chair and dropped a box of files onto the wooden seat. "Before Peter died he said he wanted to talk to me about the arrangement made with the Museum concerning Merlin's Crystal. He said it was important I know the details, but he didn't give a clue as to why. We never had that talk; he was found dead the next morning." Tabitha let out a deep breath and wiped a loose strand of hair from her face. "I'm hoping that somewhere in this mess are documents detailing the arrangement. Maybe that will help me find the mage and Peter's killer."

Trevor stretched like a typical cat and knocked over a few more papers.

"I don't need you making more of a mess than I already have here."

"I couldn't help it," he said. "My back aches." He jumped down from the table and started swatting the papers that had fallen to the floor.

"Good," Tabitha said. "You search those and I'll continue with this box up here."

Silence filled the room as she filed through folders and documents. Until now, Tabitha had never realized just how much Peter had donated to charity, or how involved he had been in securing the use of magick for good purposes only. The man hadn't deserved to die like he had. The thought unsettled her.

"Find anything, yet, Trev?"

The cat didn't answer her. Several seconds passed before she noticed Trevor wasn't in the kitchen any longer. Panic filled Tabitha's soul. Her heart pounded at an alarmingly fast pace, and her stomach twisted into knots. "Trevor? She scrambled to her feet and headed out of the kitchen. She'd never forgive herself if something happened to Trevor. "Where'd you go little guy? Trev?"

A man's garbled voice echoed from the main hall.

Not wanting to take a chance, Tabitha reached up and removed one of the swords hanging on the wall in the gallery leading from the kitchen to the entrance hall. She wrapped her fingers tightly about the hilt.

Turning the corner, she eyed Trevor sitting on the small table next to the answering machine. "You scared the living daylights out of me. What the hell are you doing in here?" She put down the sword.

"Who is this guy?" Trevor asked, hitting the playback button on the machine with the pad of his paw.

Tabitha waited for the message to start again.

"Tab, just me, Baxter..." The message went on to relay the recording made the day before.

"That's Baxter Flint, my personal assistant over at Morghanna's Maze. Why?"

Trevor hit the stop button. "I think I've found your mage."

"Don't be ridiculous. Baxter would never have wanted Peter dead."

"How can you be so sure?"

She wasn't sure of anything, but accusing Baxter didn't seem right. "Baxter relied on Peter for everything. They grew up together and shared a love of the macabre. Peter taught him everything he knows. Baxter didn't benefit from Peter's death. In fact, he suffered. I created the job of assistant just so he could stay on at Morghanna's Maze."

Trevor flicked his tail in a quick swishing movement. "I'm telling you, Tab, he's your mage."

"What makes you think so?"

He jumped off the table.

"Trevor?"

"This way," he said, scurrying across the marble floor.

In the kitchen, Tabitha followed her black cat back to the scattered papers spread out on the floor. Trevor pushed aside several documents with his paws, then dipped his head and grabbed hold of a small, yellowed sheet of paper with his teeth. He pranced over to Tabitha and sat up on his hind paws.

She bent and took the page from his mouth.

"It's a handwritten note of some sort," Trevor said. "Signed by both Peter Morghan and Baxter Flint. But the top half of the page is missing."

She read the message, the words reeling in her mind like a whirling tornado. "This doesn't make any sense. According to legend, The Merlin Crystal, if it has any real magickal powers, can be charged only by a direct descendant of the Morghan bloodline, and Peter was the last member of the family. He had no children, no siblings, and no cousins."

"Apparently Baxter is somehow tied to the legend of the crystal," Trevor said. "At least Peter must have thought so. If he was as serious about magick as you believed, then he wouldn't have trusted just anyone with the knowledge of the crystal's powers."

Tabitha tapped her fingers on the edge of the kitchen table.

"There might be more information in the secret vault behind the office."

"I'm not so sure you should go there, Tab. It's too dangerous. What if Baxter, or whoever it is, also knows about the hidden room? What if they're waiting for you there, anticipating your next move?"

Trevor was right. She couldn't just barge into her office alone, especially on a weekend. Security in the building would be at a minimum. With only a cat for her guard, Tabitha didn't think she'd stand a chance against the person who murdered Peter. "I have to go into the vault. If the other half of this note still exists, then I'm sure Peter would have had a copy for safekeeping. He'd never turn over this kind of power to someone without a backup."

"You can check the vault Monday, when the building has a full security staff."

"But Monday might be too late," she said. "And there will be a lot of people around."

Trevor meandered over to his water bowl in the corner of the room. "Lock your door. You're the boss." He bent his head and lapped up a mouthful of water.

His cocky attitude annoyed Tabitha. "Just remember, little guy, in your present form, I'm a lot bigger than you."

Trevor snapped his head to the right, a droplet of water dangling from his chin. "I was only trying to make a point. Monday would be a hell of a lot better than today." He wiped his chin with the back of his paw.

Tabitha grabbed a clean dishcloth from the counter and placed it on the floor next to Trevor's water bowl. "Here, you can use this instead of your hand."

"Thanks," he said, bunching the cloth up into a heap and then rubbing his chin against the edge. "Since we're stuck here until Monday, why don't you think over that ritual you did last night and see if we can work on changing me back to mortal form? If I can shapeshift again, I'll be a lot more useful to you than in this state."

Useful wasn't exactly the word she was thinking of, but having Trevor in human form definitely appealed more to her than his feline shape. Visions of his buff body flooded her mind. "I'll do my best, but I don't think I left anything out from what I told you already."

"Something you did or said changed me last night. You

have to do it again or at least try."

"Fine, but I'm using less flying ointment this time. I don't want to pass out again."

"Don't like waking up in the arms of a stranger?"

She didn't answer him. Truth be told, she feared herself more than the flying ointment. Waking up in Trevor's arms again was the last thing she needed right now. Hopefully, less ointment would keep her coherent and still strong enough to knock out a cat. And by the time he woke from kitty dreamland, she'd be halfway to Manhattan and Peter's secret vault.

Seven

Trevor batted around a few twigs he'd collected on the patio and pushed them over to Tabitha for use in the Chiminea. God, he hoped the woman could change him back again. He hadn't realized just how much he missed being in human form until this morning. Making love to Tabitha had renewed his sexual desires, not that he had ever actually lost them. But after spending almost five hundred years as a cat, he'd trained himself to forget about certain desires. Being with Tabitha brought them all back again.

"Are you okay?"

"Huh?"

Tabitha stared down at him, her long, black hair glistening in the moonlight shining down on her shoulders. "You seem lost in thought."

The woman knew him too well already, and he had only spent one night with her. That frightened him a bit. He had never fallen in love with a woman after only one night, but something in the depths of his soul told him he was starting to fall for Tabitha. He wasn't so sure that was a good thing for her. "I was just thinking of catnip," he lied, but he certainly couldn't tell her the truth. What woman would want a cat for a spouse? If Tabitha couldn't change him back, he'd have to find a way to escape. Being a housecat simply wasn't something for which he was ready to settle. It also wasn't something he thought Tabitha deserved.

"There," she said, standing in front of the Chiminea. "That should get the fire going."

Trevor flicked his tail and headed over to the large box where Tabitha kept her supplies. "Use the same flying ointment you used last night. I don't think you should change it."

"Do you want me knocked out cold again? What if my stalker reappears?"

He jumped onto the chair next to the magickal supply box. "I don't sense any disturbance in the area. And everyone knows cats are the best psychic animals out there."

Tabitha leaned over the box and opened the lid.

Trevor stuck his head under her arm. Smells of exotic spices danced on the air, emitting from the collection of herbs and spices piled in the box.

Tabitha reached in and retrieved two blue glass jars.

"Is it the same one from last night? You used two jars last night? I don't remember that."

She shot him an annoyed look. "I don't have enough left in the jar from last night, so I have to make up a new mixture of herbs and balm."

He lifted his paw to her arm. "You're the only chance I have to return to human form. Do you know what it's been like being a cat for half a millennium?"

Tabitha didn't comment. She let go of the box lid, letting the top close with a clunk. Then she turned and walked over to the Chiminea. A roaring fire blazed inside the clay fireplace.

Trevor steadied his paws down the leg of the chair and made his way onto the tiled floor.

Tabitha stood near the fire and had already started to slather on the thick, pungent balm she'd just mixed.

He brushed up against her calf, his tail wrapping around her ankle.

"Your fur is going to get stuck to my feet," she said.

Trevor had the funny feeling he'd somehow crossed the line with his new mistress.

Tabitha turned away from him and finished anointing her body with the flying ointment. The heady aromas of rich herbs and spices, especially clove, filled Trevor's nostrils. His cat senses went into overdrive. A stinging sensation shot through his nose and stung his eyes. He hated it when his body reacted in that way. He squinted and brushed his paw across his face. The faint taste of mixed spices even teased his tongue. Mayhap trying the ritual wasn't the best idea. Mayhap Tabitha was correct in thinking she needed to use a lighter version of the flying ointment.

His vision faded in and out, and the patio moved around him like a wavy scene. Trevor fought off the urge to stretch and curl up and take a catnap. He wanted desperately to close his eyes and sleep, but he couldn't give in to the effects of the flying ointment. He had to stay awake, be alert the moment he changed back to mortal form.

He watched Tabitha standing near the fire. With her arms outstretched and her naked body bathed in moonlight, she looked like a goddess. Trevor never remembered seeing a woman more beautiful than the one by whom he was presently bewitched. Tabitha was indeed a woman he could imagine spending all eternity with.

The patio spun again. This time he couldn't fight the effects of the flying ointment. Sleep slowly crept over his body like a silent stalker going in for the kill.

He waited for his body to change, to feel the first stretches of his bones as his world faded away. But much to his disappointment, nothing happened other than sleep.

***

Tabitha caught a glimpse of Trevor from the corner of her eye. The small, long haired cat slept curled in a ball, his tail wrapped around him, its tip touching the edge of his nose. A pang of guilt shot through her heart. She hated having lied to Trevor, but she certainly couldn't allow herself to fall asleep tonight. She needed to get to Manhattan and find the other half of the Merlin note. Switching the flying ointments when Trevor crawled down the chair was her only option, despite the fact she didn't really want to trick him. But this was her problem, not his. And she certainly couldn't risk getting him killed. If the mage she was looking for murdered Peter, then he could easily harm a small cat. She'd deal with telling Trevor the truth when she got back from Manhattan.

She had no clue as to why he'd changed back into a cat this morning. After she took care of this mess with her stalker, she'd find a way to turn him back to a mortal for good. In her view, the man's hunk status was wasted on his feline form, and that, thought Tabitha, was a sin in itself. She simply had to find a way to change him back.

Tabitha recapped the jars of herbs and flying ointment and placed them inside the supply box. She looked up at the moon and silently thanked the heavens the mixture of clove and herbs in the second jar was strong enough to knock out a cat just by leaving off the lid.

She wondered how long Trevor would be out. If he woke before she dressed and got in the car, she knew he'd never let her go to into the city alone, and she couldn't endanger him any further than she already had. She needed Trevor to sleep until she left, or at least stay occupied if he awoke before she left the house. *Catnip...* Tabitha remembered the natural catnip stowed in the supply box. She went back to the crate and opened up the lid, pushing aside the bottles until she found the one labeled organic catnip. Taking a sizeable amount into the palm of her hand, Tabitha headed over to where Trevor slept. She gathered the herb pieces between her fingers and sprinkled them by his nose. Blowing him a kiss, Tabitha headed back into the bedroom and gathered up her clothes. Dressing as she walked through the room, she reached for her purse and car keys on the dresser. She did a quick check in the mirror and then made a beeline for the hall.

As she approached the bottom step, the doorbell rang. From behind the curtained side window, her eyes made out the form of a tall, thin man.

The doorbell rang a second time.

"Tab? Are you in there, Tabitha? It's me, Baxter. Open up."

She cursed to herself. This was the last thing she needed right now. If she didn't answer, and he was indeed the mage, he wouldn't give up. Maybe he'd break in. Then what? If he found her here, ignoring him, he'd know for sure she'd figured out he'd killed Peter.

Swearing a silent oath to herself, she steadied her nerves and headed for the door. Facing Baxter head-on looked like the best option at the moment.

Eight

A burning sensation shot through Trevor's bones. The hot fiery sting seemed to be more intense than during last night's transformation, but he didn't know why. Pain filled every inch of his feline body. He twitched and shook, the unbearable sensation coursing through his veins and bones like a wild beast out on the prowl, searching for something to devour. He literally felt as if his insides were being eaten up this time.

With a final stretch of his entire body, Trevor shot back to being a man once more.

He took a deep breath and placed his hand on his chest, right where his heart lay. The rhythmic beating confirmed he was alive and hadn't died, but the soreness in his muscles hurt like hell. Thoughts of life and death collided in his brain. He cursed to himself. Maybe he was better off remaining a cat, not interfering again in the mortal realm. At least as a cat, he retained the right to have an emotionally uninvolved attitude. And not loving someone meant there was never anyone to be taken away from you. Even if he and Lady Catherine were never to marry, he still would have liked to be there to see his sons grow up. The thought that they had lived and died, and that he had no idea what had become of them, pained him. Trevor wished he could take back the past and make things right again, but he knew that was impossible, even with magick.

A second bout of pain shot through his body. He pushed himself into an upright position, every part of him aching. He swore an oath under his breath and knew if he stopped halfway he'd never get off the floor. Refusing to give in to the growing discomfort slowly taking over his bones, Trevor gave a final push and rose to his feet.

He opened his eyes and searched the patio. No sign of Tabitha. Fear filled his soul. If anything happened to his new mistress while he'd slept, he'd never forgive himself. The notion of caring for Tabitha with such a deep feeling bothered him. Since when had Lord McGovern come to care for a single female? Surely he must be slipping in his ancient age.

Trevor padded into the bedroom. The cold floor of the patio chilled his bare feet. The sound of voices coming from the hallway echoed to his ears. Tabitha was still in the house. A sense of release washed over him, calming his fears. He listened by the doorway and tried to decipher the second voice in the entrance hall beneath the stairs. A familiar, obnoxious sound jarred his memory. *Baxter Flint, the phone guy.* A sense of dread replaced Trevor's recent calmness.

He couldn't leave Tabitha alone with Baxter. But he also couldn't head downstairs naked.

He turned and made his way across the bedroom. At Tabitha's closet, he started searching through her clothes. She had to have something he could wear and yet not look ridiculous. He hadn't returned to being a man just to be dressed up in women's clothing. He searched the closet but found nothing hanging from the pole that would suffice. A top shelf offered another chance of hope. Trevor reached up and pulled down a football jersey and matching jogging pants. He pulled at the fabric. The set definitely wasn't his size, but he could make do with them.

After tugging on the snug fitting items, Trevor crossed the room, heading into the hallway. He took the stairs two at a time.

Tabitha turned and gave him a surprised look.

"Sorry, Tab," he said. "I got caught up on the phone. Who's the friend?"

He walked to her side and wrapped his arm around her waist. If Baxter Flint was any kind of a man, he'd recognize the silent, possessive message and back off.

"This is Baxter Flint, my assistant at Morghanna's Maze." Tabitha offered a faint smile to Flint. "Baxter, this is Trevor Mc…"

He cut her off. "McDonald. Trevor McDonald." He extended his hand to Baxter. "Nice to meet you."

"Likewise, I'm sure," Baxter said, his voice shaky. "Forgive the unannounced visit. I was just in the neighborhood spending some time with friends, and I thought I'd check up on you, Tabitha."

"Thank you. I appreciate it."

Trevor didn't like the way Baxter looked at his Tabitha. Something in the man's eyes wasn't normal.

"Care to stay for some tea or coffee?" Tabitha asked.

Baxter didn't answer right away. He glanced at Trevor and then turned his attention back to Tabitha. "No, thank you. It's getting late and I have to get back to the city. I just wanted to make sure you were okay."

Trevor released his hold on Tabitha and went straight for the door. He opened the latch before Baxter had a chance to change his mind. "It was nice meeting you, Baxter. Next time I'm in town, we'll have to get together. I'm sure we'd have a lot to talk about."

Baxter didn't comment. He nodded his head in Tabitha's direction and walked out the door.

Trevor watched the man get into his car and pull out of the driveway. Certain Baxter had left the premises, he closed the door and locked it. "How did he get past the gates?"

"I had the gates open." A blush of red flushed Tabitha's cheeks.

The reality of the situation hit him like a ton of bricks. "Where were you going?"

"The city."

Tabitha walked past the phone table and tossed her purse on top. The sound of jingling keys echoed in the large hall.

"I can't believe you were going to go to the vault alone and at this late hour. What if Baxter was waiting for you there?"

She kept walking.

Trevor picked up his pace and strode around her. "I'm the only one you've got right now and vice versa," he said, blocking the doorway to the kitchen. "I suggest we make the best of our situation. We need each other."

"When did you change back to human form?"

"I guess not long after you left the patio."

She bit her bottom lip.

Trevor didn't like the concerned look crossing Tabitha's face. "What are you thinking?"

"I asked the powers that be to send me my protector, and you showed up the same time Baxter did."

He pondered the thought. "So, I take on human form when you're in danger?"

She shrugged. "It's the only explanation I can think of. You changed shape when someone was in the backyard last night, then again when Baxter came to the door. And if Baxter is the culprit, then I'm in danger when he's around."

Her words made the most sense, but confirming them would only add to her anxiety, thought Trevor. "Maybe we should go somewhere else tonight. Just as an added precaution."

"I have nowhere else to go." Tabitha headed over to the refrigerator and opened the door. She reached in and took out a can of soda. "Want one?"

"No, thanks. I prefer milk."

Tabitha ducked back into the refrigerator and returned with a carton of milk in her hand.

"I think it's time you called your sister."

"No," she said. "I refuse to get her involved in this."

"But maybe she's already involved. Maybe that's why she picked me out at the shelter. Maybe her witchy senses knew I wasn't a real cat."

Tabitha slammed a plastic cup down on the table. "This is my battle. Not Maura's, not anyone else's, not even yours."

Trevor was surprised by Tabitha's show of anger. He reached out his hand and gently placed it on her shoulder. "I think it's best we go to a hotel for the night. If Baxter doesn't know what you're up to, then he might not suspect anything. We can go to the city tomorrow, at a normal time, while it's still daylight. I don't want you to go alone."

She lifted her hand and wrapped it around his. "I'm sorry. I just want all this to be over with so I can get back to living a normal life."

Her words hurt, but he didn't want her to know it. Trevor made up his mind then and there that once Baxter was caught, he'd find a way to return to his life as a stray tomcat. Besides, after Tabitha was safe, he'd probably never again turn back into mortal shape, and even if he did, magick would always be part of his world. Once the curse was lifted, he'd regain his magickal powers. There was nothing normal about a man who was a magickal mage changed to a cat then back again. And normal was all his Tabitha really desired.

Nine

Tabitha slid the key card into the lock and opened the door. The smell of carpet freshener and cheap room spray assaulted her nose. "Nothing like a dingy motel," she said.

Trevor brushed past her and placed the duffle bag on the open stand. "At least Baxter would never think you'd come to a place like this," he said, glancing around the room. "And it really isn't all that bad."

Tabitha didn't agree. From the fake red brick walls to the mismatched brown bathroom tiles, Motel Mandy wasn't exactly what she'd call "not all that bad." She pulled the bedspread off the mattress and checked the sheets. "They're clean, so I guess it's passable." Trevor handed her the two new blankets she had requested at the front desk during check in. Unfolding them, she said, "I'm going to take a shower and change my clothes. When I get out of the bathroom, we'll talk about tomorrow's plan."

"Fine by me."

Tabitha picked up her overnight bag and disappeared into the small hallway separating the bathroom and the sleeping area. She closed the door, leaning back against the plywood surface. In all her years of magick studies, she'd never imagined she could be so embroiled in a mess like this one. And to have a handsome medieval lord as her mighty protector didn't help matters any. The man was more handsome then Adonis. And he was right out of her fantasy dreams. But the idea she had the hots for a man who was once her cuddly new cat just didn't sit well with her. Even if he did stay in human form, what could she offer him? Her world was made up of all things magickal. And considering what Trevor McGovern had gone through in his lifespan, she was certain he would have no interest in a woman who lived for spells and potions. Once this matter of Baxter was settled, she'd give Trevor his freedom, even if he did turn back to feline form. She'd never try to force him into a relationship.

Overwhelmed by all that was taking place, Tabitha pushed the thoughts of Trevor from her mind. She'd enjoy what time she had with him and then deal with the emotional consequences later.

***

Trevor sat on the edge of the bed and listened to the steady streaming of shower water coming from inside the bathroom. God he wished he could be in there with Tabitha right now. She had a way of making him go weak in the knees and hard in the groin. If only she could see him as normal. Given the chance, he knew he could make amends for his past sins. If only he could convince Tabitha he could make things normal again for her, whatever normal was.

The bathroom door opened and Tabitha stepped out, drying her hair with a towel. "I forgot the hair dryer, so I hope you don't mind sleeping with someone with a wet head."

A wet head was exactly what he was thinking about, although probably not the same one Tabitha was referring to. "Um...no, I don't mind at all."

"Good, because I'm exhausted, and I don't think I can stay up to finish drying this hair."

He stared at her long dark locks, watching in awe as droplets of water fell from the ends, down the front of her nightshirt, revealing her taut nipples.

Tabitha tossed the towel across the room and it landed on the tile floor near the bathroom door. She then lifted the covers on her side of the bed and crawled in.

Trevor got up and undressed. He reached for the light on the nightstand and twisted the switch.

"No," Tabitha said. "I'd prefer we slept with the light on."

He hadn't realized just how frightened she'd become. "Fine." He flicked the knob backward and the light turned on.

"Did you lock the door?"

"As soon as we came in."

"Oh." She gave him a concerned look.

"Tabitha, as long as I'm here, in this form, I won't let anything happen to you. You have to trust me on that."

"What if Baxter followed us? What if he has a gun or some magickal powers I don't know about?"

He didn't like her being so scared. He leaned close to the bed and shoved his hand under the mattress.

"What are you doing?"

Trevor lifted his hand and revealed the boleen Tabitha had used the night before. "I took it with us just in case," he said. "Back in my day, I always carried a dagger strapped somewhere on my body." He saw a slight shift in Tabitha's fearful look. "I won't let Baxter harm you."

"No, I'm sure you won't. But I'm still not totally at ease with the situation. Why would he kill Peter?"

Trevor put the knife back between the mattress and box spring, and eased himself into the bed. "If Peter has the other half of that note in his vault, then we should know the answer tomorrow. But for now, try not to think about it."

"I can't help it."

He wrapped his arm around her and pulled her close. "You need rest."

"I don't want to sleep."

He ran his thumb over her bottom lip. "I fear you've bewitched me, Tabitha Cole."

"I know my magick well," she said, smiling at him.

The witchy look in Tabitha's eyes was all Trevor needed. He dipped his head and kissed her.

***

Trevor's lips burned Tabitha's skin. The hot touch of his body against hers set her heart to pounding. Nothing mattered at the moment. Nothing except being in Trevor's arms.

He brushed his fingers over her nipple.

A zing spiraled through her body. Tabitha inched her way closer to Trevor, closer to his wonderful hands. Her inhibitions suddenly seemed lost, as did her worries. She'd enjoy these moments, even though she knew in the deepest depths of her heart, they couldn't last forever.

Tabitha rolled onto her back and grinned. He brought out a playful side of her nature. "Going to scratch my tummy?"

Trevor shot her a wicked grin. "You think it's a joke being a cat, but I can tell you, we felines do a lot more than merely sleep and eat."

She ran a hand through his shiny black hair. "Then show me exactly what else it is that you do."

Trevor didn't need a second invitation. He wrapped his arm around her waist, rolled her onto her stomach, and then lifted her into a kneeling position. "This is how real cats do it, my dear."

Tabitha took a deep breath. Trevor ran his fingers lightly over her spine, sending a tingly sensation down her back. "How long can you last?"

He nuzzled her neck and licked her ear. "As long as you need me to."

"I meant last as a man." She rolled her eyes. Even as a

cat, Trevor was a typical guy. "Do you think there is any way we can break Old Esme's spell for good?"

He glided his hands up from her waist and cupped her breasts. "God, I hope so," Trevor groaned.

The feel of his fingers against her nipples was heaven. He tugged, he pulled, he rolled and then he did what all cats do, he kneaded her flesh with soft, steady moves. The smooth pads of his fingers caressed her breasts, lingering on the now erect tips jutting out like two ripe berries ready for the picking. Tabitha moaned and leaned back, sinking deeper into Trevor's grasp.

"We've got all night, hon," Trevor whispered. "Tomorrow we can figure a way out of this mess. For now, let's play."

Tabitha moaned a second time.

Trevor's hands now slid to her waist, one keeping a firm grasp on her, while the other wandered even lower. He reached for her labial folds and sought her clit. The pulsing button reacted to his tender touch, sending her senses spinning into a heated spiral.

The tip of his erect cock rubbed against her leg.

"I want you inside me, Trevor."

He moved his fingers away from her clitoris and teased her vagina. He slipped inside, first one finger, then two, tantalizing her, caressing her.

Tabitha pushed back and eased herself closer to Trevor.

He withdrew his fingers and steadied himself against her, securing his hold around her waist. With a slow move, he slid his hard cock inside her.

She moaned. The feel of him filling her vagina, gliding against her slick walls, sent a spasm erupting through her. Tabitha reached up and grabbed hold of the headboard. Trevor's moves increased as he started to pick up the pace.

She'd never acted like this in the past. But being with Trevor made something inside her want to be free.

He pulled back and turned her around, settling her back upon the bed. "I want to look at you," he said.

Tabitha wrapped her arms around his body and pulled him toward her. She ran her fingernails over his back in long, slow scratches.

He gave a low growl that sounded halfway between a purr and a moan. "Let me show you what else cats do well," he said, whispering in her ear.

Tabitha didn't protest.

Trevor trailed kisses down her neck and over her breasts. He teased her nipple with his teeth, nipping at the hard bud, twirling the tip of his tongue around the sensitive top.

"Don't stop," Tabitha said. The feel of him suckling at her breast shot a heated bolt of lightning through her body. A slight twinge settled in her clit.

"I have something better," Trevor whispered. He gave a final nip to her nipple and headed south.

He flicked his tongue in lapping motions across her skin, dotting her flesh with goose bumps. Tabitha couldn't remember the last time something, anything, felt as good.

He continued his trek downward, showering the insides of her upper thighs with light kisses and soft flicks of his tongue.

Tabitha squirmed. She reached above her head and slipped her hands around the spindles in the headboard. She gripped them tight as her senses heightened.

Trevor parted her lips, exposing her clit completely, and the room's cool air kissed the aching bud.

Trevor bent his head and gently ran the tip of his tongue over her clitoris. Small, pulsing spasms flowed through her vagina. She moved her body in rhythm to his flicking tongue.

Letting go of the headboard, she reached downward and weaved her fingers through Trevor's hair, the silky strands wrapping around her fingers.

He kissed her swollen clit and then returned to his previous licking mode.

Tabitha pulled him closer, wanting to feel every inch of his tongue on her mound. A ripple of pleasure shot through her.

Trevor continued his oral massage until she'd rode out the last of her orgasm. Then he kissed his way back up her body and turned her over onto her stomach once more.

She pulled herself up on all fours and nudged her pussy in his direction.

Trevor slid into her from behind, one hand wrapped tightly around her waist and the other slid over her stomach and reached down to her pussy, continuing where his tongue left off.

Tabitha let out a soft moan. The pounding of his cock against her slick walls was heaven. He thrust deep and hard, fast and slow. The increasing rhythm sent her over the edge, her body quivering in delight. Trevor followed her climax with his own several seconds later.

He leaned forward and kissed the small of her back, then settled her gently upon the bed. She cuddled up to him and didn't say a word. Trevor McGovern was her protector and for some uncanny reason, Tabitha felt the man was her soul mate as well.

Ten

Trevor waited by the car as Tabitha checked out of the motel. He scanned the area, his vision still heightened like a cat's, but he didn't see any sign of Baxter. The thought unsettled him. If Baxter wasn't in the area, why was he still in human form? Either danger had to be near or the curse was finally wearing off. The latter notion disturbed him more than the thought of danger. If the curse was wearing off, then that meant he'd changed his ways. And if he'd changed his ways, then what he felt for Tabitha Cole was more real than anything he'd ever felt for anyone else. He took a deep breath and settled on the fact that Baxter must be in the area somewhere and he just didn't sense him.

Tabitha came up to the car and unlocked the doors. "Ready to head straight into danger?"

He was already in danger. "I suppose." He lifted the door handle and slipped into the car.

Tabitha pulled out of the parking lot. "Once we get into the building, we'll go to my office. The vault is on the next floor, accessible only through a hidden staircase behind the office."

"Does Baxter ever go to the office on a weekend?"

"Not that I'm aware of," Tabitha said. "But if he did, no one would suspect anything. He's a pretty high-profile staff member, and as my assistant, he's second highest on the corporate ladder, so no one would question him. Why do you want to know?"

"Just curious to see if he was snooping around when no one else was at work."

Tabitha glanced at him from the corner of her eye. "We keep a log of everyone who comes and goes from the building. When we get there, we'll check and see if he's been visiting during off hours."

"Good. If Baxter knows about the note, then he's been to the building on weekends. And, if he is the one who killed Peter, then he'll try again to stop the crystal from passing hands. There's just one thing I don't get."

Tabitha stopped for a red light. "What's that?"

"Why would he want the crystal in the first place? The power of the Merlin Crystal is hereditary and unless he's of Morghan blood, the artifact is worthless to him."

"Baxter Flint is a strange man. If someone would kill for the Merlin Crystal, there has to be more to the item than we know. And until we find the other half of that note, we'll remain in the dark."

Trevor wracked his brain trying to think of a good reason why Baxter would want the Merlin Crystal when it was virtually no use to the man. But for the life of him, he couldn't come up with an answer. And considering the fact his soul and the Merlin Crystal both came from the Dark Ages, being left in the dark might not be such a bad idea, thought Trevor. In his time, he'd seen more than his fair share of felines brought down by curiosity, and contrary to popular belief, satisfaction never brought back a dead cat.

Eleven

Tabitha entered the Morghan building and walked up to the main reception desk. She wanted to get this over with and done. Living in the shadow of fear for several years was long enough, and come hell or high water, she was going to see the Merlin Crystal settled at the Museum of Gemology, even if it killed her.

"Morning, Miss Cole," an armed guard said, nodding his head to her.

"Morning, Timmy."

"Working on the weekend are you?"

"Just catching up on some paperwork before the museum exhibit tomorrow night."

The guard handed her a thick, opened book.

Tabitha grabbed hold of a pen mounted to the desktop by a chain of small silver balls and found the next free line available for her signature. She signed her name and Trevor's and then slid the book back to the guard.

Timmy studied the page before putting it back on the corner of his desk. "Always a pleasure to see you, Miss Cole." He glanced past her shoulder. "And nice to meet *you*, Mr. McGovern."

Trevor nodded but didn't comment.

Tabitha unzipped her pocketbook and pulled out a large, plain metal ring laden with keys. She headed toward the elevator.

Trevor followed a close step behind, the essence of his presence making her skin tingle. "You're awfully quiet," she said, as she punched the elevator button and looked up, waiting for the red flash to highlight the elevator symbol G for ground floor.

"I simply have nothing to say."

Somehow Tabitha didn't believe him. Trevor seemed to be too in tune with his surroundings. And considering he'd spent the last five hundred years as a cat, his change in behavior unsettled her.

The elevator light flashed and the doors opened.

Tabitha stepped inside and slid her keycard into the slot for the private, corporate offices. Trevor leaned back against the metal rail, his reflection showing across the mirrored walls.

God, he was handsome, thought Tabitha, even if he was a cat. Thoughts of last night came flooding back to her. Once this mess was over, she'd find a way to help Trevor stay in mortal form. Wasting a man like Lord McGovern on the feline population seemed like a mortal sin. *Sin...* She wondered what the gods really thought of her coupling with a shapeshifter. Tabitha blushed, her red cheeks visible in the mirrors.

"Are you all right?"

"Yeah, I'm fine," she lied, but telling Trevor her thoughts was the last thing she'd ever do.

The elevator came to a stop and the doors glided open.

"This is it," she said.

Trevor stepped off the elevator first and extended his arm so she couldn't pass. He stood there, his bright blue eyes shifting from side to side, surveying the area. "I don't sense anything, so I think it's okay if we head to your office."

She let out a deep breath and sighed. It was nice to have a man concerned about her again. Since Peter's death, she had forgotten what it felt like to be taken care of.

The walk to the other side of the hall seemed like an endless trek through a twilight zone. With every step, Tabitha felt her heart rate pick up a beat. What would she find in the vault? Would they have enough time to find it before Baxter figured out their plans? She had a funny feeling in her stomach, a twisting, shaky feeling, that made her feel as if she had no ability to control the world around her. A sense that she had often experienced when something was about to happen that affected her life, yet she had no say over it. A feeling she didn't welcome.

Walking up to her office door, she punched in a key code on the side panel and pushed the door open. She scanned the large, open space and found nothing amiss at first glance. Her heart rate settled a bit.

"Where's the vault?" Trevor asked.

"Behind the desk. There's a small latch on top of the third wall panel. If you pull it forward, the wall will push back."

Trevor went around the desk and stretched his arm up to the top molding on the walls.

Tabitha watched his sinewy muscles flexing beneath the tight shirt he'd rummaged from her bedroom closet. She really needed to take him shopping, she thought as she eyed him, easily understanding how the women of his time had fallen for his charm and his body. Old Esme should have cursed them all, thought Tabitha, not just Trevor. God, she was siding with a rogue! Tabitha shook her head trying to dispel the illicit thoughts that kept flooding her mind.

A click echoed through the room.

Trevor stepped back as the wall shifted and slid into the hollow space behind the other panels. A medieval-looking apothecary appeared in the hidden room.

"That's it," Tabitha said. "Peter Morghan's private domain."

***

Trevor didn't know what to think. He'd never seen such a well-equipped apothecary in all his years, and he'd been around his fair share of witches to know this room wasn't your typical sacred space. "The man had guts," he said.

"And what is that supposed to mean?"

Trevor stepped inside the room and took in a deep breath. The pungent smells of herbs and spices attacked his senses. "Mr. Morghan played with fire here. Can't you feel it? The power in this room is immense."

Tabitha entered the chamber and skirted around the main table. She pulled out a wooden crate from underneath and placed it on the marble tabletop. "Peter never did anything bad. He wouldn't use magick in that way."

"I didn't say he did. But I can assure you Peter Morghan didn't practice your basic hocus pocus in this space. He dealt with much stronger powers than the average witch would care to know or even imagine."

Tabitha raised an eyebrow. "And I suppose you know about such powers?"

"Before Old Esme's curse," said Trevor, "I lived for magick."

"Even if Peter did confront powerful entities in this room, I'm sure he used caution." Tabitha pushed the crate to the center of the table.

Trevor walked up to her side, a look of curiosity crossing his face. "What's in the box?"

"It's the Merlin Crystal."

"You kept it here all this time? What if Baxter had managed to get access to the room?"

She pulled out the large key ring from her pocketbook and slid a small, crooked piece of metal into the keyhole on the top side of the wooden box. "I told you, Baxter has never been in here. If he had, he would have taken the crystal ages ago."

The box opened, the lid lifting mechanically and revealing a set of pointed, rainbow-colored crystals arranged in a haphazard display.

Trevor studied the glistening artifact with a keen eye. Each individually wrapped piece sat in a velvet-covered holder, much like candles sitting in a candelabrum. He easily envisioned the crystals as the centerpiece to any serious mage's altar. Visions of an ancient time flashed in his mind...a shredded piece of parchment, the base of the crystals, two voices arguing...

Trevor pinched the bridge of his nose between his thumb and forefinger and squeezed his eyes shut. The energy emitting from his vision felt more intense than anything he'd ever experienced before. If he didn't know better, he'd swear his magickal powers were starting to return. He shook his head and opened his eyes. A colorful prism of light danced off the pointed tips of each faceted crystal. "I think I know why Baxter hasn't taken the Merlin Crystal."

"Because he doesn't have access to it?"

Trevor frowned, "No, not because he doesn't have access to it, but because he's waiting for something specific to happen so he *can* take possession of it."

Tabitha shot him a look of surprise. "Like what?"

She really didn't know, thought Trevor. Damn Baxter for killing Morghan before the man had a chance to tell Tabitha the whole story. "Peter willed you everything he owned, correct?"

"Yes, everything."

"Then that included the crystal."

"But I'm not of Morghan blood. According to legend, I can't access the crystal's powers and, therefore, I can't do anything magical with it."

"No, you're wrong on that account. You have the power to will it away to someone else."

"Like the museum?"

"Yes, and I bet Baxter went to see Peter the night he died to try to get him to will the crystal to him. When Peter refused, Baxter killed him. Then, since the transfer to the museum was put on hold, Baxter had a few years to work on a new plan."

"Why wouldn't he just ask me? Why didn't he think I would give him the crystal since it meant so much to Peter and he and Peter were such close friends?"

Trevor carefully pulled each crystal point out of its corresponding holder. "Because I bet Baxter thinks you know the secret behind the Merlin Crystal and wouldn't take a chance of having it fall into the wrong hands. Or maybe he thinks he'll wait and let you find the final piece of the puzzle, doing the extra work for him."

"I can't believe someone would kill over something they couldn't even use."

"Or maybe they could, with the right spell," he said, holding up a piece of torn parchment. "Peter kept the other half of the note wrapped around the crystals."

Tabitha rushed to his side.

Placing the paper on the table, Trevor smoothed out the turned up corners and read the note. "This says the crystal's powers can be accessed only by a soul born of Morghan blood, as in a descendant of the Goddess Morgaine, Merlin's adversary, or by the originator of the crystal's dark side."

"That would be the entity that sired Merlin."

Trevor heard the shock in Tabitha's voice. "My, God," he said. "Who would have thought?"

"But that would mean Baxter isn't…"

"…mortal," finished Trevor.

A dark shadow appeared from the corner of the room. Baxter Flint took shape, his previously blond hair now jet black. "Peter should never have involved you, Tabitha," Baxter said. "This isn't a game for mortal souls."

Trevor extended his arm behind him and pushed Tabitha back. "You've done enough damage, Flint. You aren't going to do anymore."

An evil laugh cackled through the room. "I gave life to one of the greatest mages of all time, and you have the audacity to believe yourself more powerful than me? Just who the hell do you think you are, little kitty?"

Why did everyone think he was little? He'd had enough. This Baxter Flint, or whatever the hell his real name was, wasn't going to get away with any more wrongdoings. "Why don't you go back to wherever it is you came from and leave well-enough alone?"

"I don't think so. The minute that crystal is willed to a non-magical being, I will never be able to access my ancient powers again. Morghan knew that, and it was his mission to see the Merlin Crystal to safety. But he failed, and I have no intention of letting a novice witch or her mutated cat get in my way."

Baxter floated through the air, slowly making his way across the room. A foul smelling odor similar to rotten eggs filled the chamber.

"My God," Tabitha said, covering her nose with her hand. "What is that smell?"

"It's the odor of evil," Trevor said. He pushed Tabitha farther back, trying to keep her from Baxter's grasp. He wrapped his free hand around the last crystal he had pulled from the box. "I wouldn't come any closer, Baxter."

"Why not, kitty, gonna scratch me?" He laughed another hideous cackle. "Aren't you supposed to be a curious creature, wanting to see what I'm really made of?"

"I see the stuff you're made of every day in my litter box," Trevor said.

"Oh, that hurt."

"You have no idea what I'm capable of. I'm warning you not to come any closer."

"Or what?" Baxter pushed ahead, his ethereal body gaining on Trevor's.

"Or you'll know exactly what this feel's like." Trevor jabbed the crystal into Baxter's stomach.

A hideous screech bellowed across the room, shattering the windows and the many glass vials lining the shelves. "What have you done to me?"

"Given you a taste of your own medicine, Baxter."

The evil entity looked down at his midsection. The crystal protruded from his organs. "You've doomed me, destroyed me with my own creation!"

"Someone should have done it a lot sooner," Trevor said.

Baxter's body coiled and curled up in a ball of dark shadows, then burst into tiny shards, dissipating in the air. The sound of a crystal hitting the tiled floor echoed around the chamber, and a quiet calm settled upon the room.

Tabitha stood in the corner, her eyes wide.

"You have nothing to fear, Tab. He's gone for good."

"I can't believe you did it."

"I told you I was good with a sword or dagger. Now I know I'm good with a crystal, too."

He reached out and wrapped his arms around Tabitha.

Timmy the guard burst into the room, gun drawn. "Are you all right, Miss Cole?"

"Yeah, I'm fine."

He looked at all the broken glass fragments. "Didn't even know this room existed. What the hell happened up here?"

Tabitha shot Trevor a worried glance.

"I insisted on trying out this concoction for a new cologne," he said.

"Wow," Timmy said. "Guess it wasn't the best mix, huh?"

Trevor nodded his head.

"Okay," Timmy said. "I'll get maintenance here in a flash to clean this up."

"No, that's all right, Timmy," Tabitha said, crouching and picking up some of the glass. "I can..."

Trevor cut her off, shaking his head. "I don't think you need to protect anything anymore," he whispered. "Besides, it would only cause more suspicion."

She looked back up at Timmy. "Second thought, this probably is a bit much for one person to clean up. Send in a crew. Thanks."

Timmy disappeared back into the main office.

Tabitha looked up at Trevor, a sparkle in her eye. "I think we better call Maura now."

"Um...I don't think so. Not yet, at least."

"But now that Baxter is gone, there's no danger anymore. I can tell Maura everything."

That was exactly what he was afraid of—women loved to talk. "Has it sunk in yet that I'm still in mortal form?"

"Yeah, so?"

"So? Is that all I get?"

She smiled a wicked grin. "What else would you like, Lord McGovern?"

"For starters, the curse wouldn't have been lifted unless true love had found me. So, I need to know if...well...you know..."

Tabitha pursed her lips and placed her hand gently upon his shoulder. "Before I answer, am I correct in remembering, you also had to fall in love yourself."

"Yes. The emotion had to be mutual."

"And is it?"

"I just put my life on the line to destroy an entity more powerful then most people can imagine. I wouldn't have done that for just anyone."

Tabitha smiled at him, a flirty look in her eyes. "Well, if I'm not just anyone, then what exactly do you consider me?"

He reached out and wrapped his arms around her. "How about the soul mate I'd like to take as my better half?"

"I think that can be arranged, my lord. But there's a lot of work to do first. Technically, you don't even exist."

He gave a slight laugh. "Well, considering the power of my title back in 1558, I think I might still have the ability to pull a few strings back home to make me legal again. Besides, I'm anxious to do some spellcasting. I didn't realize how much I missed working with magic until I met you."

Tabitha stretched up on her toes and planted her lips upon his.

"I think I am truly bewitched, Lady Tabitha," he said with a smile.

He had his life back again, thought Trevor, and it was even sweeter now that he'd finally found true love. He silently thanked Old Esme and Molly Claire for their spell, for he was certainly one lucky cat.

Don't Miss

Silk and Magic Book One

by
Rebecca York
Rickey Mallory
Brandy Lee

Dangerous Seduction
by Rebecca York

Catherine Emerson's nights are haunted by a dream lover
who introduces her to a world of passion she never knew
existed. But is her dream lover a figment of her imagination,
or a real-life man who is invading her mind and placing them
both in mortal danger . . .

Silver Dark Blue Light
by Rickey Mallory

Eva Quintana has a secret past that she no longer shares
because people think she's crazy. But when her boyfriend
dumps her because her past interferes with their love life,
she turns to therapist Dr. Seain Jones for help. However, Dr.
Jones offers her more than counseling. He introduces her to
a sensual world that makes her forget the past. What Eva
doesn't know is that Dr. Jones has a secret of his own that
will change her life forever . . . .

Sweet Surrender
by Brandy Lee

Historian Laura Linden is in love with Logan Jackson. The
problem is Logan has been dead for more than 100 years.
When Laura is transported back in time, she finds herself in
Logan 's arms. He thinks she's the "lady of the evening"
that his cousin hired to entertain Logan for what may well be
the last night of his life. Laura doesn't deny his belief
because she'll do anything—even turn herself into Logan's
love slave—to save his life . . .

Available Now from
ImaJinn Books

www.imajinnbooks.com

Printed in the United States
44655LVS00002B/448-471

9 781933 417943